CAPE *of* STORMS

ALSO BY NINA BERBEROVA

The Book of Happiness
The Ladies from St. Petersburg

NINA BERBEROVA

CAPE *of* STORMS

**TRANSLATED FROM THE RUSSIAN BY
MARIAN SCHWARTZ**

A NEW DIRECTIONS BOOK

12/99 BT 23⁹⁵

Originally published in Paris in the Russian journal *Novy zhurnal,* nos. 24–27, 1951.

Book design by Sylvia Frezzolini Severance
Manufactured in the United States of America
New Directions Books are printed on acid-free paper.

First published clothbound by New Directions in 1999
Published simultaneously in Canada by Penguin Books Canada Ltd.

Library of Congress Cataloging-in-Publication Data
Berberova, Nina Nikolaevna.
    [Mys bur'. English]
    Cape of Storms / Nina Berberova ; translated from the Russian by
Marian Schwartz.
        p.   cm.
    ISBN 0-8112-1416-8 (cloth)
    I. Schwartz, Marian.   II. Title.
    PG3476.B425M9713   1999   99-41309
    891.73'42—dc21   CIP

New Directions Books are published for James Laughlin
by New Directions Publishing Corporation
80 Eighth Avenue, New York 10011

The Cape of Good Hope. 34° 22' South, 16° 8' East.
Discovered in 1486 by Bartholomeu Dias, who called it the
Cape of Storms, because he could not sail around it.

—The Great Encyclopedia

CAPE *of* STORMS

CHAPTER ONE

I t often seemed to Dasha that inside herself it was like a starry
sky. And in fact, when she looked inward she seemed to be
standing at the brink of a great chasm. There, at her very core,
deep down, where her thoughts were anchored, reigned calm,
quiet, and clarity. The Milky Way streamed across this familiar
picture. The laws of mathematics and astronomy perhaps were
valid in this imagined place, where everything was mysteriously
beautiful and where, gazing inward, she saw her own equilibrium. Dasha was proud of this core, which had probably grown,
as had she herself, in much the same way as the world around
her, and which anchored all her contemplation, all her doubts,
and all her sleepless nights. What had seemed far beyond her
grasp turned out to be in her very blood. Sometimes Dasha felt
as if she were sitting above a precipice with the stars beneath
her; often she would linger with them for a long while. She was
thrilled and astonished that no one knew or ever would know
what counted most for her in life. This starry sky within was her
link to the universe, and she sought no others.

One dark August night she sat for a long time with her head
thrown back, thinking about herself and her destiny, about what

truly was her destiny, since by no means everything that had happened to her thus far was. She had always had an intimation of her destiny: all her senses would go on the alert, as if bracing her for a blow—a terrible, crushing, powerful blow—of luck, whether good or bad. She would feel an urgent need—not to know or guess or reason but simply to obey whatever response to this oncoming destiny surfaced in her, in those moments, like music, by way of a warning or presentiment. Sometimes, as if dragged by a slender chain, her memories would file by, among which the most fateful would suddenly turn out to be the closest.

It was a long time ago, so long ago that what were really three lives she had lived since ought to have severed her connection to the memory permanently, rendering it just as bloodless as something she might have read in a book. But that hadn't happened. She had been standing on the staircase then, a few steps from her front door, which was cracking and breaking but would not give way because the bolt had been thrown. And then suddenly the glass on top came crashing in with a great tinkling, smashed by the butt of a rifle. A large, cautious hand appeared in the black hole. It was a terrible moment. The hand slipped through the opening, felt for the bolt, and wrenched it off. It threw the bolt down on the marble floor with a ringing clatter and then cautiously, to keep from cutting itself, retreated back through the hole. Only when it had disappeared was the door flung open and several men rushed forward, yelling.

They were in full battle dress, cartridge belts across their chests and fur caps tilted to the side. One of them had his neck bound with a bloody rag; he had no nose and his chin was covered with foam. Two others dropped their rifles with an identical motion and threw Dasha's mother to the floor. Dasha heard an inhuman scream and a skull slamming against the bottom stair. At that moment she felt wings at her shoulders. She flew up the broad white staircase into someone's open apartment and through a round window on the back stairs that let out onto a neighboring courtyard. There she clung to a ledge and saw linens hanging out to dry on a line beneath her and a neat stack of firewood. Someone pulled her through the window by her legs and covered her mouth with his hand. "Hush! Hush, child!" said the stranger's voice, because she was screaming and water was pouring down her face and into her mouth. The water brought Dasha to her senses.

Now the people around her were saying she had to put on boy's clothes, which she did, her teeth chattering. These were the trousers and shirt, the boots and jacket, of the fourth-form schoolboy, Alyosha Boiko, who lived here with his father and grandmother. Dasha had seen him outside many times coming home from school, and often he would catch up with her and make loud conversation on purpose to tease her: "I know a place where they cut off braids like that, cut them clean off and shave your head, and they do it for free!"

That had been just half a year before, but when Dasha came out of the house, shaved, after a bout of typhus, he froze. His jaw dropped and he watched her for a long time, stunned, as if the joke were on him instead of her.

And here she was now, dressed like him. When she saw herself in the mirror, she stopped trembling. For the first time in her life she was seeing herself in boy's clothing, in a cap of darkness that concealed her completely from strangers. Now she could go home, now nothing frightened her, and nothing ever could frighten her, because now she was like everyone else. But wait. What if the most terrible thing in her life had already happened? What if there could never be anything so terrible again?

A strange sensation gripped her when she stood like that and looked inward: a sensation of freedom, self-confidence, self-containment, a sensation of being ready for anything, a sensation of her life just beginning.

Cautiously, clutching an apple in her hand, she crossed the courtyard, skirted the building, and stopped at her front door. It was wide open. Someone ran out without looking at her; Dasha did not notice precisely who. The smashed door, the staircase, the dirty, bloody tracks on the floor—everything was special because the silence of the air, of the walls, of the light, of the furnishings was special. Her petrifaction was such that it was as if her blood had swollen her veins to the bursting point so that she couldn't breathe. A soft, even sound, like something dripping somewhere, underscored an icy silence, so uncharacteristic of this house. Dasha made an effort to take a few steps; the sound continued. Yes, it was something dripping, or a sobbing, so very steady, too steady. . . . And then Dasha saw her: she was sprawled out, her face and neck were covered with purple bruises, her legs were spread, her hair was loose and fanned out to one side. Medorka, their rusty setter (who harked back to Grandfather Tiagin), was sitting over her and licking her dead face with an even, sobbing sound. Now it didn't sound like water dripping any more. He was licking her eyes (one of which had been poked out). He didn't seem to recognize Dasha dressed up like Alyosha Boiko.

There beyond the walls of the Tiagin home, a war was raging, a war in which no one could find the guilty party. Two truths were battling it out, because it turned out that there were many truths in the world. People had been trying to find in the history of this city, this corner of the country, the first cause of the hatred that had been prosecuting the war for two years. They had tried to figure out—or guess—precisely who, at what precise moment, had given birth to this force. Dasha stood there looking straight ahead as if only now becoming aware of this point: You had to pay and pay and pay for the fact that there were many truths in the world. There was no getting away from that.

Swaying and holding on to the wall of the building, Dasha went out and began walking the streets. Passersby, of whom there were quite a few, did not see her but looked through her. *In boy's clothes, like a beast in its hide . . . camouflage . . . I never knew you could hide this way . . . my legs feel very free, but it's tight under the arms. . . . I'm in shock, though. I haven't had time to really realize . . .* She was fifteen years old. Thick dark hair already covered her head, but since the typhus her face had remained triangular. There was shooting in the town. It was a summer evening, dusty and stuffy, and there was something black in the air and on people's faces. At the corner of English Street, in a wine cellar, voices were clamoring, and the entire street was flooded with wine, and since the pavement there took a turn and went downhill, there was champagne running down the sidewalk, quietly gurgling and foaming slightly, and it smelled of vomit.

Good or evil? Good luck or bad? How was the world supposed to divide up? Lengthwise or crosswise? Which should she choose? Right now people were slicing the world up crosswise: they were looking for good fortune but not thinking about good. They wanted to arrange the world their way. *The day has come for me to make up my own mind,* thought Dasha, and she looked around, *to make sense of this day, this today, while I'm still a long way off from any tears. To make sense of my life. Something inside me is dead, though. Something was so alive, so keen and tender, but they hit it too hard. Could it really be dead? But then why am I alive?*

By the time she got back to the Boikos', it was night. The grandmother opened the door. Whispering and crossing herself, she led Dasha into the dining room (where they had dressed her that afternoon) and with a small dry hand began stroking her head. It must have felt like stroking Alyosha's head, for they were the exact same height. The grandmother had a slight tremor, due to old age. She had thrown a fur wrap over her dark-patterned, floor-length robe, and her gray hair was combed back smoothly on her head. The large dark eyes in her swarthy face

cut deep. And suddenly something shook loose in Dasha: this
was consolation, the very thing she had never needed before,
that she was a tiny bit afraid of, and that actually, in the firm and
steadfast future, should disappear from the world. Consolation
was here, under the warmth of the grandmother's hand, in her
old-fashioned customs, in the ugly sideboard, the samovar, the
icons in the corner. This was Dasha's encounter with it, her first
encounter, and maybe her last, because all this was coming to an
end, it was no longer needed, it was over and done. *But what
about us? What about when we're sixty or seventy or eighty?
What will we be like?* she thought. *What will we have to offer
people? Without icons or a samovar, without a hand making the
cross, without this whisper and this tear falling from our eyes?
Without this memory of an intact, complete world, of a universe
that stood so firmly, without this faith.* . . . And for one brief
instant she clearly pictured a world in which there would be
nothing to fall back on.

Imperceptibly, silently, the door opened, and the head of the
household entered wearing a quasi-military tunic, Alexei Andreyevich Boiko. At the time he was a little over forty. The director of the municipal dramatic theater, he was often written up
in the papers, especially of late, in connection with the suicide of
the actress, Dumontelle. Now he was quite pale, pale blue, even.
His whole face was utterly out of the ordinary. A blackness lay
in the folds of his creased cheeks, his eyes were red, and he suddenly looked like a man who had aged. There was the trace of
something brown on his dry lips. He sat right down on the chair
by the door.

Dasha knew him but had never given him a second thought.
The actresses in the municipal theater interested her much more.
She had seen Dumontelle three times, and also once in *A Ro-
mance,* but no one was supposed to know that. From time to
time she ran into Boiko on the street. Sometimes he might bow
to her, but the expression on his face, his cold, forbidding, rather

haughty gaze, never changed. The most recent time she had seen him was one evening, right at her front door about five days ago, when she was coming home from her lessons. He walked past her quickly, his head averted. She hadn't given it a second thought.

Boiko stood up, as if he had finally made up his mind, and said something very quietly to the grandmother, who stepped aside, letting them pass through the door. Dasha and Alexei Andreyevich went down to the courtyard. Once again she walked around the corner of her building and they entered through the front door. The moon was shining everywhere now, and the steps alternated: black, white, black, white. Boiko was silent. By the indifferent way Medorka walked out past them, Dasha thought they must have taken her mother away, and she began to tremble. Boiko still said nothing but he took her arm above the elbow, and squeezed it a little too hard. Was this for comfort or his idea of comfort? Maybe he was not one of "us" (thought Dasha) and so didn't know how to do any of this, or even want to? And did the split lie not between "us" and "them" but between him and the grandmother? And consequently he had no resources left for helping either himself or anyone else?

Her mother was now lying in the middle of the parlor, on the table, covered with a muslin sheet. Two fat, placid women were sitting on either side of her and by the light of the three candles Dasha saw that they were sleeping soundly. It was the cook and her daughter, who had just been out carousing with some officers. Her mother was lying with a closed face, the face that Dasha loved so much, that had always been open; but her soul had never been open, and often she had shed tears. Her face was gone. It was hidden, and soon it would disappear altogether. By tomorrow morning it would be different than it had been; even now, actually, it was gone. Her voice was gone, too, everything was gone. All that was left were traces of her final humiliation and suffering.

Boiko wanted to wake up the cook, but Dasha restrained him. She was holding on to him now with both hands, but for some reason she kept thinking that he was holding on to her, not vice versa.

Not looking at Dasha, he said "Go to your room" so harshly that she felt that now, finally, her tears would gush. "In the morning, when you wake up, come back to our place."

She had lost control of her voice, but she shook her head and clung to him even harder. *Shame on you! You've thought about so much and learned so much. You used to despise a faint heart. Shame on you. You used to be so proud!* she scolded herself. But the tears were already coming. She couldn't stop them; she gave in, trembling and weeping. "They'll come back!" she whispered, trying to hold back her sobs. "I don't think so," he said, none too confidently. But Dasha refused to stay. In silence she slowly walked out and back to Boiko's house.

All was quiet. The grandmother was already sleeping. Alexei Andreyevich led Dasha to his room, got a bottle of port out from somewhere, and drank down a large glass. She sat on his bed and at that very moment, far away, across the river, a cannon fired over the city.

"Poor girl! Poor little girl!" he said suddenly and turned to her a changed, again somehow new face. "How horrible this all is! You have to get some sleep."

Dasha took off her boots and jacket and lay down on his bed. He sat down beside her, poured himself some more port, and drank it down, listening to the war continuing beyond the walls of his house. He downed another drink, took Dasha's hand and kissed it, but then let it go, and for a long time he looked at his own slender hands and the hair on his fingers. He could hear the shells exploding, flying across the city, and in the intervals of silence, right under the window, in the moonlight and the sweet fragrance of the flowering boulevard, a nightingale was singing, and the louder the cannons rumbled, the louder the nightingale sang, trying to finish its sobbing trill between the rumble and the explosion, while the missile was flying over the streets and gardens.

"Alexei Andreyevich," said Dasha, "give me some medicine, please, to help me stop shaking." He collected himself, stood up, and poured some port into his glass. His eyes were becoming more and more opaque to her.

"Drink this," he said. "It's the best medicine. It's good for everything. Tried and true. Get drunk and everything passes."

Slowly and sweetly, the wine began to have a numbing, dulling effect on Dasha. She was looking at the ceiling now, tears streaming down her face. Horrid plaster cupids, with legs fat as sausages, were running their fat little hands through dead garlands. *I choose good, but not good luck, and I slice the world lengthwise,* she thought. *But for now I just want to forget everything, block it out.* And the sudden lightness with which she asked him an essentially completely new question that had never interested her before astonished even her: "Alexei Andreyevich, why did Dumontelle commit suicide?"

He didn't understand her right away, or chose not to. "Who committed suicide?"

"Dumontelle, the actress."

He stood up. "Why did you think of her just now? I don't know anything about it. What they wrote in the papers was all untrue."

He drank again and poured some more for her. But she pushed the glass away. She was satisfied: *Yes this is better than any medicine.*

It's because of him, she thought.

Rather a long time passed. He sat there but did not look at her. Perhaps he was waiting for her to fall asleep. The bottle was running out.

"Poor kid," he said suddenly, looking at her. "What are you going to do now?" He moved over to the bed. "Why aren't you crying?"

He put his hand on her shoulder. And suddenly Dasha threw herself at him and wrapped her arms around his neck, and pressed her lips to his cheek. Sobs wracked her. It felt as if all that time something had been trying to push them out, and now they had finally burst through. He started back that first instant, but then quickly hugged her tight and pressed her close. "Unlucky kid! Poor kid!" he repeated, no longer conscious of what he was saying or what it meant. The pain intoxicated her more than the wine. Cautiously he laid Dasha back, himself lying down at her feet, and held her hand until she fell asleep. Then he put her sleepy hand on his face and fell asleep himself.

But before falling asleep, it occurred to him that there were days in a man's life when everything suddenly breaks, changes, and emerges from confusion and despair into clarity. The answer to everything that had happened earlier thunders out like those weapons across the river, and like the nightingale, destiny threads out its melody. On such a day, like today, you felt in your own veins, saw with your own eyes that final last straw—the drop that overflows, the thread that breaks. Afterward there was supposed to be a pause for everything gradually to fall into place.

When Dasha woke up in the morning, Boiko had already left the room. The first thing she noticed were the plaster cupids playing in a ray of sunlight. Grief weighed on her, in her breast, crushing her, unbearable, such as she could never have imagined; it was so monstrous, it had no bounds, no limit. And that moment yesterday when she had thrown herself at Alexei Andreyevich to press close to him did not stand in her memory as anything shameful or weak. She thought perfectly calmly about the moment when he, no longer a stranger, laid her down so protectively and himself lay down at her feet and she fell asleep. But what kind of man was this? And what had happened between them yesterday? This was not entirely clear to her. And why had he stayed with her? And what was that face he had, that last one, the one she saw after the first glass? Who was this Boiko?

Dasha looked at the clock. It was nine fifteen. Everything in the room was red. Light poured over the walls and floor and down Dasha's arms: the lumber storehouses were burning. A despondent bell rang a tocsin, and through it the whistle blew from the Fasovsky factories. Dasha jumped up, put on her own dress, which someone had laid out next to her, and opened the door into the dining room. At the breakfast table, in the red light of the storehouses burning across the river, between Alyosha and the grandmother and across from Alexei Andreyevich, sat Tiagin, Dasha's father, wearing an unbuttoned, crumpled but clean military tunic with a broken left epaulette. At dawn his side had taken the town.

She hadn't seen him for more than a month. His unit had not been in the retreating army that had passed through the town. It was she who made the inquiries then to be certain. She had believed that if he was close enough he would come without fail— not because of her mother, whom he had divorced six years before, but because of her, Dasha. And see, he really could be believed, he was one of those people you could count on! He had entered the town at dawn, and by nine he was here.

"Dasha," he said, and the skinny, dusty, still young face she loved so much turned toward her. "Dashenka, your mama . . ." And covering the bottom half of his face with one hand, and pushing his chair back with the other, he stood up and went to her.

But no one cried except the grandmother. Alyosha, his eyes lowered, was red-faced, as if what had happened shouldn't happen in front of other people. Alexei Andreyevich was perfectly calm, purposely calm somehow; he had his original, ordinary face back. And at that moment, in the joy of this reunion with her father, Dasha sensed at last what she had scarcely guessed at yesterday: there was between her father and Boiko, between this house and the Tiagin house, some kind of secret.

The next day, when Dasha and her father returned from the funeral, the house had been cleaned. The doors that had been torn off their hinges were leaned up against cupboards, the broken drawers pushed back into the dressers. The pile of shattered glass and china had been swept up. The bullet marks in the wallpaper, the bayoneted picture, and the traces on the floor from the wiped up filth were all that was left to remind them of the pogrom that had taken place here. The emptiness of these rooms was both terrible and sad. Was this really the old Tiagin house? That night even the nightingale boulevard was not its usual self.

Tiagin went to the window and for a long time looked out at the boulevard's splendid broad expanse, which soldiers were walking down, each on an errand of his own. Dasha was nearby and time was passing, but her weariness was such that she could have lain down and fallen asleep, although it was in fact time to go. A porter was busy at the truck and two old women, crying, passed right under the window. Time was passing. Someone had to say something. Four days earlier, Tiagin had had a horse killed under him and his knee ached since the fall. *Dasha!* he thought to say. *But no, let's wait a while. It's already three now, and it's time, it's time to gather our things and go.*

"I'll be taking you with me, Dashenka. We'll travel together, we must! Arinushka will help you collect your things. Don't take too much. After all, we won't be staying here. This evening we'll probably have to leave. And you can't stay on alone. You understand, after all, we might never come back so that's out of the question. I can't, I simply can't consent to that." There was a passion and sorrow in his voice. She was standing quite close and did not take her eyes off him.

"I'll try to send you along to the Crimea, I'll find a way. You'll get to meet your little sister there, and my wife." At that moment the clock began chiming and chiming, over and over. It was broken and always chimed like that.

"You're a big girl now," Tiagin continued, "but there's still quite a lot you can't understand. You must have guessed a long time ago, of course. Boiko is terribly guilty before me. But your mama's death reconciles everything because death is reconciling in general. . . . Any death is awful, Dashenka. And I'm so tired now that I can't feel anything for Boiko but indifference and, yes—gratitude. Forgive me, I really don't want to talk to you about this, but thank God he was here; if it hadn't been for him, you probably would not have been saved. How can I be anything but grateful to him?"

Now everything coalesced for Dasha, all her thoughts, all her feelings, in a single memory: Alexei Andreyevich emerging from their front door that evening a week ago (and she was coming home from lessons and it was as warm and dark and quiet as velvet). They had deceived her for so many years, she hadn't suspected anything, she hadn't noticed. Why was it all done in secret? Because of her perhaps? What had their intentions been? Her mother had loved him. And he had loved her. Oh, how she wished they could all be together now, all three of them, surrounding her. But that was impossible, impossible forever, for good.

There was nothing she could say in reply. Arinushka came in bringing coffee and then Dasha had to pack. Meanwhile, Tiagin stretched out on the broad couch and fell asleep, still wearing his unbuttoned tunic, and in the slit of his shirt a small cross flashed but also something else attached to the cross. And probably whatever that was attached to it was the most important thing for him. *And what is going to be the main thing for us one day?* thought Dasha.

Before their departure, that evening, Boiko came over. Yes, he knew this house well. Without asking anyone he walked straight into the room where Tiagin was lying.

"Colonel, you and I will probably never see each other again," said Alexei Andreyevich. "I have something to tell you."

Tiagin sat up on the sofa, smoothed his hair back with a

comb, and in a habitual gesture passed his hand over his chin: Did he need a shave? "I really think, Alexei Andreyevich, that you and I would do better not to talk. My gratitude for Dasha's sake is unbounded, believe me. And beyond that, we really have nothing to say to each other."

But Alexei Andreyevich sat down in the armchair and took a cigarette out of a green cigarette case with a large monogram. "You are a man who never denies himself the small pleasures of life," Boiko began, "but you could not forgive me a great love." Tiagin frowned. "You don't like the word? Are you shocked that I'm dotting the i? But after all, it did happen, *it happened,* Colonel, and since it did, why can't we talk about it?"

"I'm counting on your delicacy. I trust you'll say all this briefly, as briefly—"

"I'm a man of the old school, Colonel. Someone once said (Belinsky, I think), 'I'm not a son of my era, I'm just a son of a bitch.' But you see, when it comes to me, I'm a son of my era and never was or will be a son of a bitch. And my era—"

"I don't understand, nor do I wish to understand, your crude insinuations."

"And I love my era," Boiko continued, barely raising his voice, "I love it because, although I was born in the previous era, I have never known any other, nor will I."

"And I detest it."

"And you lay your life down for it though you detest it?"

Tiagin had been about to clean his nails with the small file he kept in his left pocket, but he decided that would be overdoing it. Right then he hated Alexei Andreyevich.

"This is why nothing will ever work out for you," Alexei Andreyevich began again. "Because you hate your own era, you don't understand it, you're a hundred years behind it, and you're still wrapped up in your reverse utopias. But that's not what I wanted to say to you, not that, nor have I come to tell you about my 'great love.' This is farewell, you might say, because you won't take the town back a second time, you know that. You'll leave for God knows where—the Caucasus maybe, or maybe the far side of the Urals. Or maybe even abroad. I don't pity you, Colonel. You're doing what you can. You can't do anything else."

Tiagin stood and walked up to Boiko. *"You're* saying this to *me? You're* talking like this to *me?* You ruined my life, broke up my family—"

"That's not true! You know the very first year after the wedding you broke up your family yourself. As for your life, it's positively flourishing."

Tiagin fell silent.

"But you continue to think that you can live any way you please. No, Colonel"—and suddenly Boiko's eyes flared—"you can't go on living any way you please. You must have a conscience!"

This was another insinuation, and now Tiagin no longer had any doubt as to why Boiko had come or what he was about to say.

"I'm guilty before you," Boiko said, lowering his voice again. "Yes, I'm guilty. But believe me, we both paid a high price for everything, both she and I. Everything worked out wrong, not the way we wanted. There was no family happiness, no life together, there was the constant anxiety—"

"The whole town knew about your liaison."

"But Dasha didn't know and Alyosha didn't know. We lived apart and loved each other in secret. My first wife wouldn't give me a divorce. We lived in this hell of wartime and revolutionary provincial life. Each of us had a child by someone else. . . . But we did have our love. We had our loyalty. And now my life is over."

Who's going to check up on that? thought Tiagin, but he did not interrupt. He himself had never suffered over women, so he felt a little awkward. Alexei Andreyevich got on his nerves. And what he was leading up to disturbed him as well.

"You and I have had occasion to clash not once but twice," Boiko began again. "This was fate—mine and yours. For you, Dumontelle was a diversion while you were on the march. For me she was a fine colleague. We worked together for a long time and were very attached to one another. For some reason my mother loved her, and she spent a lot of time with us. . . . Rumor ascribed her death to my cruelty, my coldness. You know what the reason was for her despair. Don't interrupt me! Colonel, that reason was you. You treated her like an abandoned, useless thing, after concealing the fact that you have a family in the Crimea that you would never part with."

Tiagin frowned. All this was beginning to make him angry. "Alexei Andreyevich." He spoke in a voice that had become quite nasty. "Have you come here to lecture me? *You're* lecturing *me?* I don't need you to tell me that I'm partially to blame in this story, but I'm not a child. I take full responsibility. Are you hoping to challenge me to a duel perhaps? Be my guest, I'm ready. Although I must say you've chosen a rather inauspicious moment."

"I didn't choose it!" Boiko shouted suddenly. "I didn't have a choice. You're here. That's enough. In an hour you'll be gone and I'll never see you again. Dumontelle had a child by you. That child is now six months old. And I'm adopting her."

Tiagin staggered back. He'd had a presentiment of this. Yes, he had known that this was precisely what would be said. He recalled snatches of pathetic letters written during the burning heat that drove him on to Oryol, Kursk, and Poltava. He knew how to defend himself by being cold: "I'm very grateful to you, Alexei Andreyevich," he said with a barely perceptible hint of irony. "But are you so sure it's my child? Actually, though, you're doing a good deed."

Boiko stood up. "Is that all?" he asked, looking at Tiagin with a certain distrust, as if he didn't believe that the person standing before him was still a man essentially like him. "First that cry about a duel, the vapid words; then the hackneyed question, which absolutely begged to be asked. And then a compliment. Lord, we really are crude in comparison with you. We really are artless and ingenuous! I had never thought that I was doing a good deed."

He walked toward the door, stunned. Had there been any point in coming? Away from here, he had to get away from here. . . . There had not been any point in coming. This was a different world, alien to him, incomprehensible, hostile even, a cold world of irony and mistrust. A world of empty formulas and outmoded loopholes. This man had different blood running in his veins. Once this meant chivalry and nobility, but now it was something not very well thought through, hastily understood, a touch dirty.

Tiagin walked up to Alexei Andreyevich and shook his hand.

"Don't think of me as a scoundrel," he said. "You're a marvelous man, I've always known that, and I thank you. It's not always so easy, you know. You can't make yourself over. Now other people are coming to take our place, people with a different psychology. Maybe people will live better. You and them together."

"You're wrong, Colonel," said Boiko. "I'm no Bolshevik and I never will be."

He walked out to the front door. Tiagin stopped in the doorway and, no longer contemptuously or maliciously but rather sorrowfully, looked straight ahead. And in that moment his handsome face, which women loved so much, was once again both youthful and sad. Boiko slowed his step.

"It's a girl. I think you should be the one to name her. She hasn't been christened yet," he said.

Tiagin raised his eyes. "Thank you for saying that. Call her Elizaveta. . . . How crazy this all is, Alexei Andreyevich."

"Why? Life is full of all kinds of surprises. You see plenty more in our theatrical life."

"We're about to move out, though!" Tiagin almost replied, but he stopped himself.

"Farewell, Colonel," said Boiko rather too loudly. "I hope you survive."

"Farewell. Thank you. For Dasha, thank you." He nearly said "for everything" but stopped himself in time. More than anything else in the world, he feared appearing ridiculous. This conversation, this whole horrible week, had drained him. For one instant the cause he had been serving seemed lost to him. But the habit of courage sat firmly in him, and in service—though not in life—he was strict with himself. Suddenly that inner delicacy vanished. Anyway, now he had to think in a completely different way, precisely the way he had been taught. He did not notice when Dasha appeared at the front door. All was set for departure. The signal had already come twice and the porter had finished taking out their things.

The house Dasha had been born in seemed to her so sad and old, so long uninhabited, when she stepped across its threshold. It was a shell that had been shed for good, a stage set that had been moved out and had disappeared. Had this house really been her home? And what and where was "her home"?

CHAPTER TWO

Zai, as Elizaveta was called, was fourteen when she found out she was essentially living with strangers, that is, people not related to her by blood. Up until that time she had thought that Alexei Andreyevich Boiko was her uncle, her dead mother's brother, and that the grandmother was her own, blood grandmother. One day, though, they called her into the room she had called "ours" and said that she would have to go away and leave them both. Where? Why?

She had always thought that of the three people among whom she had spent her childhood, one was like a book of fairy tales, the second like a trembling insect, and the third like an intricate sailor's knot. Grandmother was like the book of fairy tales. She was very old, and when she came in at night to make the sign of the cross over Zai, dressed in her long patterned robe, tiny and thin, a halo of gray hair over big black eyes, she would say: "Dear heart! It's time I died! God forgot me!"

But Zai thought Grandmother might never die, she couldn't: she had been readying herself all her life for death; her entire existence, truth be told, had been one long preparation for the life eternal. Grandmother proceeded from one thing to the next with

astonishing faith in the future, constantly setting and secretly re-
solving certain tasks for herself. It was as if she already lived in
eternity without ever having crossed over, as if life eternal had
begun for her on the day she was born. Everything that might be
there was already known, familiar, and ordinary to her, and
everything that was *here* had been forgiven and accepted. Her
soul was made up in such a way that nothing could frighten or
shock her. She had an answer for everything, and that answer
was God. She lived in marvelous concentration. She wore wings
through life and every day she knew precisely what she needed
to do. Her main business was humility and prayer.

The trembling insect was her grandson Alyosha Boiko. His
name would come up in the house (he had already been married
and living in Moscow for two years) as the mischiefmaker and
bully who teased girls like Zai. But that was long ago. During
the years Zai knew him, he gave the impression of a man be-
numbed by questionnaires and political literacy tests, preoccu-
pied with obtaining certain papers, coupons, and passes, constantly fearful of being dismissed from his technical college or
construction site, involved in meetings he naturally never said a
word about. He was afraid of everything. For him there was
nothing but today, with its rain, kasha, and obligations. He had
married, and now he was afraid of his greedy, sharp-tongued
wife. The only surprise was that he hadn't yet been crushed or
borne clean away by a whirlwind.

The third person, who was like an intricate sailor's knot,
was Alexei Andreyevich Boiko. He too had probably been different once, like Alyosha, but no one ever spoke of this, and only
Zai liked imagining him young and cheerful, healthy, smart, and
happy. Now he was old, though not in years, as Grandmother
used to say. He was simply an old man. He worked as a
prompter at the Workers Theater, brought a food ration home
from the cooperative, and everything he wore had reached such
a state of tatters lately that once on the street a Red officer gave

him alms. At age twelve, Zai realized that Uncle Lyosha belonged to a generation that was particularly fond of knotty romantic liaisons, that he had left his wife long ago, and that there had been another woman in his life who had been killed during the Civil War, either by the Reds or the Whites (you were supposed to say the Whites, of course, though it was the Reds). He had never been able to live with her for some reason, and that too had been fashionable.

Everything Zai knew about life and the world she had learned from him, because for as long as she could remember, he had been by her side every free moment he had. He would take her on his knee and tell her stories, and she would doze off, having heard her fill, and when she woke would find him somewhere nearby. But in the last two years, since his son's departure, Boiko had changed. He seemed to be waiting for something. The tension in the house was such that it became quite melancholy at home. As Zai understood it, Boiko was expecting to be fired and the theater shut down. He was anticipating some misfortune for himself and all three of them. Grandmother could barely drag herself from room to room. One day they called Zai in and told her that she might be going away soon, going away alone and forever.

At the time she was studying dance; she had a light, flexible body and a small round head. She had her own mysterious thoughts about what was happening inside her and in secret— but not from Boiko—she was writing poetry.

No one answered her questions about where they were sending her or why. Her grandmother told her to get on her knees in front of the icon. "I don't believe in God," Zai insisted, but her grandmother replied that all that was nonsense, made the cross over her, and promised her the day would come when God would reveal himself to her. In the meantime, Zai had to kneel next to her and repeat the words she said, and submit wholeheartedly, always submit, above all, and also to remember always that revolution, bread rations, arrests, and dance schools were just the specks and trifles of life, but what was genuine, great, terrible, and merciful was God and only God.

Zai, mainly not to distress her, obeyed.

Grandmother asked God (as Zai understood it then) to show Zai the way of wisdom for the rest of her life. "If a letter arrives, that means that is Your will," she said, the tears running down her cheeks, and Zai, at the thought that instead of rebelling and demanding she should submit, felt like crying, too. "If it doesn't, that means that's the way it should be." But a letter did arrive, a couple of months after that evening, and Zai found out she was going to her father.

"Why should I, Uncle Lyosha? He doesn't know me," said Zai.

Alexei Andreyevich chuckled. "So you tell him everything you know about yourself."

"What can I tell him? What do I know about myself? Nothing!"

"Well, tell him him how once when you were six years old, you kissed all the flowers in the garden."

"Is that really interesting?"

"Very. Or how once you took a bag along on May Day to catch the fireworks."

"I took a sack, not a bag."

He chuckled once more. He had no teeth in front and his mouth stretched open long and thin, but his eyes looked at her sadly.

"Zai," he said. "I con't think of anything else for you, no matter how hard I try. Grandmother is completely old now. And me, what am I good for? The dump. I'm going to be completely old, too, pretty soon and no use to anyone."

She hugged and kissed him. Yes, she realized he wasn't sending her away because he wanted to, he was submitting, or, if he was rebelling, then he was doing it in his own way. He wasn't saying goodbye to her so that someone else could take her place.

On the day of her departure, Grandmother pinned a piece of cardboard to her chest with Alyosha's address. She was going abroad via Moscow. Boiko had been arrested just two days before. They came for him one night and took him away, along with two others from the same building. He left perfectly calmly, saying goodbye to Grandmother and to Zai. "Don't forget," he said softly right into her ear, and then he pointed to himself. She watched from the window as they put him in the van, her hand pressed to her chest. He did not look back.

"Dear heart, God forgot me!" cried Grandmother. Was she starting to rave?

Zai boarded the train with the cardboard pinned to her chest. No one could keep from looking at Alyosha's address, Zai most of all.

Another piece of cardboard, this one with a Paris address, was pinned to her by Alyosha at the Moscow train station. The week had passed in a frenzy. She had come to a clear realization of what was happening to her, as if she had been woken from a deep sleep she'd been sleeping up until now. On Christmas night she left the land of blue snows where everything was so frightening. Most of all, it was the immensity of the country that was frightening, and the deep, mournful, remote, and impassable blue of those snows through which Alexei Andreyevich had sent her to a strange place.

Entrusted to the conductor, she sat in her own corner, a blistered finger bandaged up and immobilized. She was carrying away her future, her entire self, her entire lot. For the first time in her life she was alone, among strangers, riding to a strange land, a strange father, a strange family. Boiko was so far away. Grandmother . . . this was a different world already. What world she herself was from, who she was—she still didn't know

any of that, let alone why all this had happened to her. There was
something tremulous and the least bit pathetic about her face,
her darned stockings, the faded ribbon woven into her hair. She
was given a seat by the window, and in the evening she crawled
into the upper berth and lay there, but the train kept moving,
rocking, shaking, telling stories, shaking some more, telling the
same story over and over: *Once upon a time there was Grandmother, Zai, and Uncle Lyosha, the clock in the dining room
had stopped working long ago . . . time to die . . . the ara-
besques . . . the cardboard is bothersome . . . her papa
. . . the poem in which she had recently sung the praises of
doing the laundry . . . Alyosha's wife . . .* At the last minute
she had taken away Zai's warm jacket at the station: "You don't
need it but it will come in handy for little Vasya."

In Warsaw a man with a large round face and completely
gray hair walked into the train compartment and sat down opposite Zai. He looked at her attentively, at her cardboard, at her
basket of provisions, and then opened up a small fat book that
resembled a dictionary and read it for a long time. They spoke a
little in German, and the man told her he was going to Belgium
and he already knew all about Zai. He slapped the book, as if he
had read everything it had to offer him.

The train went on and on, telling the same story over and
over, a story so familiar she could cry. Zai looked out the window at the snow-drifted fields, the jackdaws, the distant horizon.
The man sat opposite, dozing. "We have a three-hour layover in
Berlin," he said, glancing at his book. Zai did not dare ask what
kind of reference book it was.

A change of trains. The second night. All the customs and
checkpoints were behind her. Zai lay down on the upper berth
again. The man went out into the corridor and spent a long time
standing at the window, which you couldn't see anything out of,
only the reflection of his round face, his white hair, and his
hands pressed up against the frame. The night light swayed and

shuddered over Zai's head. She decided to take off the cardboard.

In the morning—Berlin. The man looked at his book and said, "Today is Friday." How strange it all was! He conferred about something with the conductor and Zai guessed they were talking about her. She took fright. The man wanted to take her to the city. He had noticed her torn shoes.

She gave him her arm and they walked down the street, bought newspapers, cigarettes, and chocolate, ate a sandwich apiece in a store where there weren't any waitresses and everything popped out of some kind of opening—an apple, beer, ham. Zai was pleased to be amazed. So far in her life she had had so few occasions to be amazed.

They walked on. Zai was cold; there was a wet snow falling. Her jacket was back with little Vasya and all she had to wear was a wool coat she was terribly ashamed to have grown out of. She saw herself in the mirrored walls of the stores and felt she was not like other children. "Here we have the Museum and this is the Avenue of their Victory." said Zai's companion. "but we aren't going there, but in here." And they walked into a shoe store.

Zai's stockings were completely intact, only heavily darned, and when she tried on new brown shoes with flaps, she almost leapt up with joy. They led her over to a complicated apparatus that looked like a large scale. Through her new shoe, through her darned stocking, through her foot, Zai saw five bones lying evenly and separately—it was the skeleton of her foot She looked and could not believe her eyes, but the man was once again searching for something in his mysterious book. Zai wanted to look at her foot, then her hand. . . . She had never seen herself like that before, from the inside out.

When the train started moving, they set out the food they had bought in their laps and began to eat.

"What kind of people live in your country?" asked the man,

who had become ruddy and cheerful since their walk and the shoe store and the food.

Zai pondered his question. She wanted to give the best answer possible (evidently his reference book didn't have the answer to it). She remembered Alyosha and his wife; she remembered her grandmother and the men who had come to take Boiko away. How far away all that was!

"There are two kinds of people," she said. "Some are like insects. They are half transparent, you can barely see them, they tremble in the light. The others are like carpenter's nails, you can't break them with a hammer no matter how hard you try. They just get stronger. They're scary, especially when they come at night. But the first kind you can squish and not notice! Should I tell you? I myself am more like the first kind."

"Might this be because of serfdom and the Tatar yoke?" asked the man.

Zai didn't answer. She was thinking, and when she was thinking about something, worry appeared in her scrawny face.

In the middle of the night, right before Liège, the man woke her up and gave her his address.

"If you think of me at New Year's, send me a card," he said, and he nodded to her.

"Why just New Year's? I might some other time, too."

"It's the custom to remember one's friends at the New Year," he said, smiling. "I wish you happiness, dear girl."

He took his suitcase off the shelf. The train was already braking hard. "If not for New Year's, then some other time. It doesn't matter," he added.

"Tell me, please, what is that book you have that you're always reading?" Zai got up the nerve to ask.

"It's a special kind of a book." He smiled. "It has everything in it, everything. Very handy."

He waved his hat from the platform, standing under a street lamp, as she looked out into the black night, having pulled back the curtain. She felt like writing a poem about love. She started thinking about what would have happened if she had gotten off with him and moved in with him, how they would have lived. . . . Then her thoughts plunged into disarray, swinging back and forth, to the knocking of the train. And suddenly something stabbed her in the heart: Paris. Her father. Her sisters. Her father's wife. A strange city. A strange country. Her mother's homeland, where her French surname would immediately fit in.

The conductor helped her down the steps of the train car. The Moscow cardboard was hanging around her neck again. In her hands were two baskets, one with linens; the other, books. She stood in the scurrying crowd, in the din of the huge train station, deafened, paralyzed with terror, and she felt that here she was in her entirety: with her very own soul, which she herself didn't know completely yet, with her small body, with all the little bones like those that had been lit up in the shoe store the day before. And everything was so mysterious, both inside her and all around her, in this gray air, in this noise; it was as if a completely new universe was on the verge of opening up to her, with its new laws and puzzles. . . . Before her she saw her father.

"Liza Dumontelle?" said Tiagin. He came up to her and wanted to pick her up. He hadn't expected her to be so big, so tall. He could only hug her, squeeze her shoulders, press her close. He kissed her on the eyes twice. He was dressed rather sloppily and seemed to her very old. He had a nose like an eagle's beak and a beard. Removing his hat, he said something to the conductor and crumpled the money in his hand before giving him a tip. Zai dropped her baskets and looked at him, her eyes full of tears. She was afraid of him.

The day passed and it was no more. It passed, like all the rest, but it seemed so special, so unusually important, difficult, and new. It was no more, as if it never had been. Her stepmother rebandaged her finger and drew her a bath. Zai got the doors in the apartment mixed up and took fright when the gas ignited in the kitchen. Nothing could make her change clothes in front of her sisters and she opened her baskets with excruciating shame. Then everyone went somewhere and only her stepmother Liubov Ivanovna remained. Zai sat in the kitchen for two hours watching her iron the linen and listening to the clock tick.

"And what did you eat?" asked Liubov Ivanovna. "What could you buy on his salary? How much did he earn? Was he still handsome or was he already old? Was he directing plays? Acting himself? What about the old woman? Did she beat you?"

Zai replied that they had plenty of everything—potatoes, kasha, even bread—that Uncle Lyosha was very handsome, though he was missing some teeth and so skinny that Grandmother said he was frightening to look at. And that no one ever beat her. Just the opposite, everyone loved her an awful lot, even Alyosha, who was married in Moscow now. And that Alyosha was really embarrassed when his wife took the jacket off her for little Vasya.

"She took your jacket off you?" asked Liubov Ivanovna, and suddenly she froze with the iron in her hand.

"Yes, Liubov Ivanovna."

"I'm not Liubov Ivanovna to you, I'm Auntie Liuba," she said, and she dropped the iron on the plate with a clatter.

I've made her angry, thought Zai. *Lord, if You exist, please help me!*

She spent the entire evening alone with her father. She struggled with her terrible shyness. She told him about Boiko, about what he had been like in the last few years, what kinds of plays they were doing at the Workers Theater (but without him now), where they often went with the tickets he was able to get.

"Did actors come to visit you? Actresses?" asked Tiagin.

"No, no one came to visit."

"At one time he had ideas of his own, interesting ideas. He was talented and left-wing."

"He never talked about that."

"Did he suffer over being a prompter?"

She didn't know whether he suffered or not. He never talked about that either. What did he talk about?

"He used to tell me stories about different things. All sorts of odd things. I used to study dance. They didn't tell me about anything there."

"Do you speak French?"

"Yes. And a little German."

Her grandmother had taught her that. They had read Hugo, *L'homme qui rire*. It was very boring.

Tiagin said, "Everyone here is going to love you. Even Sonia. You have not come to strangers. This is your country, your mother was born here. And please, eat properly, you're so skinny. You are going to feel more at home here than anyone else."

Zai was finally left alone. There was one more bed in the room they showed her, but she didn't have the nerve to ask which one of her sisters it belonged to. She got down on her knees beside her bed, laid her head down, and started thinking hard. She was trying to remember the prayer Grandmother used to make her say. Yes, "it was His will," the letter had come, and here she was, but she couldn't remember a single word. She crawled under the blanket and turned off the light. They had taken Alexei Andreyevich away from her and Grandmother had let her go. Alyosha had such a greedy wife. The man from the train had taken his marvelous book away with him forever. He had given her the shoes, as if she were a beggar, and her bones had been lit up—so still, so frightening. The bones were still inside her. And her soul too sliced through her body, and yet it was still and frightening. Next she pictured a big transparent trembling insect crawling across the floor on bent legs and straightening itself up with the help of its stub of a tail. "Could that really be me?" The door to the bathroom wasn't closed all the way. Someone was washing up there, brushing her teeth, and then started singing softly in French.

It was a long song about some prince galloping through the woods, in the days of knights; his feet were in golden stirrups, and his steed was covered in foam. In a castle a princess was waiting for him. He was returning from a campaign; he had left a year before on a campaign with King Renaud. The princess was standing by the tall window looking out into the distance. The road was dusty. The prince was racing in the early dawn to his beloved. . . .

Dasha stopped singing and entered cautiously, but Zai made a movement to show she wasn't asleep.

Dasha sat down on the low stool alongside Zai's bed. She lit the lamp on the table. She was wearing thin-striped pajamas. Zai was all eyes looking at her.

"I guess this means they arrested him?" said Dasha. "But what for? What do you think? Was he working against them?"

"Of course not. They didn't arrest him for anything. Though now I think he must have had a presentiment. Otherwise he wouldn't have started trying to figure out a way for me to leave. It was obvious he assumed this might happen. That's why he wrote here."

"Did he love you?"

"Yes. A lot."

"And is Grandmother still alive?"

"Yes. And she's still saying it's time to die."

"And what about Alyosha? Is he still the same smart alec he always was? Once he wanted to cut off my braid. You must have had it pretty rough from him."

"Alyosha? What do you mean! He's as mild-mannered as can be. He's afraid of every little thing. I have no idea how a man like that can be alive."

"Is the Tiagin house still standing?" asked Dasha after a pause.

"What house is that? I guess so. A communal cafeteria has opened up there now."

Dasha lit a cheap cigarette.

"So," she said. "Well, tell me more."

But Zai didn't know what else to tell her. She didn't feel like talking about Alexei Andreyevich or their evenings together.

"Was Boiko afraid of everything as well?" asked Dasha.

"No, he wasn't afraid of anything. He was just very sad. And always very lonely. He liked my poems."

"Recite a poem."

"Maybe later. I wrote one about the laundry. I always liked it a lot when Grandmother and I were hanging the linens out, and I always tried to make it as colorful as I could."

"Didn't he ever talk about me?"

"No, never. Only when the passport came, he said he knew Papa and you well. He said he'd never seen Sonia."

"He was my first love," said Dasha, smiling. "Afterward, when we went away. I had such a crush on him! I wanted to run back. . . . Have you been in love yet?"

"A little, just now. With someone who was traveling on the train."

Dasha laughed softly and said that it really was long past their bedtime.

"I'll recite a poem," said Zai. "Listen!"

Sitting down on the bed, she recited, not without a certain pride:

The Laundry

How pleasant in the midst of work
And cares befitting us alone,
To feel on hands all pink from laundry
The touch of warm and soapy foam.

I know there have been other times,
The most magnificent of worlds,
That in the springs we used to see
The gentlest of women, wives and girls,

And in the hour as noon approached
The tsar's young daughters, humbled yet,
Brought hands to face and smelled their palms
The air of the sea, the salt and wet.

Dasha took the cigarette away from her lips and stared at her sister. A rather long silence ensued.

"What an odd girl you are!" she said. "And what fine poems you write!"

Later she walked around the room, moved the lamp closer to the head of her bed, chose a book off the shelf, crushed out her cigarette butt, and lay down.

"What pretty shoes you have, and brand new," she said. "Where did they buy those for you?"

"In Moscow, Alyosha's wife," said Zai without blinking. She turned to the wall, pulled the blanket over her head, and suddenly fell asleep, the way only children do.

CHAPTER THREE

Sonia Tiagina's Notebook

I walked over to the bookshelf in Zai's room and stood there for a long time trying to find something to read. The Russian classics are magnificent—but they weren't written for me or about me. I've tried to find their virtues, not their classroom merits, but the other ones, and I can't. So I stood there looking at the spines of foreign editions of our writers and thought: I don't want this one—he laughs at what isn't funny at all; or that one— he died young and never had the chance to become wise; or this other one—because there's a lot of moralizing about family happiness and unhappiness in him; or the fourth one—his heroes are bored and so is he; and this next one always has too many heroes and they talk too intelligently; this next one is always lashing out at something: that leaves me completely cold; the seventh goes on and on about nature, what do I know or care about nature; the eighth is a foreigner, plus which he's so strident that his poems crack like nuts. So I walk away from the bookshelf. I even start feeling sorry for myself, my ugly old self, though at the bottom of my soul I feel utter self-satisfaction at my originality and the daring of my opinions.

Meanwhile, the only thing I want in life is happiness.

Not tranquillity or freedom but happiness. I'm not looking for moments to plant and cultivate—I want an assured, nontransient state of happiness. Absolutely, constantly complete. Totalitarian happiness, so to speak. And my task, my goal, the entire meaning of my life, is to find that happiness.

But what is that absolute? Of what does it consist? A pile of gold coins? A handsome, broad-shouldered, intelligent boy? A cozy nest? An immortal masterpiece I create? Communion with God?

My happiness has nothing to do with any of those things.

My happiness I still haven't found—it would be unquestionably real, palpable, indisputable harmony with the world I came out of and to which I will return. This world is more than God who is part of it. For me this world is everything, the only happiness that seems complete and perfect to me is being in tune with this world, merging with it, sharing its common storms and common harmonies.

When I find this absolute, I won't just keep it to myself. I'll tell people about it, and those who want to will hear me. I'll show it to them—and I'll show myself to them. Happiness for oneself alone is too possible, too attainable, too temporary, not absolute. Only harmony with the world is absolute. But the world doesn't want me!

About a year ago I faced a certain temptation. It seemed to me then that my solitude was happiness and harmony, that somehow I had achieved the absolute. I was stunned, crushed. It was all inside me: good (because I love good more than evil and virtue more than sin); beauty (my own); and truth (for me any truth is higher than any lie).

I was equal to the world.

I lived inside this temptation for a while. But I couldn't go without the world—without my connection to it.

I couldn't not reflect its tortured rebirths, not follow its unresolved issues, its dirt, blood, and beauty. Its malice, depravity,

unbelief, and greatness. Solitude turned out to be merely the
form of my existence—which I liked more than other forms—
but it couldn't be the content of my life.

I see a map of hemispheres, I listen to the noise of the city, I
examine a new strain of infinitely small cells, I read social laws.
Man kills man; man kills himself for the sake of man; in the
steppes of the East a new tyrant is born; a comet crashes into a
star.

Everything going on in the world, the universe, affects me. I
don't feel Russian or French; I don't feel like a woman, or a
man, or a person, or an animal.

I want to be a part of the world, the way people may once
have been a part of God. They sought a connection with God—
God was them, they left God and returned to God, they trembled
close to Him and finally were taken into His lap. One day, I'll go
away like that into the lap of the world, but first I have to feel
like a part of it.

I felt like explaining all this to B. one day just this spring,
when we were walking along where everyone strolls on the
quay. He had offered me a job in the bookstore. To work for him.

"What do you live on?" he made himself ask. A question
like this goes completely against his upbringing.

I made myself answer him: "Mainly I live off my father and
sister. Sometimes I work as a model for 'art photographs.' And
last year, as you know, I defended my dissertation in the History
Department."

Answers like that are very Russian and flabbergast the
French—but they get a big kick out of them all the same.

What flabbergasts us are the streets of our shame, and we
are silent. The streets traverse all of Paris, and we walk them:

avenue de Malakoff,
boulevard de Sébastopol,
place de l'Alma,

rue de Crimée,
and so on and so forth.

But I didn't say that.

We were walking along the river, down where the city feels like it's somewhere high above you, like a first sky. I was going on about how a creation is greater than its creator—about how we all know this perfectly well but hypocritically won't admit it. B. immediately moved to religion, on religion as opposed to belief, on the connection among religions, including my "religion."

I defended myself.

Then he switched to the books of the New Testament and said that a few days ago he had read the Epistle to the Romans, which had depressed him. He said that if you replace "circumcised" with "Party" and "heathens" with "non-Party," and then also "Father, Son, and the Holy Ghost" with those other names (which B. hated), it turned out that a highly placed individual in a certain international organization was writing a memorandum to his subordinate "apparatchik" supporters: he promised the same speedy ruin of capitalism—"Soon God shall crush Satan"; the same command, "Do not reason overmuch!" ("Do not bandy sophistries"); the same cry, "No disputing of opinions!" and the same firm counsel to submit to authority (it comes "from God"). He said there's even something about being civil to one another, about discipline and self-criticism. But most of all: everyone should think and say the same thing.

For me, of all the holy books only the Gospels are precious, so I listened to B. with interest. At one time the Gospels played an enormous role in my life—back in the Crimea, after Papa was wounded and Dasha arrived. (At that same time I felt inexplicably driven to mean tricks. It was as if I wanted to test evil, or test myself in evil. I had no compunctions about making petty compromises with my conscience—I didn't treasure its purity at all. I didn't treasure myself or my unsulliedness.)

The Gospels revealed the beauty of goodness to me, but the full significance of this revelation I didn't understand right away; I was still my old self for a while. Later, after I came to Paris (not long before Zai appeared in our house), I suddenly saw that despite all my sinfulness, I love the truth more than anything in the world. I shouted it out to myself—what joy: I love truth more than lies! That was the day of my resurrection. Now I believe that all my pettiness, irresponsibility, and insensitivity to what is good, noble, lofty, and beautiful is just the legacy of my childhood—just what I brought with me into this life and now have outgrown. How could it be otherwise? (And I also wonder—why did I outgrow it all so forcefully—yet not altogether consciously—mysteriously even?)

I remember myself at twelve—and at fifteen. I could be a tattle-tale, inform, lie, steal, be a coward, hide from the truth, spoil things maliciously, wish death on my near and dear, and hate without rhyme or reason.

That's all over. Everything petty, base, and false has fallen away from me.

A sense of responsibility has come—and for this I am indebted to my era: if I eat chicken, it's only because I know I could slaughter it myself.

Responsibility. Who ever knew its sweet burden the way we do? In other times a commander might have been responsible to his emperor, a head of household for his offspring, a free man for his conscience. But the world has grown old and wise in the last half-century; responsibility is more valuable than it was in our fathers' day: then everyone lived just that little bit haphazardly, slipshod, however God predisposed them. The fear of God was on its last legs. Our era brought with it Responsibility. Awareness. The dream of our fathers and mothers may still be dragging itself out, but we are living in reality, we are wide awake—we have a hundred ideas. And no wonder. We were shaken awake by a world war, the Russian revolution, the fall of empires; we were woken up by words like "equality" and "collective," "freedom" and—in unprecedented proportions—the loss thereof; we were woken up by our love—and our hatred— for the world, our love and our hatred for mankind.

B. and I talked about all this that spring evening there on the quay, below the city, beside the water, during those months when I read and worked in my room for nights on end and slept in the daytime, let my opportunities slip. In the evening we walked there. I didn't have a coat because my last one had been singed on the stove in that cramped atelier on the rue Boissonade where we danced so much. I was ashamed of walking around with a patch on my side so in April I was wearing just a jacket and skirt—no stockings, no gloves, no hat—my teeth chattering and my hands blue. (A bit later I picked up some tutoring, Latin and Greek, a moron stuck in the fourth form, and extricated myself.) B. asked me what, in my opinion, made our times different from all the ones that came before. I replied:

"Human consciousness. The last quarter-century has suffered so many changes and in so many respects that it's become unlike anything it ever was before. A few completely new elements have come into the picture.

"First our awareness of our own worth—almost universally we have outlived slavishness—and that used to be the privilege of only a few.

"Second is a feeling of man's universality. Despite nationalistic theories and dogma, this feeling, once incomprehensible, once familiar only to individual geniuses, is now gripping more and more people—it's getting to be the norm.

"Third is the weakening of blood ties—the voice of the clan—not universal, of course, but a hundred years ago anarchy seemed like a paradox, and it frightened us, whereas today it seems as natural as the voice of blood.

"In fourth place let's put the expiration of shame—not just bodily shamelessness but an inner liberation, knowing yourself, fearlessly judging yourself. Everyone may not admit it but each of us knows.

"The fifth element is the rift between individual belief and the Church, a rift accepted as fact by individuals if still rejected by society.

"And last, our attitude that our own death is one of the moments of our own life that we can control."

In three or four minutes I had laid out everything I'd been thinking about every day—and maybe every night—for the past ten years. It was as if a knight who had loved a lady in secret for ten years had gone down on one knee and declared at last: I love you.

We were sitting on one of those benches by the water which reflected the tenderly green trees, young and old. The sunset blazed under and over the bridge, and my thoughts flew into this bridge-split sun. Having said the "I love you" that had been searing my lips for ten years, it was good to be quiet now and not expect an answer.

B. took off his jacket and pullover and put his jacket back on, while I, at his insistence, put on his soft warm pullover. We remained sitting on the bench a little longer. At the opposite bank was a barge, and on it a radio was playing and a woman was innocently looking at the same sky as we were.

I don't know whether B. said anything in reply to my words, which had cost me so much. I think he found it all very interesting, curious, worthy of attention. . . . He was already very distant from me then. Now I've nearly lost him from view. I still have his pullover. He has plenty of others.

He might have objected. Half a year has passed now since my conversation with him, and I'm disagreeing with myself. All this *newness* was of course anything but. You can stretch a thread of thoughts, presentiments, and intuitions from genius to genius; the predictions they made about the future and us have now come to pass.

But I'm not interested in geniuses or their prophesies.

I think about those who have barely left a trace, ordinary people whose names are known to a very few and who will soon drown in oblivion. These unremarkable people, simple mortals, walked ahead of their time, lived and died in obscurity, and, what is most important, were never recognized by the very geniuses, their contemporaries, who had prophesied about them. What Dostoevsky spoke and wrote about was in part already alive all around him. He didn't know it, but it was there. Might he have been afraid of it? This refers to his correspondence with Kovner, which I'm rereading.

I regard everyone who seems coarse and primitively cruel toward themselves and others, everyone who shocks me or evokes my disgust, disbelief, or hostility, with great caution. The new always seems coarser than the old. The old has worn thin to the vanishing point.

It is autumn now. I'm sitting in my room in front of two open books, which I took from my own shelf, not Zai's. This is how I read: two books simultaneously. And often one author has harbored no suspicion of the other's existence.

I am reading two books simultaneously and I am listening to two people simultaneously: myself and Zai, who is sitting in her room. A ponderous discordance—a deafening alarm—keeps mounting inside me. Where is my world, my intact and only world? Might it never be revealed to me, never absorb me? I treasure my connection to it more than I do my own self. There everything is straightforward, holy, and harmonious.

Through the open door I can hear Zai singing. She is sewing something, very quickly; her hair is down. She is singing some French song. I've heard it a few times already. Someone is galloping through the forest on his steed, in the moonlight. The horseman is racing to a tall castle where his beloved awaits him. She is standing by the window and watching the road. . . . For me, this marvelous old song is France, unattainable and beloved France, which will never realize what it has meant to me.

No, I don't want to die. I still want to live.

CHAPTER FOUR

D asha was working in a bank as secretary to the director. From the very start of her life in Paris she had sailed with the current. Almost immediately after her arrival she had had to earn her own living, and since she didn't feel a calling to anything in particular, it was especially easy for her to choose.

For the first years after his arrival in Paris, without two coins to rub together, as the saying goes, Tiagin dabbled in speculation and over the course of more than ten years would fly high and then plummet, without ever having anything reliable. Depending on the prosperity that first disappeared and then reappeared, their domestic circumstances would change, as would the appearance of Tiagin and Liubov Ivanovna themselves. The colonel would look crumpled, sullen, and demeaned one day and calm, self-assured, and with the remnants of gentility in his manners the next. People said either that he was rather tedious and pathetic or else that he still had his wits and his good looks.

It so happened that Tiagin's partner in many of these enter-prises was the owner of a small bank on the Grands Boulevards, a man who had arrived in Paris before the others and, perhaps for that reason, had succeeded. Dasha began working for him, at first gluing stamps and answering telephone calls, but after about five years, when she had finished night school, she moved to the large building across the street where things constantly hummed, as in a factory, and she took a seat behind a broad desk. A double door, upholstered in fabric like the door to the holy of holies, led to the office where Leon Moreau's father had once sat, where Leon Moreau himself sat now, and where, in the future, Leon Moreau's son was supposed to sit.

In recent years Tiagin's speculating had not gone badly. An apartment was bought on a back street on the Left Bank that was unlike other Paris streets: the entrance to the blind alley began at the gates of another building and the place was hard to find on a map, somewhere between rue Saint Dominique and the Ministry of Industry. Some land was bought outside Paris, wooded land, albeit rather poor, and for a while it seemed that things would always be this way. Suddenly, though, his affairs took a nose-dive. For a few months the entire household lived on Dasha's salary and the country wasteland was sold. Tiagin was prepared to work as a guard in a garage if he had to, but soon things took another turn, everything fell into place, their debts were swiftly consolidated, and for Christmas Liubov Ivanovna bought herself a large, highly polished wooden radio.

They lived in a spacious but dark apartment. The windows looked out on a street that was more like a courtyard or a huge hall with overhead lighting, especially if you walked through it at twilight, crossing it on the diagonal, across the deserted pavement. In the silence of stone buildings, steps resonated as in a cathedral.

Tiagin had extricated himself from the situation with an alacrity no one had expected. He had greatly changed over these years: there was not a trace of his youthfulness. He was completely gray. Women, whom out of habit he continued to court sometimes, thereby evoking his wife's passionate jealousy, thought of him as one of the last representatives of the "old school." He simply could not get used to his false teeth. His eyes were lifeless, and you could tell from his face that he had already given a lot of thought to death. His skinniness hinted at some concealed illnesses, but like a well-trained mount, he maintained his old habits, was still at times even loquacious and witty, and chose not to notice that at home they looked on him as something fragile and perhaps even not long for this world.

A year before Zai's arrival, Tiagin had lost a large sum of money for something like the sixth time, only this time it wasn't just his own. Everyone realized there would be no more getting back on his feet. Sonia displayed her utter indifference to the changes that had come about at home. Liubov Ivanovna let the maid go and began cooking and cleaning herself. Tiagin had to take a job for a mere two thousand, and there came to reign in the house that troubled spirit of concern when there is never enough money from one month to the next.

Still Zai felt as if there had never been poor or hungry people in Paris. For months she could not get used to the idea that there was always enough bread for everyone, that there was wool in the house for darning holes, that for a franc you could be in a cheerful large store where music played all day and buy a pink comb that turned soft in hot water, and for two francs, a sky blue toothbrush. And when Dasha tried to explain that the pink comb and in fact all those things bought to music were dreadfully unattractive and embarrassing to have in the house, Zai didn't understand. For her these things held so much poetry and joy and she loved them so tenderly! She even wrote poems entitled "Floor Washing" and "Shoe Shining," and how she reconciled all this with her fear of the gas stove when lit in the kitchen or the gates of the Prefecture where she had been taken several times to straighten out her papers, was beyond all understanding.

Dasha told Zai frankly what she thought of her poems: "I like the fact that you talk about yourself as a bee, about the wax for the floors, and as an ant on the subject of turpentine and shoe polish, but I find it odd that you never write about anything but chores and that they all turn out so cheerfully."

But Zai couldn't explain why other things failed to inspire her.

Three years later this phase had passed and a year after that she couldn't even make herself remember "about the chimney sweep who is like Father Christmas because he comes to the house once a year and cleans the chimney, like a musician in a wind orchestra." At one time even Sonia liked that poem.

When Zai turned eighteen, she did not like to study. On the other hand, she did like being at home with Liubov Ivanovna and also she liked walking up and down the streets by herself.

"Where do you go walking?" they asked her.

"Around," she replied. Nonetheless, she did have to study and she did so reluctantly.

She went outside in the winter at twilight and in the summer at the very end of the day, when the lights were being turned on in all the buildings but not the street lamps yet, at the hour when it was easy to look into strangers' windows. She would have liked to have known everything about the people she saw through the windows. Oh, that parlor with the half-circle of window above the darkness and rain of the rustling boulevard! In there, a chandelier cast a wide circle above a woman, a fine-boned and stern woman, who was waiting in an armchair, erect and motionless. *I will come stand under this window in ten or twenty years. What happiness to know that the world stands firm and eternal, that the chandelier burns night after night, for years, centuries, millennia, and the woman sits under it all the time, her gaze riveted on the darkening city sky.*

Turn the corner, and on the first floor of a large new building children were gathering around a table: two boys and two girls. They were doing something—studying their lessons or playing or drawing . . . she couldn't tell. But they were living and growing. They would live for a long time, forever. A hundred years from now they would be leaning around the table in exactly the same way and doing something quickly with their hands and a woman would bring in four glasses of milk and four rolls on a tray. *Oh this stable stone world I've landed in! You don't know me, I'm learning how not to be afraid of you. I come from a world that has collapsed, cracked, smashed to pieces, frightening me for life. It's a secret. Not a word to anyone.*

In a dark side street, in a half-cellar—they were just about to notice her and close the shutter. But no! This summer's evening the window was wide open and a dark hand in a faded sleeve was holding a glass of red wine—like yesterday, and the day before yesterday, and last month. *So drink, drink that wine. What are you waiting for? What's the hurry? No one is going to take it from me, no one can come in and see me. I'm at home and it's mine. A piece of Camembert on a plate, a fish tail moved to the edge. I do what I want. It's up to me! Tomorrow we'll make our demands and the day after we'll go on strike. Oh joy, joy eternal! No one can take away your wine or Camembert, your rights, or your freedom! It's time for me to stop trembling at every knock on the door.*

This was how Zai walked up and down the streets, until the street lamps came on. Then it was all over. Shutters slammed, curtains were drawn, the buildings became blind and mute and the streets came to life. Zai returned to her own blind alley, which resembled a courtyard room, abandoned, echoing, and dim.

Sometimes there were guests at home, and then Zai went into the kitchen, where she had loved sitting since the day she arrived and where she listened to the voices and the sound of the dishes. All these people were complete strangers to her and she had nothing to say to them.

Dasha arrived in time for tea, gave her a hug, and said, "You know, this year *it* definitely has to happen."

And Zai knew she was talking about their trip together in

the summer, when Dasha had her vacation. She had talked about
it last year, too, and the year before that, but they hadn't gone.
And now here it was again. Zai waited: she knew one day it
would happen.

And this year they did go. And although Zai had never seen
the sea, they did not go to the sea because Dasha had decided to
go to the mountains. She had three weeks of freedom, something
she had not had for a long time.

They settled in a large and noisy pension on the shore of a
cold clear lake where they swam in the morning and where there
were flat pink stones on the shore over which it was very pleasant to step barefoot. There were two sailboats and several row-
boats one could take out in the late afternoon to watch the sun
set in the narrow slit between the two mountains. Some young
Danes staying in the same place often took the sailboats out and
when Dasha and Zai went for their afternoon walk, they could
see the boats scudding far off over the water. The higher up they
went, the tinier and more vivid were the two sails flashing on the
water's deep blue.

The mountains smelled warmly of heather and pine. Dasha
and Zai lay on the dry pine needles, looking at the sky, or they
leaned over a chasm and ran their gaze along the whole lengthy
mountain path they had taken: the stones and bushes burnt by
the sun, the worn stone steps here and there. This path took them
to a half-ruined medieval castle, which from a distance looked
perfectly round, majestic, and gloomy—and dead. There,
through the narrow embrasures, they could see the contours of
the stern, sun-beaten, hazy landscape, which opened up to them
from the flat roof, and far away, even higher up and even more
severe, there was another castle they could not walk to. It was
nothing more than a stone outline.

Dasha especially loved the descent through the forest: suddenly the broad road opened up and down it a toylike red bus
would roll or a tiny automobile, though they couldn't hear them.

All around was the same hot, hovering, turquoise silence. The road led to a village where there was a small church and a low-slung mayor's office. From the bakery came the aroma of hot bread. Striped ticking hung above the butcher shop. A dusty boredom spread around the post office; there were chickens and flies. And here was the lake and the big house where the left window on the third floor was their room and on the window sill two bathing suits were drying, green and red like the Italian flag.

A group formed very quickly around the Danes (two young men and one young woman). Dasha joined them, as did two French women, one of whom was expecting a baby, a man of indeterminate nationality who spoke all languages, and a cellist from the Bordeaux opera along with his wife. In the evening they danced in the big hall, which had windows looking out on the lake, and in the day when it rained they played ping-pong and were noisy. Often they took pictures of themselves sitting astride the verandah railing or in the wicker armchairs when they were waiting, hungry and half-naked, for the dinner gong.

The man of indeterminate nationality was not Russian. Dasha immediately became convinced of this when she saw the mail that came for him. His newspaper was in an unfamiliar language, and his letters had colorful stamps unlike any she'd ever seen. When they asked him where he was from, he said that he himself didn't really know, since the state he was born in (some thirty-five years before) had not existed for a long time, and now in its place there was a completely different one with which he was not on good terms. Moreover, he said that he had four different kinds of blood in him and he could never decide which was the real one: Hungarian, Norwegian, Irish, or Polish? He still didn't have a passport, he still needed one more document. All this was very interesting, and everyone sat around him on the shore, Turkish fashion, and listened to his story. His deep blue eyes could not be seen behind his dark glasses, but his mouth was always smiling.

One evening, Dasha danced with him and then they strolled along the shore until late and laughed a great deal when they admitted to each other that they considered this shore, this castle, this corner of the earth sort of their own property.

"It's as if we possessed one undivided property together," said the man, whose name was Jan Ladd. "But, when the rightful heirs come back, we'll be left empty-handed."

"You mean we're not the rightful heirs?" asked Dasha. "As long as the world lasts, isn't this ours?"

"It's not going to last forever."

"Perhaps, but still . . . But what is forever then?"

"There used to be God. Now there isn't anything."

"But now there's the world."

He picked up a silvery pink stone. "I am bequeathing this to you from my property. And I warn you that the world is going to fall apart very quickly. And what kind of a world it is now, I'll be damned if I know."

"I like it."

Ladd shrugged. "I've been in London. They have these neighborhoods there. In the mornings children rummage through the trash, and when they find meat scraps—raw, of course—they eat them up then and there."

They went as far as the reeds and turned around, in silence. Gradually the conversation turned to something else. When Dasha returned to her room, it started to rain and she had to close the window, which woke up Zai. But by morning everything was shining and bathed in sun once more. No one could have predicted what would happen to Dasha that day.

Around four o'clock, Ladd was carried back from the path that led to the distant mountains. He had slipped into a chasm and hurtled down about thirty meters, clutching at stones and bushes. A young Dane and the baker's son, a sixteen-year-old giant, lowered themselves down on a rope to get him and brought him back on their shoulders. Ladd's shirt was in shreds and he was unconscious. He came to on the floor in the circular vestibule and began moaning loudly. There was no doctor in the village; the one who lived fifteen kilometers away was on summer vacation, and the owner of the pension could not get a telephone call through to town for a long time.

It was hard to figure out what exactly Ladd had broken, but the worst danger seemed to be the possible internal hemorrhaging, the pain in his head from the blow, and concussion. Ladd lost consciousness several times before they put him in his narrow white room. Before nightfall the doctor arrived, examined Ladd, gave him some injections, and said that his ribs were intact but the head wound had not been washed out carefully enough and he had rebandaged it. He promised to send an ambulance in the morning and made a telephone call to the hospital in town.

Dasha found out about what had happened later than everyone else. That day she and Zai had taken a boat to the other side of the lake, where the shore was flat and deserted and nearby cows tinkled their little bells. They roamed around for a long time and found white mushrooms, a gurgling brook, and thousands of flowers. The sun set early. Returning for dinner, Dasha went to her room to change and Zai came up a few minutes later and said that the man Dasha had taken evening walks with to the reeds a few times had been hurt in the mountains.

When they went down to dinner, Dasha listened to the Dane's detailed account of Ladd falling into the chasm. Everyone was shaken up and conversations were muted. Dasha kept going up to the upstairs hallway with the others to listen to Ladd moaning. In the evening, they all sat on the terrace for a long time smiling and sipping iced lemonade through straws. It was hot and starry, their tanned faces merged with the darkness, and all one could see were the men's white shirts and the women's bright dresses, as in a photographic negative.

It was around midnight when Dasha went to her room. She

felt completely unlike her usual self. Everything inside her was tensed, as if in addition to her ordinary senses—hearing and sight—there was something else within her that heard and saw something different in some other way. Both her usual and her new senses were focused on the single point that was her soul. Her fingers were suffused with an unusual heat, but her head was clear and she felt strangely confident that nothing was beyond possibility. She sat down on her bed.

Ladd's room was upstairs, directly over hers in fact. She thought she could hear his moans. She stood up. It was like a summons, though not his summons. She didn't know whose summons it was, but it was very strong. Still, she hesitated. Should she go upstairs or not? And if she did, then how could she do what she was now totally ready to do?

She had never known such a state before. Once, five years ago, she had been present when Liubov Ivanovna had had a bad kidney attack, when neither medicine nor injections had helped, and Dasha, distraught at the sight of her stepmother's sufferings, put both her hands on Liubov Ivanovna's forehead. And the pain abated. Dasha never told anyone about this and gradually forgot about it herself, that it had happened at all, let alone how, but now, for the first time in her life, she felt conscious of a power. It wasn't scary in the least. It was like an unexpected happiness. Quietly, she went out into the hall and up the stairs.

When she opened the door to Ladd's room, he was lying on his back dressed in his pajamas with his head bandaged, half-covered with a sheet. A lamp burned in the corner of the room and it was stuffy. Without making a sound Dasha opened the window. The night air drifted into the room; in the deep silence you could hear fish splashing in the lake and a bird begin sobbing in response. It was the night world and Dasha was at its center. A light wind ran across the tree tops. Then, everything fell still.

Through clenched teeth, Ladd was making a strange,

whistling noise. His tanned face had a greenish cast and sweat was dribbling down next to his ear. His half-closed eyes seemed to protrude too much under his eyelids and the gauze bandage went around his face and covered his forehead. Dasha unbuttoned his pajama top. There was a large black bruise under his right nipple. She bared the entire right-hand side of his chest and placed her large, calm, and very hot hand on it. Inside her everything was taut, like a sail in the wind.

Just today she had been admiring the Danes' boat racing along in the distance. The main sail slanted ever so gently to one side, as if it wanted to wrap in its sail embrace the slender and likewise bowed jib. Without touching, without even the chance of touching, the main sail and the jib raced in the blue and nothing could have been lovelier than their tandem flight. It was as if the large wing was sheltering the small one, as if the small one was flying its heart out to cling to the breast of the large one; a tack, and the two slender white parentheses took a piece of blue, pieces of water, air, and sky into their grip and once again they flew along side by side, stretching toward one another the way clouds sometimes do. The large sail, which had something swanlike about it, inclined and curled, loomed up and flew above the small one; the small one beckoned to it and would not relent. It flew ahead, tracing the gentlest line with its curve. The same wind was blowing them. Faster, faster! A light fog was racing over the water, the sky was clear, the wind coming up. The wave was parted in two and foam played behind the boat's stern. The distance drew near, the far distance, impossible and unattainable; the distance flew toward them.

Quite a long time elapsed. The light wind passed softly by the window again. Ladd was breathing calmly now. His eyes were completely shut; his face, pale and moist. Suddenly he opened his eyes and saw Dasha. "You're here?"

She covered him up with the sheet and stood silently by the bed.

"Why are you here? What time is it? What did the doctor say? Are all my ribs broken?"

But she was still silent.

"I'm thirsty," he whispered, weakened again.

She smiled.

"I'll ring for the maid," she said, giving him a glass of water. "I don't know anything about tending the sick." And trying to step very quietly, she walked out of the room.

Downstairs, Zai could not sleep. She lay with her hands behind her head watching the door for Dasha. "Is he dead?" she asked quietly.

"Heavens, no!"

"What were you doing there? It was so quiet."

"I may have healed him," said Dasha. "Only not a word about it."

She threw herself on the bed fully dressed, exhausted, glad that it was dark and Zai could not see her face. No sooner had she stretched out and felt alone with herself, than she became sober and peaceful as never before. Deep inside, at the bottom of her soul, where her thoughts anchored, she saw the same starry sky.

She pictured the meaning of her life opening up gradually like a fan. Here was her aloneness that concealed her harmony with the world, which she did not completely understand; here the memory of her two-week marriage; and her difficult debate with her own conscience before deciding to leave—or rather, flee—escaping the man she had thought she loved who had suddenly terrified her, and with whom she could not live. And here her mother's end, which had nearly dealt her a mortal blow; here her childish crush on Boiko, which had come as a kind of salvation; here, everything that had now vanished like a dream; and here also, certain attempts to be happy like everyone else.

And the present. This power she had, which, as it now seemed to her, she had always suspected without knowing its precise application or who needed her and why. Could this power turn her world around and herself along with it? Or stop time? Or banish any suffering? Or only the small bodily suffering of certain good friends? A child's cold? A puppy's mange? What had she done to Ladd? Had she given him a quarter-hour's respite or put him to sleep? Would he go out hiking in the mountains tomorrow, as if nothing had happened? How far could her miracle-making go if, for example, a man's rib were broken?

A thousand questions burned inside her. She was waiting for the morning. She had to be prepared for no one—not Ladd, not she herself—finding out about the result of last night's experiment. They would simply take him to the hospital in an ambulance and heal him there and she would never see him again. But they might not.

She did not feel herself falling asleep. The gong for coffee woke her up. Zai was gone, but the shutters were still closed. My God, how she had crumpled her dress, which she had ironed only yesterday! She changed her clothes, washed, and went downstairs. There the sun had laid down a stripe across the dining room, as it did every morning: the orange canvas blind was too narrow, and at this hour there was nothing to be done with this importunate sunbeam that invaded the room.

"He refused to go to the hospital," the Bordeaux cellist was saying. "I was in his room. He says he feel much better. He's really quite unhappy that we called the doctor."

"But yesterday he was in such a bad way," someone said, "and it was essential. After all, at first we all thought something was wrong with his spine."

Zai whispered: "You healed him. You. But no one except me knows it."

Dasha pretended not to hear. The maid serving the coffee said cheerfully: "You've been asked to come upstairs after coffee."

She was in no rush to go up to see Ladd. He was lying as before, his head bandaged. Seeing her with a tulip in her hand, he held out both hands: "I figured you would come at this very moment. Tell me quickly, must I keep what happened last night a secret, or do you want people to know about it?"

"I don't care one way or the other," she said as she put the tulip in a glass of water.

"I've been keeping it a secret because I wanted to ask you first. How can I ever thank you?"

"Did you sleep?"

"Of course I did. And now, well, my side still hurts, as if there were just a large bruise. My head hurts very badly, but not like yesterday. I was waiting for you and didn't take a single powder. You seem to have forgotten about my head last night."

She nodded in embarrassment. "Imagine that, forgetting about your head!"

"A subject not even worth mentioning, though my head has always seemed rather important to me. What happiness that I'm not in the hospital!"

Dasha sat down in the armchair. They both lit cigarettes.

"Does this happen often with you, like yesterday?"

"That was the first time," she replied and she lowered her gaze. "And now I want to try again. Are you staying here?"

"I sent the automobile back. I was already up a little this morning and asked them to send me a nurse for a few days, to change the bandages."

"Yes. I don't know how to do that."

"Amazing. And you don't want to learn?"

"No, I don't."

He fell silent. She sat down beside him on the bed and put her right hand on the bandage, through which she could feel his stiff hair. With her other hand she took the tulip out of the water.

"Have you ever looked inside a tulip?" She brought the flower toward his face. "Imagine you're entering this tulip. You're entering its very heart. See how yellowy green, and wet, and sticky it is. You take a step and you're stepping into a place where no one before you has ever been. This is the heart of the world and the door to it is through this flower. Everything there seems new to you at first because you've never known the flower way into the universe before. There are aromas, quiet, mystery, and gradually you forget all about the laws of time and space. You're wrapped in the flower's warmth, and the light there is also the flower's, and gradually the flower's secrets are beginning to be revealed to you, they are the laws of the universe. You are going from joy to joy, from lesson to lesson, and you know that at the end of this flower journey, you will discover at last what has been tormenting you. Here in the flower's heart you will find a harmony greater than happiness. Step in, on this flower road. . . . Don't be afraid. . . . Look: the tulip is waiting for you."

Ladd was looking not at the flower but at her wide open eyes. He felt a little like laughing at her nonsensical story or simply just laughing because he felt relieved. Then he closed his eyes and evidently fell asleep. He did not hear her go out.

By that evening he was already sitting downstairs, playing with the straw in a tall glass in front of him and watching her dance with the others. And it seemed amazing to him that no one else seemed to notice her charm, her fragile neck and soft shoulders, her beautiful arms and wide gray eyes. But then he remembered how three days ago everyone had admired her when she was running along the shore with a ball after swimming, and suddenly he was filled with both joy and jealousy: joy that she was his and would be his completely and jealousy that she could be both his and someone else's, that she could love him and someone else as well. Ladd had not known this sort of stormy and sudden emotion in a long time.

About four days later, when he had recuperated, he went to see her in the evening, borrowed some magazine to read, read

Zai's palm and then—her foot, and Zai laughed merrily and read
his, too, until Dasha showed him out, saying their neighbors had
long since gone to bed. They stood by the elevator for a long
time talking until they went to the stairs and sat down on a step.

"What was it about the tulip? Did you think that up yourself?" he asked suddenly.

"What tulip? . . . Oh, the tulip!"

"Yes, yes, the tulip."

"It could have been any flower."

"But you thought it up yourself?"

"It's my way of thinking. The flower is just a pretext."

"I don't like flowers," he said, suddenly serious. "I've always thought them an utterly useless beauty. What can you do
with them? I've always liked vegetables more. At least you can
cook them. Fresh bread, a hot stove, and a place, my own place,
a numbered seat, on the train."

She made no reply.

"I don't like uselessness," he continued. "That's just how I
am. I'm a crude man. I don't like memories either; I don't know
what to do with them. For instance, the way my mother used to
. . . There's just no point in going into it. What for?"

"I never discuss my mother with anyone," Dasha said.

Even that one statement was too much. She had never uttered a word to anyone about the fact that her life bore such an
intolerable burden. But within an hour he knew about it and her
whole life, and they were still sitting on the step on the upper
landing of the stairs. The entire house had long been asleep, and
it was quiet and cool. She heard a cricket in the elevator, which
was hanging in the air next to them, motionless. A small green
light was burning inside it as if it were a streetlight signaling that
Dasha could go somewhere she had never considered.

At last, drained by this nocturnal conversation, Dasha stood
up and started walking down the broad red carpet, past a dark

window. She went down to her room and at the same time, with a barely audible sigh, the elevator began to drop, slowly, into the darkness: someone had returned and pushed the button. And this seemed like the wrap-up of a long evening, a motion that put an end to something, rounded it off, like the wave of a kerchief in a train car window or the fall of a curtain.

CHAPTER FIVE

That autumn Dasha experienced a grave melancholy for the first time in her life. It was as if everything inside her had been turned around by something vague yet grievous. At first this sadness was very ordinary, even prosaic. Life's trivialities suddenly began showing her their awkward, boring, and onerous side. Something deep inside her was stirred. That vivid world she had connected herself to so naturally for as long as she could remember may have been forcing her to relive something difficult and sad. This melancholy began early in the morning, before dawn, when Dasha was still waking up, though she hadn't been able to sleep for an hour or more. This was essentially the only time in the entire day when she was really alone.

Lying in bed, she thought long and calmly, as she had been accustomed to thinking for many years, as the books she had read had taught her to think—not the old ones so much as the new books by her contemporaries. These were different from the old ones because it took real effort to read them and also because when you read them you never asked, What's going to happen next? Each page seemed to start on its own and have its own special goal. But the main thing that distinguished the new

books from the old ones was the fact that they were telling stories not about Peter and Ivan but about Chloë and Emile, about
herself, and Ladd, and Sonia, and even about Zai.

But who was she really? And what had these years of matu-
rity brought her? Strange though it might seem, what was most
important to her had changed very little. Here, in Europe, what
remained paramount was her Russian essence, which she had
brought with her: experiences engraved in her soul—maybe in
her childhood, maybe even before she was born, as if here in
France she had only learned a way, a style of life but not life itself about which, in some miraculous way, she had always
known.

When she was young, she thought she was like other people,
that all people were somewhat alike and everyone was connected to the world in the same way she was. Lately she had
begun to doubt this more and more. After all, no one was really
the least bit like her, and even if someone in the world did have
the same moments of full and absolute harmony that she had,
she suspected that people arrived at this harmony through suffering, trials, doubts, and defeats, whereas she had been presented
with it as a kind of gift, a grace, a blessing. But didn't this gift
involve a duty not merely to carry it on through life but also to
develop it?

Up to the present time she had been aware of this harmony
when she woke up and at night when she was falling asleep, but
one recent morning, doubt arose in Dasha's mind: What was actually behind this sense of fullness and peace? Was there anything to it? Was there some meaning, some faith or power?
Would this marvelous feeling last forever or would it become
muddied and diluted? Would it fall apart? Would it desert her altogether? Would it change over time? Or would it lead her to
something, either noble or base? Should she leave everything as
it was or would she have to fight for it?

This autumn morning for the first time she perceived her life as an assignment to be completed and she was concerned about her own powers.

She didn't keep track of the present. In this past year memories of her childhood had been almost completely forgotten and in their stead thoughts about the future surfaced. It was as if she had room for either the past and present or the present and future, but not all three. It wasn't only books that had taught her how to think. She had taught herself, and since she wasn't talkative, it seemed perfectly natural to her that no one really knew anything about her: her vague melancholy, her great equilibrium, her destiny, if she had one. Such thoughts, which nourished her and on which she nourished herself, eventually got lost somewhere, unclarified and unresolved as if they had drowned in a deep blue sea that was full of light.

September's smoky orange dawns were gentle and slow in Dasha's window. Stretched out on her bed she looked straight at the sun rising in the pale window, in the sky she couldn't see. And while she lay there the fundamental, tortuous, paramount question arose that she seemed to have had a presentiment of in her sleep: Had she healed Ladd because she could heal anyone, or had she healed him because she loved him? Were there hundreds of Ladds, all of them waiting for her help, the same help she had once rendered to Liubov Ivanovna as well? Did she have a power, secret and mysterious, that could fill her entire life or was this an accident? Was it all due to the tenderness of the strange feeling born in her after saying goodbye to Ladd that was now turning into love and longing? Aware that she had confused herself completely, she got up very quietly, walked over to the window, and pulled back the curtains.

The second floor was like a dais for delivering a speech to a crowd of people. *Listen, listen to me! What will happen to me and all of you along with me? What is all this for? What is my life for?* By this window, early in the morning, she always felt as if she could stop the sun if only she and everyone else had not lost the connection between the sun and the power that resided in her. It was strange and mildly ridiculous to be standing here, looking at the quiet street, knowing that she might have . . . Actually, it was more of a feeling than a knowledge or memory that at one time she might have done more than now. In the future she might be able to do even less. *Then* it had been as if there were no time. Everything had been different then. The past could become the future. Now, though, what remained of that power and faith? Did it apply to her present life at all? To human suffering? Or to her own love?

On Sundays, everything at home was completely different. Liubov Ivanovna and Tiagin, in their old robes, both uncombed and unwashed, took a long time over their coffee, listened to the radio, smoked, and talked. He was an old man now and looked much older than his years; he still retained his old-fashioned ways. She had changed markedly in the last year, with her full pale face and faded round eyes, her curling papers wound too tightly. She suffered from boils on her throat and so a piece of woolen lace was always bound under her chin. After coffee on Sundays they began drinking tea, and they were even cozier together. They would listen to the mass from Notre Dame or Hawaiian guitars or the news. Through the open door one could see their untidied bedroom and unmade bed, yesterday's papers, which they always read before going to sleep, on the floor; in the kitchen something was boiling and overflowing its pot, but no one cared. They were taking great pleasure in discussing how they would go to the chrysanthemum show in the Bois de Boulogne, from there to friends for a christening, and in the evening to the cinema to see their favorite celebrity. The actress's name did not have to be spoken.

When Dasha went into the dining room, neither of them paid any attention to her. All Liubov Ivanovna, who was scratching her head, said was: "The coffee's cold. The tea's hot."

If I could make it boil right here on this table wouldn't they be amazed! thought Dasha. And she was immediately ashamed of herself.

Tiagin raised his eyebrows when she started dunking her croissant in her coffee. He watched with disgust as the bread got all squishy in Dasha's fingers.

"Citizens of the Canton of Uri!"* he said. "Quickly and painlessly. Lost for the homeland."

Dasha laughed. "Spare me the grand statements, Papa. People have said and heard enough of them in their day, and even the gallery gave only a smattering of applause."

Liubov Ivanovna broke in. "Don't make him feel bad. Papochka has a cold."

That's her logic. And that's his pathos, thought Dasha, and she fell silent.

"My children are citizens of the Canton of Uri," repeated Tiagin. It was so mellifluous. Pity he hadn't thought it up.

It was a theme the three of them felt like discussing, however. Liubov Ivanovna stood up and closed the door to the hall. "Yesterday Zai wrote a poem in French," she said, addressing them both. "Long, melodious, very beautiful." (Liubov Ivanovna did not understand French very well.) "About a parrot who picks slips of paper. In her childhood, Zai said, for a kopek, a parrot used to pick out a slip of paper with your fate written on it. But now, she said, so that no one is ever frightened, they have an automat in every train station: horoscopes jump out of them. And this, she says, is much better, because when you buy a ticket to go somewhere, to ride or sail or fly, you find out then and there what awaits you and you're not afraid of anything any more."

Dasha smiled. So did Tiagin.

"With rhymes?"

"That I can't say," Liubov Ivanovna whispered readily. "I don't know the language that well. But Zai put it all very nicely."

*The Uri Canton of Switzerland rejected the Reformation.

This was a domestic event in which even Dasha took part. "All girls her age write," she said distractedly.

"Sonia says the same thing," Liubov Ivanovna hastened to add. "She thinks it's time for Zai to meet others like her, to listen to them, and to get out in the world. . . . And your papochka says so, too. What are we going to do with her, he says?"

Tiagin frowned. "Where is she going to go? Who is she going to meet? What else have you dreamed up! The kinds of morals out there, and she's only eighteen! Cocaine and opium."

Dasha took away the basket of bread he'd been digging in. "Eighteen isn't all that young," she said indifferently. "It's a whole, long eighteen years. And naturally Zai herself knows very well what she should do and where she should go."

"Uri!" Tiagin muttered again, and he stood up. This time, though, Zai opened the door and stopped on the threshold.

Zai never woke up early; she had to be woken up. Today however everything felt new; she even felt like styling her hair differently, but she didn't know how. Last night she had had a dream that left behind a little taste of freedom. Until now, her world had consisted mainly of dreams she never told anyone. She had carefully safeguarded them, suspecting that everyone had their own mysterious and special dreams, except for maybe Tiagin and Liubov Ivanovna, who shared one, which was probably very boring. For a long time she thought everyone in the world lived in the same way, just like Tiagin and Liubov Ivanovna. It turned out, though, that there were also the woman who sat under the chandelier waiting, the children she had seen at the table and whose life she knew so much about, the worker holding his glass of wine—all had opened up an entire world to her. It was now clear that people were different from each other. They lived differently and she too would live her own way once she stopped being afraid.

She paused and surveyed the table. Everything seemed new this morning. She herself was new and different.

"Listen! I was standing on a sharp cliff. There was nowhere to step either forward or back. Down below was a chasm, a deep chasm, bottomless, actually, though there's no point telling you, you wouldn't understand. Dasha, listen! I stood there and I knew that this was the end for me and there was nowhere for me to go. I was on the verge of falling. And then suddenly I had a thought, just the least little bit of a one at first. This was a dream! I could put my foot in the air and . . . nothing would happen. No catastrophe. Because this wasn't real, it was just me dreaming, and since I was dreaming, that meant I could walk freely into nothingness, into emptiness. And as soon as I thought that (are you listening to me?), it was gone and I stepped out as easy as you please over an even, smooth parquet floor."

Where had those words come from? She started telling them about how yesterday she had seen a sky above Paris that was like an "overturned shell" which she "would never forget," that the trees by the Invalides bridge were the color of cigars, and there was nothing more wonderful in the world than the windows of flower shops and sausage stores.

"What stores?" Tiagin asked, thinking he must have misheard.

"Sausage," repeated Zai.

"Don't you get fed at home?"

"This is completely different. They're so wonderful!"

Silence reigned. You could hear Zai slurping her coffee. And all of a sudden Dasha realized that today she would go to see Ladd. She would walk through those sunny autumn streets, full of these ponderous and troubled thoughts and this oppressive feeling, the hopes that had tormented her all month and questions that would not leave her be.

Meanwhile, Zai kept dunking her croissant in her coffee. Tiagin watched her sadly and reproachfully, and with a blissful smile Liubov Ivanovna, her gaze resting on the wall calendar, ascertained for the hundredth time that morning that today was

Sunday. The time was passing in utter serenity, and there was a light in a window beyond which stood an empty hall where formal balls had probably been held two hundred years ago.

A door slammed somewhere and the taps in the bathroom started singing in two voices: one higher, one lower.

"At last!" said Liubov Ivanovna as if she had just woken up. "Now she'll splash around until we eat."

This was about Sonia, and Zai laughed. She liked the fact that Liubov Ivanovna was stern with Sonia and kind with her. It was nice. Dasha calmly pushed her cup aside and stood up. She had no desire to run into Sonia today.

She would go to see Ladd. Through the sunny streets. Full of hope, questions, and love. She had memorized his address. He lived in a hotel on the rue Jacob. That evening when she said goodbye to him (had she really been mistaken in her presentiment then that this person would bring her great joy as well as great suffering?), he had said: "Don't visit me. My place is cramped, uncomfortable, and dusty. I'll certainly visit you myself and very soon, and we'll take walks to places you don't know at all."

"I know all the places," she said. "I know where the chestnuts bloom in September and where they bloom in December. I know where the first snowdrops appear in March, and I can take you to one magnolia that has blossoms in early October. I know when the mama elephant at Vincennes has a baby and the shortest route to the rhinoceroses, of which there are now only three because—"

"Listening to you, you'd think Paris was a forest, not a city."

"Paris is a forest, a field, mountains, a river, canals, and pasture," she replied.

And it was true, the buildings and palaces, monuments and arches, could disappear, especially the apartment buildings Zai so loved to peek into. For Dasha they didn't exist. They were simply stone—her attachments lay elsewhere.

The rue Jacob. A small hotel; in the reception office a pile of linen to be mended on the table and the smell of cooking. The concierge's lean look at the key board: "Yes, he's in his room. Fourth floor, a door like all the others." Ladd's voice: "Who's there?" Through the door, Dasha visualized him, but when he appeared he was all wrong: unshaven, skinny, red-eyed, wearing a sweater with a torn elbow.

"It's you!" He seemed less than thrilled and his surprise seemed fake.

Cigarette smoke lingered in the small, colorfully upholstered room. The hotel regulations on the door were covered with flies; there was a cotton curtain behind which you could hear the water running in the sink, and the table was stacked with books, papers, and newspapers. There was something impersonal about this disarray.

"I missed you very much, Ladd. I wanted to see you. How unfaithful you turned out to be."

"No, I'm faithful. I did come to see you, more than a month ago it was. Just as soon as I arrived. But you didn't get back to me, and I decided you didn't have any use for me."

She thought that this too was untrue, but it was the truth, and she sat down.

"Today's a horrible day," he said, not looking her in the eye. "All these days are horrible days. I'm ashamed of the mess, but I'm in this bad, awkward state. . . . Yes, I did come see you but you weren't home. Dear Zai wasn't there either."

"No one said anything to me."

"And after that—I was worn out. I just couldn't tear myself away." And suddenly Ladd started flipping through the newspapers looking for matches. "I had a talk with your other sister, she opened the door. We introduced ourselves, but she must have forgotten." He uttered the last word firmly, and naturally you couldn't not believe him.

Enough of this! But Dasha couldn't see his eyes. Either he

had his back to the window or was sitting sideways or was walking around the room in search of something, putting books on the shelf, pulling up the coverlet on the bed.

For a few moments Dasha didn't know what to think. All was not well there. Then she thought she should leave right away, but she stayed.

At the same time, not only was it clear to her that she should go, but even Ladd himself seemed to be begging her with his eyes to leave. The conversation followed its course, Ladd even said "it's still early" once, which might have meant "stay longer," but somewhere, one step away from the room, on another plane, everything was crossed out and destroyed.

Ladd, however, attempted to keep up a conversation and when he couldn't think of anything to say and there were gaps of silence, Dasha listened through them to the continuation of his thoughts, which kept flowing with incredible power, screaming at her to be convinced. But they seemed cold and obscure to her.

Two portraits were nailed to the wall over the table, two faces, and she thought it would be impossible to find, not only in the entire nineteenth century but throughout history as well, two faces more different from each other. The one on the left had something angelic about it. In its tenderness there was an asexuality; its eyes, its features did not have anything you could call either intellectual or wise. In the youthful sketch of the chiseled cheekbones there was a great charm. One couldn't help but feel moved by the sketch of the mouth. Could such a mouth chew, kiss, smoke? Could one imagine this face when its time came to lie in the grave, turning black and decomposing? It was Novalis. He was nailed up purely for his face, of course. It's unlikely Ladd had ever given any thought to Novalis's poetry, or at least not for a long time.

The other face was fleshy, heavy, and bearded, and the eyes under their fat lids and the thick dark blue hair were ominous. Dasha did not immediately recognize Bakunin.

Dasha looked attentively out the window. Had she really once placed her hand on Ladd's chest and talked to him about a tulip? He was filled with some kind of despair and had no idea himself what he was talking about.

"It's very hard, very hard not to have your own country," he interrupted himself suddenly (he had been talking about how he was writing an article in three languages at once), "and especially for me, someone like me, because I don't have a homeland, no homeland at all. I never did and I never will. It means I can't have any genuine purpose in life. Nothing but nervous strain going from one foreign corner to the next. And everything being not quite right, not quite right, and so on, until my hair turns gray. The hopelessness. You can't understand that, can you?"

She did not sense a question in his words, only an assertion, and she felt no urge to reply. She did have an opinion about this, but she felt no need to reveal her thoughts to him. She had seen irrevocably, as if he himself had said it in his loud dry voice, that there was no place for her in his life and struggle. He felt her to be an utter stranger and even if she did think it indisputable that in her and her alone lay his salvation, that it was not her fate that had led her to him but his to her, that he was blind and deaf to his own being—she had to stand up and leave. A cloud was crossing over the dried-up field and pouring rain stormily over the ocean.

After all, in the language people speak in, in which Papa and Liubov Ivanovna, Sonia and Zai, and everyone I know expresses themselves, this is called thrusting yourself, foisting yourself on someone as a friend or lover, she thought and she stood up. Ladd immediately followed her to the door, repeating: "Yes. There you have it. I should have left. Why am I in Paris at all? But where am I supposed to go? It's time to choose. Things are just getting tragically futile. I'm still fighting for my life, but I don't have the foundation everyone else has, I'm only half a man. You really came at an awful moment in my life, you know, when everything is going haywire and you despise yourself in the morning so that you can love yourself in the evening."

She said: "If you feel like seeing me (which I doubt), scribble me a note."

"Oh yes," he said, shaking her hand over-solicitously. "Without fail. That time I was at your apartment (and didn't find you), I was a completely different person, more like my summer me."

"Sonia can be very forgetful," Dasha interjected. "Especially when it concerns my affairs."

"Don't say anything to her!" exclaimed Ladd. "I hate it when there are fights because of me."

Dasha was amazed. "Fine, if you're so much against it."

Having freed her hand, she began descending the stairs. Ladd leaned over the railing. "I sat with her that time for a while, waiting for you. . . . She's nothing like you."

"We have different mothers," Dasha said calmly without turning around and feeling suddenly that the meeting with Ladd was becoming utterly superfluous, losing its outline in space and melting in time. . . . Stairs had once before played a big role in her story, but now it would be good to take a long walk somewhere far away and long ago, somewhere near Athens, in the third century, drawing her cloak across her chest, stepping barefoot across the flat pink stones, among the dragonflies and bay laurels.

CHAPTER SIX

Sonia Tiagina's Notebook

Yesterday Ladd told me he was leaving for Hungary, hinting that he had some sort of political assignment. This has been his way out of all our long conversations for the past month.

"If I were going to go somewhere," I replied, this time without any ulterior motives, "it wouldn't be Hungary." He said I was reproaching him for not going to Spain when he could have.

I had no reason to reproach him. But I do have my opinion. If someone wanted to do something, of course it wouldn't be to go to Hungary. "Hungary is one of your four (how many do you have?) homelands. It's a fact that in the final analysis you prefer working on that without realizing you could work on that and the whole world in Spain."

But of course he didn't agree. He said Rudin's* life and death would have made sense if he had perished on the barricades in Moscow, not Paris. Anyway, I think it has a beautiful meaning. The main thing is to perish on the barricades—where they are doesn't matter.

*Rudin is the protagonist in a Turgenev novel of the same name.

"One of my four homelands," Ladd repeated, something bitter in his face. "How evil you are!"

I was lying down and so couldn't shrug my shoulders, but I shrugged them mentally and raised my eyes to the sky, also mentally.

"There's that old saying: Go ahead and die, just do it for a cause."

Ladd came over to the sofa, his fists clenched, his voice mournful: "I sacrificed the most precious and mysterious thing I had for you. It was unique and would probably have changed not only my life today but my entire destiny, which may well turn out to be simply insignificant, like me."

I didn't ask any questions because none of that holds any deep interest for me. He was talking of course about Dasha.

"But I have no regrets. I love you."

I've heard this so many times. Each time I feel sad for a bit but I can't be his echo. (And if I could, would I feel joy at being an echo?)

I like the fact that he talks this way, though. I like him. I took the first step the way I always do. Once upon a time that was considered impossible, later merely awkward, but that's a holdover from some forgotten prejudice that expired a long time ago. Once people thought the man was more righteous and direct and the woman was evasive, elusive, capricious. That's all erased now. I take the first step. I don't care what kind of person he is. I only know that I'm righteous and direct.

When I take his head in my hands, I think about merging with the universe. I brush my lips on his forehead, he's so happy. He says he was once a cheerful, lively, enterprising man and when he was around twenty he had a hundred opportunities. But suddenly they began dropping by the wayside one by one, melting, vanishing. Everything around him ran aground, he clutched at this and that, racing around the world. I don't think there's a country he hasn't been to. And he's grateful to each one because he owes each one something.

"Yes, you are the happiest man in the world," I tell him, joking.

He doesn't have a place or a cause of his own in the whole wide world, and now he's searching for them in fits and starts. As if he was under a deadline. His last chance to choose. Still, it seems to me that Ladd is more at home in the world than most of us. In the kind of world we live in now, maybe he's in more of the right place than anyone.

I was lying on his sofa in the overheated room of his tiny hotel, and I was asking him questions, my questions, which I invented for him. I like to know what's going on in his thoughts. He was cutting out paper dolls with curiously soft outlines and laying them out around himself, and answering me. It's a game—you can't stop to think for a second:

I walk—Down the road—You walk—From cloud to cloud—He walks—Over the Notre Dame bridge—We walk—Across a tightrope—You walk—Down the Metro escalator—They walk—Arm in arm, in the twilight . . . You can't take time to think—You have to answer immediately, automatically, letting out all the signals from your subconscious.

I die—Holding a glass of poison—You die—Alone, in the desert—He dies—By hara-kiri—We die—Attacking the enemy—You die—In your own bed—They die—In a train wreck.

I stopped and lay there for a long time without stirring.

We die attacking the enemy. I hope so! But that's just how it seems to him. He'll never attack an enemy.

Everything I think about love, all my experience with it, I have to hide from the person who loves me. It's as if I had stolen something: everyone knows I've been a thief except the one I stole from, who mustn't know anything. There's a conspiracy all around him.

But today I decided to tell him that he is not the only one for me. *And if we live, there'll be others, that's for sure.*

There he was sitting close to me, looking at me with such suffering in his eyes that I started reassuring him that it was a joke, a quotation . . . What happiness—the possibility of always telling the truth. But I don't know this happiness and I feel terrible. My rare attempts to be truthful never work out. If I was honest with him, he'd suffer more. Once I told him I loved him not because I felt it but like an incantation, to evoke, or try to evoke, the sensation of being one with him. It didn't work . . . it just sounded like a lie that didn't fool anyone.

Words. I say some as if they were like prophetic formulas that could perform miracles, making a whole out of broken pieces. The world is split into the me and the not-me. I want everything to grow together, to unite, to coalesce into a single answer. This is a key, not an incantation. In my dream someone tells me: first find the key, find the key! Then you can look for the door. And I walk off in search of the key.

At first Ladd seemed to be suggesting I go with him. Where? To the ends of the earth, naturally. At first he thought he would be able to glue a toy together for me, give it to me for my very own, then I'd be so grateful I'd follow him. That didn't happen, it couldn't. I don't need glued-together toys. Solving the Ladd problem (for him the world is split simply into rich and poor) is just a small part of the enormous task I face and that becomes more and more terrifying, more and more onerous, with every passing year.

"The rich," I tell him, "almost always live in a state of boredom, longing, despair, bad conscience. Anyone who achieves fame or power pays for it with their freedom—passions, loneliness, more boredom. Ordinary happiness, in the final analysis, strips man of his human image so that he's just like a beast of burden. But if he isn't happy, he plunges into a savage, dim hell that may not end with death."

I was lying on his sofa playing our favorite game of questions and answers with him. But he knew and I knew that both of us had a life before us, a whole difficult life. And that we couldn't afford to lose.

"Right now," said Ladd, "there must be somewhere in the world where you don't have to be superfluous, where you might even be essential."

"Byron, where is your Missolonghi?" I said in reply. *I hope he goes! If he doesn't go, what am I going to do with him here in Paris? Ultimately he's just going to make things harder for me. One day this whole burden is going to be the death of me.*

The world is split, and maybe in fact there isn't anything to be done about it. All you can do is split along with it and maybe that'll give you the harmony you're after. The way I am now, I'm still complicating everything, just by existing I'm complicating the system, the universe. But what if it is beautiful? That's something I don't know. I've always wanted to be in harmony with everything. Ten years ago I made a decision which at the time seemed like my salvation, and even though it wasn't, I still rejoice that I followed it through.

I decided to take a close look at the history of the world— not the history of its wars, the fate of its rulers, the migration of its peoples, or its economic systems, but the history of its spiritual movements, the chain of those ideas. I decided to recapitulate this journey myself. Graphically it can be depicted like this: Imagine a chain of high mountains, the Alps or the Himalayas. Each peak in the chain is one of the "leading ideas of mankind." I am going from peak to peak. It's as if I settled 2000 meters up and began living there. That is my starting height. I take a step, from one peak to another, and from that one to a third, and then a fourth (never descending below 2000 meters). I might ascend to 5000 and then descend to 3000. A few times I've been as high as 6000 or 7000, and then I dropped back to 4000. But I live high up and breathe that air. I'm retracing the path traveled by the world on its spiritual plane, the journey of human thought. My assignment has taken many years. Now it is coming to an end.

From the sources of world spirituality, the Chinese Book of Changes, the Orient and the prophets, through Greece, Rome, the New Testament, Alexandria and the Middle Ages, I reached the Renaissance, the Reformation, the eighteenth and nineteenth centuries and now our day. I've grown older and wiser, I've lived the world's history.

I'm not saying I've read everything ever written on history, philosophy, religion, all the poetry of the last twenty-five centuries. A human life isn't long enough for that! But once I started down this road, I followed it without so much as a glance at anything else. I spent ten years learning the journey the world took and making this journey my own. I have never had any doubts that my calculation was correct. The university has been my whole life. For me, getting my license, defending my dissertation meant not only overcoming obstacles but also one of the few great joys I have ever known. My work on Xenophon, my dissertation on Philip of Macedon, Alexander's father (and how I loved Daedelus and Icarus)—all this carried me through the ages, made me understand the course and grandeur of what I dreamed of merging with.

The main thing was not merely to learn, but to submit inwardly to those influences, those profound movements, that the world has submitted to for thousands of years—and not always willingly. There were times when philosophy and literature, art and sociology, each interested me almost equally. I let everything that stirred the world spiritually pass through me so that I could follow its "curve." Yes, there's that word: I wanted the *curve* of my development and the *curve* of the world's to coincide.

People will say that a human life doesn't last long enough for studying the world the way I wanted to. Well—I did what I could. Keeping strictly to the basics I wanted to experience all the same influences as the world.

At the time my father, Tiagin, was busy speculating and getting rich, then losing it all and being unable to pay for my education. Sometimes I didn't even have Metro fare and I would dash out of the house hungry, barely washed, but gripped by my idea, to the lecture hall, if I wasn't sitting over my books. Tiagin and my mother tried a few times to talk me into learning how to sew and stuff dolls, and once they even tried to get me to study hairdressing (which they consider among the most profitable trades). My sister, Dasha, neither gave me advice nor expressed disapproval. She belongs to that group of people who don't care about anyone else and are happier on their own. Actually, I may be being unfair to her. Well-balanced human beings! They all end up the same way: they get fat and die surrounded by grandchildren.

I've lived haphazardly, I'm not terribly honest, and not terribly pure. I stuck to my goal though. When B. would give me some money, I was grateful—I could eat as much as I wanted. I tried to eat at home as little as possible.

All that's over with. I can get a job as a *professeur d'histoire* in any provincial town in France, but here I've spent a year in Paris lying on one sofa or another. Now, it's Ladd's. I lie around on his sofa until twilight. Novalis and Bakunin, two old friends I once gave quite a lot of thought, are side by side now on the colorful wall in Ladd's room. Better to die like Novalis than Bakunin. But better to live like Bakunin than Novalis.

"If you're searching for an action," I told him, "then you're saved. And you have nothing to fear."

He hugged me and kissed my hands. "Let's go together," he said. "Then I'll be safe. Come away with me."

To distract him from sad thoughts, I told him a fairy story: "On a faraway island a long long time ago there was a very small nation. They had their own culture and a high civilization, they had arts and laws, there was no poverty or war. And the people lived in harmony. They did not have disputes or calamities, epidemics or tyrannies. Their rulers were honest and farsighted, the women hard-working, the children faultless.

"Not far from this island nation there were other islands where greedy, coarse, stupid, and criminal people had lived from time immemorial. They had decided to attack and wipe out the small nation to get rid of their way of life so that there would be the same poverty, disease, lies, fear, and boredom everywhere.

"When the little nation found out about this, all its people came out of their houses in profound grief. It was clear that none of the inhabitants would survive this unequal battle. So the little nation decided to choose from their midst the worthiest person and send him to tell the people of Earth about their island and civilization so that what they had achieved would not be lost to human memory. They knew their beautiful country was doomed and they wanted at least the legend of their existence to survive.

"The chosen man sailed off, taking with him models of his native country's lightweight and durable machines, its flying machines, its amazingly effective medicines, which gave them long life. He took the scholarly books of its sages, its musical instruments that emitted the sweetest sounds, and its state laws. He took fine fabrics, drawings of bridges, and models of astonishing buildings. When he was gone, the little island nation started anticipating its fate. Its entire life changed. Everything that had had any significance lost all value or meaning. And instead of all that had been so beautiful and perfect, something hitherto unknown—for which they did not even have a name—arose. As the barbarians came in relentless hordes on their rafts from all directions, the more vividly this nameless something burned in the little nation's people, the brighter their faces and the purer their thoughts became, and the more expressive their eyes and majestic their movements. Their hearts blazed up, their thoughts shone, their souls became pure—in anticipation of death. Something immortal and special took hold, a brief dying magnificence that was a thousand times more valuable than what the chosen man had taken away. This new something could not be compared to their material things—books, machines, designs.

If this chosen man could have returned right then, he would not have recognized them, and they in turn would not have understood why he had taken those things. What was the point of living in people's memories as some kind of legend?

"Of course the little nation's people perished. There were three hundred times more barbarians than them. And their time had come."

I left Ladd's place after seven o'clock. The street smelled of ashes and a damp fog swaddled the city. What Himalayas were my thoughts striding through? The sense of my own freedom intoxicated me. I could go left or right, I could stop, I could live or die. I could come back to life, resurrect my past, and create my own future. I went into a bakery and from the eight kinds of golden brown rolls chose one and asked them to slice it in half. In the grocery next door they put a thick piece of rather dry, hard ham into the roll. I walked down the street, taking bites and chewing. My head was spinning from this sense of limitless freedom. No one was looking at me, no one saw me. I was walking along and chewing, drunk on my solitude and will. I could choose anything at all, and I chose the whole world because that was the hardest.

What path did I need to find to merge with the world? A fine rain was drizzling in my face, the sky on the other side of the river was turning a dark crimson. I didn't know where I was going, across what bridges, down what quays. I was scared and sad, overwhelmed by the recurrent thought that there was no way out for me, no meaning and no answer. The thought that it was all in vain, that there never had been a merging of I and not-I, that I had nothing in common with this city, this country, this continent, this planet, and never would. The dark crimson sky was one thing and I and my freedom were another: Should I have a glass of wine in the corner café, at the bar? Or should I order coffee?

CHAPTER SEVEN

The light had yet to appear in Dasha's window. This morning the sun was dawdling, still making up its mind about rising. Somewhere it probably had, but not over Paris. At six, seven, and eight o'clock things were still the same: a dark gray frame around a white window (the curtain had not been lowered), as if it had been whitened with chalk, or a stuccoed wall had appeared outside overnight. There were no sounds, no ticking of the clock, which she evidently had neglected to wind the night before, which meant there wasn't any time. Dasha, eyes open, was lying on her back, in the silence and gloom, and thinking, as was her wont.

Everything that had happened was for nothing. Essentially nothing had happened. The feel of his chest, his little nipple under my hand, healing a man. Only that healing was a reality; all the rest was intangible, imponderable. He knew, of course. Now he's suffering over Sonia's indifference. I wish she would die. You can wish anything. Or maybe I, especially, can't? What idiocy! Wishing doesn't make it so. I wish there were no Sonia, not to change the past—it can't be changed—or the future (you have to say goodbye to that idea). I wish she didn't exist: my life would be so good without her.

Life sometimes turns out this way: presentiments go smashing into a wall and omens go up in smoke. They're futile. Everything is futile. Signs, prophetic hints—that's all vanity, there's nothing behind them. It's all a trick to be mocked and forgotten. For this man, Ladd, I found within myself the words and the powers, and a month later he doesn't remember my name—and in a year he won't be able to recall my face. The tricks fate plays on me—what good do they do? I didn't choose them or agree to them. I don't understand them and I don't want to. All this just ties me up in a knot, and I can't live like this. Something completely different is dear to me and nobody dare touch it!

I like my inner tranquillity. Without it, I wouldn't be me. And I preserve it, through it all, at all costs. People might say it's utterly futile, but I'm doing it for it in itself, for its wholeness and fullness. It's a part of me. And if ever I feel that heat in my hands again, that power coming from me, well then, I'll know that fate is trying to trick me again, but I'll take the bait anyway, I'll heal some suffering, if only my neighbors' cat. . . . But man is deceitful, and it's a mistake to get close to anyone. The more significant what's said is, the more emptiness lies ahead and all around. What an empty life! And yet inside me everything is so clear and calm.

No. What lives deep down inside me is full of profound meaning that I don't understand. It's inside me, only I can't understand what it's for. Time is passing and life is gradually chipping away at this meaning, and eventually it will be meaningless because I couldn't understand it. Things might have been different. I might have been given not only this power but the ability to comprehend its meaning, it purpose and significance. Like a mandala. . . . If things had been different, life might have let me blossom, let everything open up and grow fragrantly into something grand and beautiful and, most importantly, meaningful, powerful, significant. Maybe the fundamental sin is that I was given tranquillity and perception instead of action, instead of concern, holy concern, and a capacity for suffering. *I ought to have taken a difficult and dangerous journey to become wise, but I didn't. The way I am, I always had inside myself a refuge from everything. Truth be told, I was too content too long.*

I want Sonia to die, I want her not to be. No one loves her anyway. It just seems like they do. She's impossible to love. It's hard for me to think about her. I'd rather think about myself some more.

At this point Dasha suddenly realized that the silence she found so pleasant was unnaturally complete, that her clock had stopped and it was probably late. She got up and began dressing. The window was just growing light.

When she arrived at work Leon Moreau had already been sitting for a while behind his upholstered double door. The management of the bank where Dasha worked had been anticipating major changes in the near future. The old man's son had been taking his place for a week, as had been expected. His father had not died but he had serious liver and heart disease so now Dasha went to his house at the end of the day with letters and papers. Moaning and calling her "my child" much too often (something he had never done before), he dictated while he sipped some healthful liquid from a glass and two other secretaries deciphered what he had dictated to her during the day: the next chapter in Moreau's book about the future of European finance.

Sometimes Moreau's son drove Dasha to his father's house in his own car. He was a calm, rather unattractive, balding man whose left arm had been amputated at the shoulder (a wound suffered in the last month of the war in 1918). He was in his forties but looked older. When his father fell ill, he had been called back from Oran, and he was supposed to leave again soon for Africa, which he liked very much. Paris left him cold. He steered deftly with his one hand (the front assembly had been special-ordered) and drove past the parc Monceau or down the boulevard, and while the automobile was stopped at red lights, he would talk about Oran, Tunis, and Algiers, about how "if anything happened to my father" he would not take over his office or move back to Paris. On the contrary, he would go even farther away: to Addis Ababa, Johannesburg, Madagascar. Not because he had any love for adventure, exotic tiger-hunting, or anything like that but because he found life there much more comfortable and pleasant. He had many servants, two cars, and a breathtaking collection of the rarest gramophone records. In short, he was quite content with his life.

Stifling a yawn, Dasha would get out of the car and an hour later she would be going home alone, usually oblivious to what was going on around her, oblivious to the weather and the streets, automatically descending and ascending the Metro stairs. They were holding dinner for her. Feltman often came to see her father and had dinner with them as well, or popped in later and sat with them for the evening. And then Liubov Ivanovna and Zai would run out to the cinema and Dasha would stay sitting in the dining room by the cleared table and listen happily to Tiagin and Feltman's stories about the Crimea, Odessa, Petersburg, Constantinople, Belgrade, and Prague, and she would tell them something about Addis Ababa or Johannesburg.

Feltman was getting on in years. He was a cozy little man, once a lawyer in St. Petersburg. A year ago he had had a strange adventure, and although almost everyone who visited the Tiagins' home had had out of the ordinary things happen in their life, Feltman for some reason was considered to have had the most original fate of all. After many years of impoverished living in France, he, who had never been a composer and did not even play the piano properly, out of the blue composed a tango that gradually made its way all around the world. The sheet music was published, records were cut, singers dressed up like Gypsies or Spaniards wailed the song to a guitar in Russian nightclubs, orchestras played it, and in one American film a diva with a huge operatic voice sang it with an orchestra. It was translated into every language and street urchins whistled it. Now Feltman still lived modestly but not in poverty, and there was the sense that he had provided for himself to the end of his days. There was also the sense, however, that he would never come up with anything else, that his sole accomplishment in life would be his "Star Eridan."

Feltman's face was covered with an array of wrinkles that fanned out from his nose past his eyes, to his temples, giving him a permanent smile. He liked to say that he was starting to look like Repin,* except that "he looked like a much better person," which was probably true. In recent years he had started shielding his blue, slightly faded eyes from bright light and tried to sit outside the circle of lamplight. That evening, leaning on her elbows, smoking slowly and blowing rings, Dasha asked him about his ballad. For the hundredth time he told her the story of how he had composed it. He now thought that he had written it, but in fact one evening, when he was over sixty years old, a melody had simply come to him (later his fellow countrymen had pointed out to him more than once that it resembled a certain Jewish song), and he went to his neighbors', where there was a piano, and picked the tune out with one finger. Then that same night, lying in bed, he made up words to go with the melody—poor, sentimental words that made him cry. He made them up by thinking about his wife's leaving him five years before. He had planned to live with her until he died and had been mostly faithful to her all of his life, but she had left him for his best friend, though that didn't matter anymore. It didn't matter whether it was his best friend or someone he barely knew because disappointment over the friendship was insignificant in comparison with the nightmare. Someone sent a Moldavian

---

*Ilya Repin (1844–1930), Russian painter, foremost representative of realistic style.

guitarist to learn the melody from him and its fame began with this guitarist, that is, the tango's fame, because who ever knows the name of the person who composed any fashionable tango?

Dasha already knew all this, but she'd forgotten.

"But why 'Star Eridan'? What is Eridan?"

"Because," replied Feltman, beaming with tenderness, pride, and regret over the past, "because she left and I decided to search for her at the other end of the earth, where there's a star called Eridan." And he started singing in his tremulous tenor, which quickly became a whisper since he had no proper voice.

In the hall cupboard there was an old gramophone, owner unknown. Sonia had brought it into the house the year before and had not yet returned it. Dasha took it out, wiped off the dust, and brought it into the dining room. She found the record, too, which Feltman had given them once. A small piece was broken off the edge. On one side, a Gypsy sang "Star Eridan" in Russian with a guitar ensemble; on the other, the same Gypsy sang it with a chorus. First they put on the Gypsy and chorus, then guitars. Feltman listened with obvious satisfaction and Tiagin whistled along softly. Dasha was standing next to the gramophone and listening intently to the words. They really were not all that insightful: *You left, I took your portrait from the table . . . And now I'm going to search for you to the ends of the earth.*

> *Where through the fog,*
> *Where all is gone,*
> *I see a flickering Eridan.*

For some reason all this captivated her. She did not think it strange anymore that the whole world, in its most far-flung corners, was singing and listening to it.

"People nowadays don't understand this," said Tiagin. "Nowadays everything's more about saxophones and drums."

"But they did!" Dasha objected, cranking up the gramophone for a second time. "If tens of thousands of records were sold, that means they love this, too."

She was embarrassed for Feltman when the door slammed just as the music was starting. It was Sonia's way of showing they were bothering her. But Feltman was smiling and watching the spinning disk. His thoughts were obviously very far away.

When Liubov Ivanovna and Zai returned, Tiagin and his friend were conducting their endless discussion of the past and future, the old war and the new, which would certainly come, and Dasha was putting papers in order under the lamp. Ever since Leon Moreau had fallen ill, she had had much more work than before.

"They ought to give you a raise," Liubov Ivanovna said as she walked by, glancing over Dasha's shoulder.

"Well, how was the movie? Good?"

"Zai liked it, which means it was good."

They heard Zai walking down the hall from her room to the kitchen and back. She had been hungry evidently and was drinking milk as she walked. Then she went to her room, listened to hear if anyone was coming, opened her tan purse with the strap, which she wore across her shoulder, and took an envelope out and a piece of paper out of the envelope. For the tenth time she reread the invitation printed on the flimsy green paper: Tomorrow evening, for the first time in her life, she was going to go to a certain meeting, and right now this seemed like the greatest event in her life.

She had never been to such a gathering before—it wasn't easy to break into this society. The green paper had been given to her by a new acquaintance, who said she must come, and this acquaintance's girlfriend, a young lady who had been a total stranger to her the night before, had smiled at her patronizingly when he'd said it. This had all happened last Thursday, at three o'clock, in the café opposite the Church of Saint-Germain. Zai was reading a slim book of French verse she had just bought in the store opposite, on the corner, occasionally glancing from side to side at the square, at the church illuminated by the pale December sun, at the signs, at the opposite side of the street. She was sitting on the terrace, the afternoon was quite warm, and the terrace was half full. Zai's table was right by the sidewalk and suddenly next to her appeared a child's carriage: the mother, evidently looking for someone, had dashed into the café, and the child, a little boy about two, was smiling blissfully and clearly had something on his mind. Slowly, efficiently, and with evident satisfaction, he started unwrapping the newspaper around the package lying on the little blanket at his feet. He got comfortably seated, spread his little knees, and all of a sudden Zai saw several slippery, silvery fish in his hands. They were large sardines, evidently just bought at the fish stand. They shimmered in his pudgy hands, leaving a fine bloody trail on his blue blanket. The child's face was screwed up with satisfaction and from time to time he let out an ecstatic, not very loud cry. The sardines (they may have been small herring) kept slipping onto the blanket; one was already wedged between the side of the carriage and the mattress, another he was poking between his knees, and the third he was attempting to stuff in his mouth. Two of them, their heads torn off, fell on the sidewalk.

"He's about to swallow it!" someone said loudly. All heads turned, but no one budged.

"Dinner for an entire family!" The lady sitting behind Zai laughed.

"Where's his mama? There's going to be a spanking!"

The baby had already bitten off the tail and was pulling at the slick shiny fish body with both hands. Zai jumped up, grabbed the sardine out of his hands, picked up the fish that had fallen to the sidewalk, gathered up the one lying on the blanket, and quickly wrapped them all back up in the paper.

"Don't you dare touch that!" she said sternly and returned to her place. At that moment the woman returned and pushed the carriage away with the bawling child. Everyone around her looked at Zai for several seconds. *What have I done?* She was horrified. *I never should have done that.*

"You can tell right away she's a foreigner," said the young man sitting with a young lady at the next table. "She meddles in other people's business so sweetly and naturally. We are incapable of that, even if he'd been playing with dynamite."

Zai turned around. "I'm French," she said. "And who are you? Now you've gone and meddled in other people's business." All of a sudden she felt very hot and she worried that she was blushing.

The young lady burst out laughing, and the young man said: "I'm French and I meddled out of a sense of contradiction. No one here would have gotten up even if he'd been choking. There's always that doubt: What if his mother came back and said, 'You have no right to touch my child or talk to him. You insult me that way. Are you trying to tell me I don't take good care of him? Maybe I gave him those fish on purpose and it has nothing to do with you. Maybe it's my way of raising children. Everyone has his own ideas on this subject and mine have nothing to do with you.' Have you ever noticed, Denise, that nothing ever has anything to do with anyone?"

Denise took a sip from the straw in her tall glass. "You exaggerate."

"Not a bit. There was no reason to jump up and take the fish tail away from him. The mother certainly left him those herring on purpose: 'It's time you learned, my sweet, not to be afraid of anything. Fish today, kittens tomorrow, and tigers the day after that.'"

Now the three of them laughed merrily.

That is how they became acquainted. At the end of this first encounter, Zai was given the green invitation.

But no one even asked her for it when she walked into the
packed cellar hall, or rather, room, which was already thick with
smoke and a noisy crowd. She was let in by a very young boy,
hoarse and excited, his eyes bulging, his collar unbuttoned. He
laid his hand on her shoulder, as he did to everyone who entered:
"To the left, there are still seats at the far end!" She pushed
through to the left. The garçon who walked in after her with a
large tray deposited it on one of the tables and passed out the
glasses without making a single mistake: beer, coffee, wine,
brandy, tea, lemonade, apple juice, grog, and a few other colorful liquids whose names Zai didn't know. A shout went up. The
tables were pushed back. One of the girls sat down on the table
but she was pulled off immediately. About six people came in together. "Make way, gentlemen," they shouted from the door.

"Make wa-a-ay!" the whole crowd chorused, and the entire
back row moved to the left. Zai was crushed. Denise and her
friend turned out to be jammed into the corner and someone was
sitting on the floor.

"They pushed me out!" she heard from somewhere. "This is
my place, but they pushed me out."

"Quiet!" a skinny good-looking boy of about eighteen
shouted in a loud voice. He had a long neck and a sharp profile.
"In view of our success, the next meeting of our club will take
place in some other more spacious establishment."

The response was a terrible racket that was supposed to sig-
nify approval of what he had said.

"Quiet!" he repeated. "Has everyone given the garçon their
order? He demands to be paid right away. Then he'll leave us in
peace."

The clamor, this time twice as loud, was supposed to show
that the gathering was displeased with this demand. The garçon,
grinning, waved his towel.

Zai looked around wide-eyed. There were nearly as many

girls as boys; many of them were sitting with their arms around each other. Almost everyone was smoking. Two or three young men were a little older, about twenty-five; the rest were very young, wearing colorful shirts, no ties. The young women were dressed modestly and had on almost no makeup. Many of them had utterly childlike faces and hands. Obviously the idea here was to effect an air of gloomy jollity.

Her neighbor on the left, with a swarthy narrow face, suddenly roared: "Start! It's time!"

And Zai cried out: "Start!"

Quite a few picked up the cry and someone began clapping.

The first to come out to the center was René, the one Zai already knew. He surveyed the audience, took out a sheet of paper, and cleared his throat. The place became quiet.

"I'll read my latest," he said and the self-confidence vanished from his face. "It's called 'Fish.'"

He recited a rather long and clumsy poem that repeated the line: "A live child playing with dead fish."

When he finished, Zai felt a little awkward, as if something had been stolen right out from under her nose. She glanced over at Denise, but she was clapping madly. Shouts rang out: "Useless! Boring! Flat!" René, endeavoring with all his might to maintain his dignity, returned to his seat.

Next was someone in the opposite corner, then Denise, then a young woman with long, very blond hair that hung loose over her shoulders. Someone read something endless and lofty, and they shouted at him that he'd "milked Musset dry," and another whose poem was strewn with obscenities was greeted with the silence of the grave. Zai kept looking around wide-eyed and alert, not wanting to miss a word. The boy working the door recited something about soccer that everyone liked a lot.

"Who else? Who's next? Whoever hasn't recited, raise your hand!" they shouted from the opposite wall, where she could see the leaders were sitting.

A few people raised their hands. Zai raised hers.

"Come out in the center."

At that moment Zai felt like she was flying off a cliff, into an abyss. "I'm only dreaming that I'm walking across the parquet," she told herself, and indeed, stepping out from behind her table, she took two steps over the smooth floor.

"Who's that?" shouted a chorus of voices. "Your name?"

A bulky, hairy man who she hadn't noticed before dove out from somewhere, leaned toward her, and asked her a question she didn't hear but guessed.

"Dumontelle," she said, barely opening her lips and trying to stop trembling inside.

"Dumontelle!" shouted the hairy man, whose beard started just below his eyes.

Zai swallowed some air, looked over the faces aimed at her, and suddenly it all became easy and simple. Not only had the fear vanished, but so had her trembling. She felt she had the voice and the desire to speak in this voice. She recited:

Elle regarde dans les yeux son Destin
Qui la regarde.
Etre ou ne pas être?
Oh, la belle, la douce, l'heureuse,
La notre!
Celle, qui a donné aux batârds
Plus qu'à ses propres fils.

Ils dorment sous la pierre,
Sous le marbre,
Sous les lauriers,
Sous les saules et les cyprès
Ceux, qui ont donné leur souffle à cette terre.
Nous respirons encore. Avec quelle peine!
Il est dans nos poumons,
Le dernier,

Le plus précieux,
Le plus triste
Des derniers âtomes de ce souffle adoré.

Nous tous, convoqués à un festin tragique,
A l'heure du depouillement,
A l'heure terrible,
Nous avons vu sombrer une autre patrie,
Animal sauvage, jeune, barbare, cruel et inconscient.
Nous sommes convoqués. Et le rideau de la grande histoire
Est levé devant nous.
Mais les spéctateurs deviennent les acteurs.

Si je reviens dans mille ans, je trouverais un petit pays
Faisant le commerce des homards et des vins râres,
Ou la population—quelques millions d'habitants—
Conserve dans sa mémoire
Le secret des parfums,
Les traces des idées,
Qui ont été données au monde,
Gaspillées, massacrées, anéanties,
Tandis que le grand Pérou
Se bat contre un peuple qui n'est pas encore né
Pour une mine de métal, encore inconnu.

There was a storm of applause. Someone let out a piercing whistle. A voice from the far corner shouted: "Why *batârds*?"

Zai had started toward her seat, but she turned quickly around, and without seeing anyone in front of her, answered in the direction of the question: "Because I'm a *batârde*."

There were a few seconds of silence. Then everyone began talking at once.

She sat down. Her heart was beating so hard it seemed to be trying to jump out of her throat, and she could barely breathe. The swarthy young man silently moved over to let Zai sit in her former seat. She squeezed in between him and Denise. He was mulling something over in his mind, then he freed his arm, extended it over Zai's head, and put it around her shoulders. She didn't budge. Glancing to the side, she noticed the fingernails on his slender fingers were clean. *He didn't recite a poem,* thought Zai. *Why is he here? Who is he?* And pressed close to each other, neither of them moved.

CHAPTER EIGHT

Through the dark streets, down the rain-lacquered boulevards, under a cold and steady December rain, both of them
in damp raincoats, their faces wet from the night fog, they
walked for a long time and his hand lay on her shoulder all the
while.

"Right here," she said at last. The tall archway of the darkened building led to an urban backwater that was not quite a
garden. He walked under the arch with her.

"Wait a minute, stand here, don't go away," he said.

She made a cautious attempt to free her hand from his.

"Take a very good look at me, or else tomorrow you won't
recognize me. Will I see you tomorrow? When?"

She wasn't afraid to have a stranger so close to her at night. A
bicyclist swished by through the puddles. "If you like. Why didn't
you recite anything? Don't you write? Don't you write poetry?"

"No. I just like to listen. I'm studying medicine. But I want
to quit and go to drama school. I go to all their meetings when I
have the time. I get around, generally. . . . Shall we go hear
Edelbrenner together tomorrow? But the day after is Sunday and
I train at the gym. . . . Will you come?"

She didn't know who Edelbrenner was—a philosopher, a pianist, or someone who had read a poem today. The training caught her completely off guard. She had never known anyone before who trained. And so she stalled and didn't answer right away. Suddenly he became terribly embarrassed: "Don't come! You don't have to! All this is probably completely uninteresting to you. I'll go alone."

They stood silently there in the courtyard. "I'm very happy being with you," he said quietly. "You won't vanish without a trace, will you?"

"No."

They heard footsteps. Someone was walking down the street, splashing in the puddles, getting closer and closer. Then he came even with them and went past. The footsteps faded away.

He was holding her hand and looking closely into her face with his big dark eyes. In the darkness his skinny face was lively, serious, and agitated, completely different from what it had been in the cellar, and Zai sensed that she would remember him as he looked now, but even better would be her memory of his voice.

"I'm afraid you'll disappear and I won't find you," he said. "What street is this? What is the address? I'm going to wait for you here tomorrow, in this place, all right?"

"At eight thirty."

"If I may. Now I'll go."

"On foot? Where do you live?"

"In Passy. Yes, on foot. It's good to walk across the city alone at night. It would be even better with you."

Zai smiled and pushed her damp, straight hair away from her cheeks. Gently, he moved a lock from her other cheek. When Zai pulled her hair behind her ears on both sides, the oval of her face was suddenly revealed—her uniquely high, sharp cheekbones and her wide-set eyes.

"Do you write a lot of poems?"

"I used to," she replied, though not immediately.

"You're not going to write poetry any more?"

She shook her head. "No. I don't think I will."

He wanted to ask why, but intrigued with her face, he forgot what they'd been talking about. Something meaningful passed between them from eyes to lips. No words were spoken, but he realized that something had happened to her this evening that he might find out about very soon because it might be connected with their meeting. Zai was quiet because she didn't know how to define the new sense of liberation she had just found. She raised her eyes to him a second time and for a second time they made a connection with each other. Suddenly Zai vanished, without a sound. She had run lightly across the alley toward a dark entryway.

A whole night and a whole day, and again it was evening and again he was standing at the same gates. He glanced in: What was there, behind the gates? An enormous dark enclosed space, four street lamps on the four corners, a nighttime dampness forming clouds between them. A few windows were lit here and there, and through the closed shutters and drawn curtains stripes of light shone. A dark pink sky above; a metallic star peeking out from behind the clouds; someone's footsteps; distant music. He stepped into the space as someone walked past him. All was quiet. An automobile pulled up to the curb, a light shone over the number one thousand nine hundred twenty, which seemed like a year—the year of Zai's birth maybe? She was walking slowly forward, into the empty dimness. What amazing places there were in Paris. He might never have known about this blind alley, probably the courtyard of a lord's private manor from long long ago, and now there were likely to be a lot of cats here and the alley had a name. At its end was a wall, the windowless wall of a building whose front faced some distant, completely unknown street, and wet leafless ivy wound up the wall, under the street lamp. Slowly he returned to the gateway.

They had stood here the night before. He read a sign he hadn't noticed then: Gilding, Mounting & Framing. . . . Someone shuddered under the sign and stood up. It was she. Her hair was pulled back tightly with a ribbon at her nape, her cheeks were pink, and her eyebrows flew up like a swallow's wings.

She could pass under his arm, which was why it was so easy to hold her around the shoulders. "Where shall we go? To hear Edelbrenner?" he asked, and she laughed gaily, "or to eat oysters?"

"Thank you. I already ate."

"To see *Embankment of Mists*? To a café? Wherever we wind up?"

They went to a café and to *Embankment of Mists,* and after the movie they ate oysters and heard Edelbrenner (who turned out to be a violinist) and walked through the bare Paris gardens or along the fences if they were closed. These days it was sometimes dry and frosty (it was almost Christmas) and in the mornings hoar frost covered the roofs. A crust of ice crunched under their feet.

For days and weeks they spent every evening together, and every evening under the framer's sign she would appear swiftly and soundlessly, as if wings had brought her to the gate. Without speaking, he put his arm around her shoulders, afraid these very wings would bear her away from him. "Let's go. Let's go somewhere, just the two of us. We don't need anyone else. We can go to my place if you like. It's winter now and cold outside and the gardens are damp. You're not afraid?"

"Of what?" she asked.

"Of coming to my place. I don't live alone. I have my mother at home, and she has all kinds of people coming to see her all day long, endlessly—you'll see. But they aren't going to bother us. I even told them about you at home. Let's go!"

It now occurred to her that he had never told her he lived with his mother and that in fact she knew as little about him as he did about her. Actually, they had just been making each other happy. There was so much to learn about him and so much to tell him about herself! They jumped on a bus and hung from a strap near the exit; he shielded her from others with his body, pressing her up to the railing. She was merry, she was laughing, they didn't need words. They could forget words. She could smile silently, shut her eyes for a second while he brushed the hair above her forehead with his lips and unintentionally—with the lapel of his coat—her face. He helped her get down at the stop and they started off quickly, nearly running side by side, and turned a corner into a narrow lane. The wind was whistling. They stopped at a small private house with four windows and a chipped, noseless caryatid supporting an overhang with broken glass over a darkened door. He took out a key.

Words deserted her and Zai made no effort to catch them, to call them back. They walked into the house. A tiny vestibule, a parlor all in gilt and silk, with dolls and porcelain; the gilt chipping, the silk fading, the porcelain full of cracks and the dolls moth-eaten. A steep staircase, creaking floorboards singing on all notes, a half-open door to someone's bedroom filled to the ceiling with boxes and trunks, the door to his room, a toylike one with a toylike window, a bookcase, a desk with an ink spot in the shape of Australia, a bed covered with an old worn quilt.

"Sit down. It does feel like we're very far away from everything. If you only knew how quiet it can get here—in my nook, I mean, because there's always someone downstairs. And no matter how much you air the place out, there's always a slight musty smell."

The air wasn't musty as much as it was filled with the smell of tobacco, certain herbs, and medicines. Zai dropped her coat on the chair and sat down on the bed. He had barely closed the door before he fell on her greedily and she flung herself at him with equal abandon.

The books on the shelf in front of Zai seemed to be part of a new landscape that stretched out before her, stretching a long, long way—all the way to the horizon—in which a window had been precisely cut. Through that window swung a branch—that was a different world—and she could hear the wind gathering strength overhead and ripping through the stove pipe.

Here, very close to her, long black eyelashes, dark masculine eyes; she bent to look at them and saw herself reflected in his pupil, which shone with kindness. His even, smooth, cool lips, whose taste she now knew, gleamed, they smelled like almonds and were parted in a smile; his youthful chin, his fragile neck. She placed her hand on his face.

"How curled your eyelashes are at the tips and how long! How old are you? Wait, don't answer, don't say anything, you don't have to! I'll tell you: life is liberation. Don't laugh, I know now what life is. At first everything is so frightening, the world around you, and the people, and even you yourself, because you don't know yourself, and as you find out, you're afraid. You tremble and you don't know whether you have a right to live, a right to choose, desire, demand, or fight for anything. Everything is so frightening, your thoughts are so frightening, and just one thing keeps you going: Where can I hide? You despise yourself and you despise other people, too, because they should be just like you, how come they are bolder? Time passes, though, and you grow up, and your freedom keeps drawing closer! Your life can unfold gradually, opening up like a fan—or it may strike like lightning. Sometimes it happens when you're dreaming. Oh—listen, let me tell you how easy it is to live and be alive, to move, breathe, want, and love in this world. How easy it is to exist, to know what you want, to dare, to think and grow! Hold me tighter. You know what dreams can be like? The kind that when you wake up you come out of them as if you were being freed from a cell where you were locked up without light or air.

And then everything you do, everything leads to traveling down the marvelous road of emancipation, coming out of life a free person. Are there really people who stay imprisoned in themselves until old age? My happiness, we aren't going to be like that, right? My happiness, you think I'm going to go on writing poetry, composing, making things up? Not one bit! It was one of my phases. And now I'm free of it. I was free of it that evening, remember, when I went to that place the first time and recited for them. . . . I don't care whether they liked it or not. The main thing is that I went through that on the way to my liberty, and something different and new started that's going to set me free all over again. And today—kiss me again!—I've been freed once more, and the fan has opened up one more slat, and after this there are others that will open up, too. I know that living is about freeing oneself, through poetry, through prayer, through whatever. Listen to me! Oh what happiness this would be if only you would believe me!"

He wanted to tell her that her voice sounded like the gurgling of a brook and that he had not heard what she was saying and he didn't mind not knowing. He laid his cheek on hers. "I believe you. I've been listening to everything very closely. But you still haven't told me you love me."

Zai's hand played over his face. "But that's exactly what I've been telling you for half an hour!"

And they both burst out laughing.

Downstairs a door slammed, voices rang out, there was running on the stairs. Someone knocked at the door.

What happened afterward was not very important to Zai: she met Jean-Guy's mother, a jolly, talkative woman with dyed hair, and her two friends, one fat and one thin. Tea appeared from somewhere, and everyone went down to the dining room. They drank the tea with rum and there was a pile of sweet pastries on the table, still in their papers. Zai and Jean-Guy looked at each other gravely and the ladies were loud and cheerful.

They pushed the dishes to one side and sat down to play *belote,* smoking and pouring themselves liquor out of a black bottle. The radio played

> *Voir briller l'Eridan*
> *Dans un ciel inconnu,*

and the clock said it was after midnight.

"I know the man who wrote that," said Zai. "I'm going home. It's late."

They went out. It was quiet in the lane except for the wind storming along the roofs and in the undersized trees behind the fences with all their naked branches hunched up. Zai and Jean-Guy walked to the Metro. He embraced her and held her close, she returned a long, happy kiss and ran—flew—down the stairs, not noticing the people or the posters or the ticket taker, talking to herself nonstop as if she were talking to him:

I love you, I love you because you free me from myself, from the fears that settled in me when I was a child. You free me from the doubts and hesitations, the sense of humiliation that I've had inside me, and my loneliness. With you, I become strong and free; through you, I've found my place in the world—and it's by your side. And because there is you, I know, at last, that there is a God, because there is my love for you and yours for me.

She strode through the darkness, passing from time to time through strips of light from shop windows that stayed lit all night. In one of them, a jewelry store, behind a mesh grating, a pair of pearl earrings sparkled. Zai stopped. The entire window depicted the bottom of the sea, and in the middle lay a large half-open shell with a long strand of large gray pearls crawling toward it—back from whence they'd come. If she had still been writing poetry, Zai would have put this in a poem, but all that was long passed. "Life is liberation!" The thought was imprinted once again so clearly and simply in her thoughts. And she ran on.

Trying to make her voice sound convincing and stern, Liubov Ivanovna, her hair in curling papers, pushed Zai through the door to the kitchen. "Every night you're out gadding about. It keeps getting later and later! You papa is right when he says there's no controlling you. What am I supposed to do with you? Tell me, what am I supposed to do? I can't spank you, you're eighteen. Lock you in? I'm not your mother. I pray to Christ the Lord: hold on for three more years, and then you can do anything you want!"

"Three years!" Zai was horrified. "But I'm not doing anything. Oh, Auntie Liuba, I've wanted to tell you for a long time: I know how much you love me. More than the others. . . . Don't protest, please, it's true. This is what I wanted to say: No matter what happens, I'll always be with you, I'll never abandon you. No matter what happens to Papa or Sonia. Or to Dasha. Listen, I'm not doing anything. I was afraid of everything, and now I'm not afraid of anything, or almost anything, because I know that life is liberation. I'm happy, Auntie Liuba! Don't you go thinking that we're all so brazen, smoking and drinking and sitting around until all hours. It's very complicated and hard for us, too, and lots of people are afraid, and they're cowards, and they get confused. There are a lot of very unfortunate, utterly lost, and very shy people. And now I believe in God."

Liubov Ivanovna was struck dumb. Instead of hearing her out, Zai had delivered a speech, and everything that Liubov Ivanovna had been preparing for the last two hours, all of it simply flew from her mind.

"What does that mean: 'I'll never abandon you'?" she repeated sternly. "What is that supposed to mean?"

"If something happens . . . I meant to say, if you're left on your own. Because it can be important to know sometimes that people love you and won't abandon you. It's the most important thing in life."

"Silence!" Liubov Ivanovna broke in harshly, trying, however, to keep her voice down so that the others in their rooms wouldn't hear. "What kind of raving is this? I'm not interested in your ready tongue. Please get home by eleven. And kindly keep all these speeches to yourself. It's Dasha who got you going on like this."

She doesn't think anything of the kind, of course, Zai told herself as she got into bed. *After the holidays, if there's a chance, maybe I'll show her Jean-Guy. Then we'll see.*

She thought Dasha rustled in her bed, but she didn't call out to her. She didn't feel like talking. She'd talked enough for one day, to herself and to him—as never before. Things were so clear to her, she had no interest in anything else.

Dasha usually did not go to bed before Zai came in, but today she felt tired from the cold she'd been fighting for the last few days. She took two powders, drank some hot tea, and bundled up warmly. There was something out of the ordinary about today which had been bothering her. What was it? Loaded down with all kinds of letters and papers she had gone from the bank to see the director. It was five o'clock and the automobile had been waiting for her. She was used to that. Over the past few days Leon Moreau had been somewhat better, the liver specialist and the heart specialist called on him on alternate days. He was sitting now in his large study in an armchair by the window, the bottom of which was covered with a rug to keep out drafts. The entire wall facing the window was hung with Flemish primitives, which he collected and now spent hours admiring. The other two walls of his study were filled with books real and fake, that is, one wall was a real library and the other had shelves filled with empty bindings that pulled out to reveal files with all kinds of business papers, innumerable old checkbooks, and appointment books covering the last thirty years. On the bottom shelf, camouflaged by dummy book spines, were bottles of old Cognac and crystal glasses.

Moreau sat like a Chinese emperor in his big armchair, fat, perfumed, unusually unattractive, but with intelligent, piercing eyes and magnificent, well-groomed hands, wearing a quilted Bukharan silk robe and a skull cap embroidered with gold thread brought back from one of his many trips to Afghanistan. He smoked special harmless cigarettes and perused one newspaper after another. Dasha read him the mail she had brought, recorded his replies to the letters, put through his calls to ministers and academicians, and left—usually at seven o'clock. The unusual thing about this day was the fact that when she came out the automobile was still waiting for her. Moreau the younger (his left arm, the prosthesis in a black glove, tucked into the jacket of his coat) offered to drive her home. She accepted.

They talked very little. About how the old man was better, how he might be able to go out soon, how it wasn't particularly pleasant to fly to Oran at this time of year and that the automobile would go by sea. In general, as far as Dasha could tell, comfort played a very large role in the life of Moreau the younger.

"Have you been to Madagascar too?" she asked.

"Oh yes, many times," he replied, "After all, we do business there. And in Johannesburg as well. Didn't I ever tell you about that? It's a very comfortable life there and such interesting nature, all kinds of rare birds and flowers and fruit trees. . . . And the landscape has completely different colors from here" (*Is that so,* she thought, looking out at the December evening) "and the sky is different."

"Are the constellations different?"

"The constellations are completely different. Remember what they once taught us? Southern hemisphere: Argos and the Southern Cross. And the star Eridan. I had that on an exam once. I have to tell you that I was a very good student."

"Eridan?" Dasha echoed. "I thought that was just made up."

Just then the automobile came to a stop. "All my life I've dreamed of living on a small street like this. How did you ever find an apartment here? It's an utterly special corner of Paris," he said, trying to make out the arched gates.

"We've been here a long time."

She got out, closed the door, and nodded at him, smiling. All this now seemed to her like a question mark in an otherwise ordinary, gray weekday.

Returning home, she envisioned Feltman sitting there with her father and how she would walk in and say: "Why didn't you tell us all this time that . . ." But Feltman wasn't there. Tiagin, disheveled, gray-haired, wearing a well-worn jacket with frogs and loops down the front, was writing a long letter under the dining room lamp. Liubov Ivanovna was in bed with a migraine, in her darkened bedroom. Dasha went to the kitchen, where dinner had been kept warm for her. Zai wasn't home.

Dasha was lying sleepless, obsessively going over the day. It was clear to her that she was putting up no resistance to certain forces. Instead she was becoming increasingly weak and spineless.

Was there really any point to listening to yourself and believing in yourself so much? Wouldn't it be better simply to yield to the flow of life? It took courage to admit that when you're just starting your life lots of things seem like deep and important mysteries to be figured out and that there is something magical about people's fates—especially your own. Wasn't all this false, deceptive, imaginary, or had she simply failed to figure out the puzzle? Had she lacked the wisdom and instinct . . . something else? Integrity maybe. There was definitely something lacking in her.

I carry this equilibrium of mine around like a camel's hump, she thought. *Yes, there is tremendous joy and beauty in it, but there is a kind of inertness, an inflexibility, and I don't know what to do about it. Where am I to go, who am I to go to? No great joys, no great sufferings. I'm not capable of them,* she told herself. *My joys and sufferings weigh exactly the weight the scale was made for. Not too much and not too little. And inside me—peace. The star Eridan, which you don't have to sail anywhere to find.*

The following morning the city seemed festive to Dasha, full of cheerful bustle: the new year was approaching. Trees, sprinkled with shimmery artificial snow and hung with toys, sparkled brightly in the shop windows. *It's an entire forest in the windows. Paris is a forest, as I once joked with Ladd,* she thought walking down the street. *I wonder where he is now. Why did we ever meet?*

Her thoughts about Ladd shifted to Sonia. Not long ago she had wished her dead. Now she didn't care. Yes, she was completely indifferent to Sonia and her loud voice and sharp, albeit handsome, face, her slender and quick movements, her short curly hair and waist so slender it seemed as if it might break.

Dasha was in a hurry. On her desk a stack of letters was waiting for her as well as the day's appointment calendar: seven telephone conversations in the morning, telegrams and letters to dictate, someone was supposed to come in at ten thirty-five, and before that instructions were supposed to arrive from Moreau. First thing, she reached him by phone: he felt quite well today, he had spent a marvelous night.

Suddenly the door opened behind her and she looked around. The empty sleeve (no, not empty, a polished piece of wood probably) was carefully tucked into his jacket side pocket. The arm had evidently been amputated high up near the shoulder because the shoulder itself was smaller than the other.

"You're here so early today?" she asked, greeting him politely. "Or am I late?"

He stood by the window. "Sit, please. Do you have a lot of

work? As always . . . You are amazingly conscientious. I have something to ask you."

She did not turn toward him; against the backdrop of the window he saw her profile with the knot of dark hair at her nape and the curled line of her eyelashes.

"Please give me the pleasure of having lunch with me today."

She thanked him and called in an employee to whom she handed a large envelope with the morning post for delivery to Leon Moreau. "Take a bus or a bicycle," she said, "but be quick about it."

"When the French say 'thank you,' it means 'no,'" Moreau said. "When Russians, Germans, and Englishmen say 'thank you,' I think they mean 'yes'—am I right?"

She smiled and raised her eyes to him. "Thank you. That means 'yes.'"

"I don't have much of a sense of humor, you may have noticed," he said, meeting her glance. "To my tremendous regret. I would like to always be saying something funny to you, to make you smile more often."

The telephone rang and Dasha picked up the receiver.

"But what would it be like," he continued, paying no attention to the phone, "to see your smile, to hear your laughter in response to something perfectly serious   something thoroughly thought through beforehand . . ."

"For goodness sake," she said quickly, covering the receiver with her hand, "I can't hear a thing. It's someone calling from Casablanca. For you, more than likely."

But he went on: "Something very important that's not always easy to say, especially for someone who is not usually very good at subjects like this . . ."

"It's Casablanca," Dasha repeated. "I'm here. Who's calling? Yes, he'll pick up right away"—she held out the receiver to him.

He took it with his only hand, held it for a moment, and put it down on the desk. Dasha was standing two steps away from him. She could hear the impatient crackling of a distant voice in the receiver. He took Dasha's hand and raised it to his lips without taking his eyes off her face.

"For several reasons you probably guessed long ago," he said, ignoring the telephone, "I do not feel like someone who has the least bit of confidence in himself. But I've gathered up the courage . . . Yes, that's it exactly, the courage to tell you . . ."

She picked up the crackling telephone receiver and put it to his ear, and while he was talking she walked out of the room, took the elevator to the third floor, went into the big room where the typists were typing, and seeking out fat, pink Jeanette, dictated two telegrams for London.

"This Jeanette has been sitting in the same chair for twenty-one years, just changing the piece of carpet she has on her chair when it wears out," said Dasha in the restaurant, "but I don't see anything so terrible in that constancy."

"Nor do I," he replied, beautifully managing both the food and the drink with his hand. "When you come right down to it, I've been sitting in the same chair for years, too, and I'll go on sitting in the same chair (or one very much like it) for many more years to come. There's even a certain pleasure in that. And very possibly my son will do the same."

She knew he had two sons, that he was a widower.

"And if we are speaking candidly, this pleasure actually comes down to one thing: my stable position. I value that very highly. I could not live on a volcano."

In a way, the restaurant looked like a giant aquarium: the same green light, the perfectly quiet garçons, the passers-by moving silently behind the tulle curtain of the big picture window. But neither of them had much time; Dasha had to be back by two.

"I still haven't decided," he said, pushing a tiny cup of fragrant coffee toward her, "whether or not I'll go home for Epiphany. I shouldn't leave the boys alone too long. Christmas has already been not really Christmas for them, and they love me though they're terrible scamps and quite a headache for Miss Mill. Still, I'm afraid I'm going to have to stay on here."

"I thought you said a few days ago that you had a seat reserved on the plane."

Deftly, he lit himself a cigarette (his right hand was trained like a sensitive, intelligent animal). "I'm not sure of anything at this point. I've returned the ticket for the time being. Didn't I tell you that yesterday? I must have forgotten."

When the bill came, he unexpectedly said: "What calm, confident, warm hands you always have. Don't you wear rings? If you had a wedding ring, if that ever happened, would you wear it?"

"If that ever happened," Dasha replied, rising to her feet.

CHAPTER NINE

Sonia Tiagina's Notebook

S now blanketed us one morning, and by midday it started to melt, turn black, run off in streams down the streets which lost their ordinarily unsociable look. Everything became black and white, fluid—the city was coming apart before my eyes. When I went out, the landscape was wintry; when I returned, it was autumn-spring again, so typical of Paris. Winter hung on in our alley until the following morning because not many people went here, let alone drove. Fat black stripes, the trail of the one automobile that turned in here all day, made a loop in front of our entryway.

In the morning when I went out, the whole city was white and there weren't any automobile tracks in the snow, it was so thick. People cursed the weather and assured us all this had something to do with war. You could hear the first pinging of drops of water falling from the roofs and the streams gurgling softly here and there. I realized that I actually like snow, I like this blinding whiteness of the city and the clean air, which I breathe so rarely, this whole precarious city landscape—which won't last more than a few hours. I like spring, too. There's something about it I can't put my finger on—maybe its warm power. Maybe I've been on the wrong track doing what I did for so many years. Instead of delving so into books, maybe I should have traveled "over the face of the earth," from country to country, gotten to know the world. This might have been difficult, but not a great deal more so than what I in fact did. It might have yielded more—who knows!—than the knowledge I did amass, which I wanted and which I pretty much mastered. Because coming to know the world in breadth is getting to know its beauty.

I say I don't like nature, but that's because I don't know it. I'm not interested in butterflies and bugs, I don't melt at the sight of a sunset over the sea, I'm bored in the country. I'm afraid of big black cliffs (something connected with Crimea's Diva and Monakh). To tell the truth, nature leaves me cold. It doesn't even make me ask questions or wonder the way beauty makes me ask questions, questions I can't resolve. Above all: What is it? What is it for? Where is it in the world *right now*? There's something here I haven't been able to figure out.

Before our era beauty resided in nature, religion, art. We have come a long way from nature now. We think up our own religions, not always successfully. As for art, ever since romanticism ended and classicism moved to the back shelves in libraries and adolescents started studying abridged versions, art definitely has not known what to do with beauty. What is the artist to do with a beautiful face? The sculptor with a beautiful body? The musician with a beautiful combination of sounds? Things of beauty are suspiciously soft, sweet, ridiculous. Having lost all content, a form falls apart and ceases to exist. It is decay. But I could be wrong. Beauty might not have anything to do with religion or nature or art; it might exist for its own sake. But what is its purpose? Bereft of content, how can it last? It would have to become transient, like fashion.

For most women, this issue of beauty never comes up in an abstract way. Too often it becomes the issue of their own beauty.

If I could devote myself to the cult of my own appearance, like most women, I would probably survive, but as it is, I won't. I don't know what beauty is or what the world needs it for.

You see the inequality. I don't mean the inequality among free people—some rich, others poor, some sick, others healthy—but the inequality among unfree people because that shows you what has become of the world. In France or America someone locked up in prison for holding different views runs the prison library, whereas in Germany and Russia he hauls rocks. And if that's all you saw, it would still be enough to understand today's world. But the universe is still the universe and I'm still me and I can't even find my way as it is.

If someone came to earth from another planet, we would show him the marvelous and terrible things we have created. We would tell him how once the wisest of men gathered to speak of love, but even wiser was the woman who told them about how music's greatest genius was deaf and how a storm can turn into hope. We would also show him the inequality of those who aren't free. Most people worry about the inequality of the free, but it is the inequality of the unfree that is at the root of our social tragedy. This past year, in my total outward idleness, my shame and guilt have crushed me.

If I could find a way to act, maybe I could merge with the world at last, but I don't even have the words to talk about it, and I am left alone with myself. In my melancholy I feel it's my fault, and my hopelessness and despair increase. I want to do something—the one single necessary act. But my cry is my silence, and the time has not yet come for me to act.

After an entire day's work when I left the university library to go home, the roofs were still white but the rest of the city was black, and in our alley in the deep wet snow two streams gurgled in the tracks of the automobile that had turned in. It smelled of spring, as it does sometimes in Paris at the end of January, where January is so often more like March, October like May, June like

September. Everyone was home, and there were even three others for my mother's birthday: Feltman and the Sipovskys, husband and wife. All seven sitting at the table, drinking and eating. I said hello and sat down, too, between the Sipovskys and Zai. Zai seemed odd. Father, Mother, and their guests comprise a single whole in my mind, but the three of us don't combine at all— that's probably natural.

They're of no interest whatsoever to me. Feltman has a pseudo-profound gaze, Sipovsky-the-husband a pseudo-genial expression on his face, and Sipovskaya-the-wife a face like a plate or a saucer—blank, without personality or intelligence. My mother's face, once so sweet, now reflects constant worry and the effort of concealing that worry (especially from guests); my father's reflects weariness and, more and more clearly, the hidden disease that is consuming him. I don't believe anything about them, not their faces or what they say, not anything at all. Everything about them is vague, limp, full of compromises, spiced with tedious heroism (they've all had hard lives). You get the feeling that they never chose anything but just yielded to circumstances, reconciled themselves to the headlines—not thinking things through. The hardest reproach for them is to say someone "shines but doesn't warm," as if light weren't a thousand times greater than warmth! Sipovsky uses ringing, completely empty words (about the international situation) that sound thrilling but are not supported by any deed of his own (he thinks there should be a war, but he himself won't go—he's too old). Fiery talk and a body gone to fat—who would ever believe that fiery talk with that belly and that appetite? When the time comes to decide, act, and choose, such a belly leads to ambivalence and compromise. My father loves him though, he says Sipovsky saved his life once, that he is the most unselfish, energetic, and cultured man. Perhaps . . .

Sipovsky's wife has such an awful face you can't take your eyes off her. It doesn't express a thing, not even tranquillity or contentment or boredom—nothing. She starts every sentence "Ah, my dear!" They say those first years in exile she worked as a day maid, did everything she could to give her son an education (now he's somewhere overseas) until her husband got a job. My mother invariably talks about her as a heroine (once she seriously lost her temper with me and called me a parasite). This woman once said to me: "Why do you keep thinking all the time? Everything's been thought out already by other people, before you, when people were better and life was easier. What's there to keep thinking about?" At the time I felt like talking back, but I held my tongue so as not to shock her.

Feltman's theme is art. Everyone considers him the most refined expert on music and poetry and a connoisseur of painting. He likes to opine cozily about all this and is a symmetrical complement to Sipovsky, whose theme is politics. Feltman is embarrassed, he has a new weakness—when he has money, he spends it on old books—"I know, I know, it's unforgivable. A sin! Frivolous! What can you do? It's my weakness! I'm ashamed myself, there are so many needy people everywhere." I told him once that in his tango (which spread all over the world) he had stolen from Blok. He looked at me sad-eyed, smiled guiltily, and answered softly: "You're right. But who in his life has never stolen anything? Even Goethe."

Without any smile whatsoever I replied, "Me, apparently." But he shook his head and said that I had no sense of humor.

People like Feltman aren't cannon fodder, of course, but rather prison camp material for the world catastrophes of the future. They won't survive. They can't. To survive you have to be a commander and a rank-and-file soldier all in one. They're neither.

Amid this entire company sitting at the table, Zai continued to seem odd to me. Her face was distracted and wistful and she barely raised her eyes. My father was talking smoothly and expansively the way he does. His spirits get up in front of people, he forgets that when he and my mother are alone together he plays the old baby a little because he often has something hurting inside. When he's among the three of us he gets gloomy, as if we were asking him a riddle he has to solve and he's in no mood to laugh and could never solve it anyway. When he's with others like him, he blossoms with memories of the past and about himself and what he was once like; he gets voluble, the old gestures return. The familiar ideas act like a narcotic on him. I think of the portrait of him as a young man. He was handsome.

My mother watches him with delight and humility. She won him with her delight and humility. Why her and not one of the hundreds of other women he'd had in his day? He could have gone back to Dasha's mother; he could have dropped everything and stayed with that actress Dumontelle. And there would have been no me or at least there would have been no me as I am now. Imagine—something midway between Dasha and Zai.

Impossible. There are images you can't imagine. You don't lack imagination but there's a mystical fear about letting your thoughts dwell on them. I wouldn't dare open my granny's closed coffin now, twenty years after her death: an aged beauty who starved to death, she lies there, maybe not fully decayed. All I would have to do is raise the coffin lid. I can't imagine my own conception, I avoid thinking about it. I'm afraid of the old icon covered in human excrement that was found after Dasha's mother was murdered, the day after the pogrom.

The main reason my father stayed with my mother was me coming into the world. Neither Dasha's nor Zai's births tied him down. Whatever it was, he stayed with my mother. Maybe because I looked so much like him. I united them. They're happy together, they love each other, their lives are bound together to the grave. Dasha and Zai couldn't do that. Indirectly, I'm the one who gave Tiagin and my mother happiness; the further I moved away from them, the more attached they became to each other. They complemented each other. All they gave me was my name.

My mother is placid and ruddy from pie baking. She admires the bouquet of carnations Tiagin brought her this morning. There are people, especially women, who have an almost religious feeling for flowers. Not everyone can throw a live, fresh bouquet into the garbage. I can—yet I can't throw out a dried flower pressed in a book, even someone else's. When someone else's dried blade of grass falls out of a book, I piously reinsert it. It's dead and so it must live. There are actions I cannot take, just as there are images I don't dare look at. I hope no one finds out, but I can't crumble a dried flower in my fingers.

The carnations shone, their faces shone, you could tell it was a holiday because Dasha was trying to fall in with the general mood; actually, she may have done this quite naturally. Zai, however, was embarrassed and bored, and finally she found a convenient moment and went to her room. I waited about five minutes, during which the conversation went on as before about people I didn't know and events that didn't concern me—nonetheless I listened attentively,with a pleasant expression on my face—actually, two or three times a year it doesn't cost me anything to put on a face like that!—and I may have been infected by Dasha's example. She was being particularly sweet and gracious—and, as always, self-confident. Now that Zai was no longer in the room, my attention turned to Dasha.

A few minutes after Zai left, I slipped out of the dining room unnoticed and went to my room—small, narrow, looking out on a dark courtyard. I switched on the light and perked my ears. Soon I heard footsteps in the hall and Zai came in. She closed the door behind her and sat down on my bed. She looked utterly crushed.

"It snowed," she said softly.

I didn't answer. I was sitting by my desk, doodling weird faces on a piece of paper.

"It hasn't melted yet. You can see it from our room," Zai went on. I still didn't say anything. Utterly stupid to carry on a conversation with her about the weather. I drew the street and the black tracks from the automobile tires. The apartment building. The gates. The tracks make a semicircle and go back. It's too sharp an angle—you can't make that turn. Back up. Straighten the wheels. Inkblot. That means the pen is out of ink.

"You can still see the automobile tracks—that was Moreau coming by."

"Well, what happened?" I asked at last. "Wasn't he dying last week?"

"He's never been ill. That's the old man who was ill, his father. It was the son who came."

"He has a son? Why did he come by? For Dasha?"

"Yes, for Dasha."

She fell silent and flopped down on my bed. "Dasha is marrying him. She's going to be Madame Moreau."

We looked at each other for a minute. Finally I caught my breath. "Why aren't you rejoicing then?"

Zai didn't know. She said she'd never anticipated this kind of an "end." She'd been expecting a miracle from Dasha! She thought Dasha's life would be special and now it was just like everyone else's. In short, the news came as a total surprise to her; to me too, for that matter.

I teased Zai at first. I told her that, on the contrary, I thought it was a great happiness for Dasha and quite suitable—actually amazingly suitable for her to become the wife of an honest banker, a widower with two children, armless and noble. That is exactly what we might have predicted for her. My God, Dasha has an inner harmony. . . . Haven't I always envied her that? Her future will be perfectly harmonious, too: more children, lots of money, she'll have a house, servants, a bank account. Naturally, she'll be happy. And undoubtedly Mr. Moreau will be happy with her, too.

"You have a deaf soul, Sonia. It doesn't hear what's going on around you, and it may not even be your fault. You're not angry at me for saying so, are you? You and your deaf soul don't understand that some people have been different from you since they were born. And different from me. They might not be as smart or as beautiful as you, they might not have any talent, but they do have a power. Don't laugh! I don't know what kind of power it is, but I do know it's good and very strong. And it comes from their equilibrium. And Dasha has this power, she's one with the world. And I'm not!"

"Go on," I pushed her cautiously. "This is all very interesting."

"I think she's already performed small miracles. Once I thought she'd perform a big miracle someday—walk on air or raise the dead or . . . Now I don't think she will. There's something so ordinary about what's happened today. That's why I'm sad."

I burst out laughing and couldn't stop. I'd been anticipating this moment for a long time: here was Zai's soul laid out before me, defenseless and utterly innocent.

"Bravo!" I exclaimed. "Not badly thought out! But, poor girl, you forgot one thing: people who are in harmony with the world from the moment they're born are unflappable, they don't go getting themselves into hurricanes. On the contrary, they all end well and live comfortable lives full of warmth and family feeling, and they stay young in body and soul until they're seventy. Anyone who is in balance like that floats through life without mishap, finds a rich husband, to the delight of their papas and mamas, and is universally liked. Some people skirt all the reefs, oblivious to their existence; some smash up on them. That's the whole difference. Did you really imagine Dasha suffering for love, standing on the brink of ruin, struggling, doubting? And it's been a very long time since anyone walked on water."

During Zai's long silence I drew a small ship with the ink left in my pen.

"Is that really true?" she finally said sorrowfully. "The last thing I want for her is any more suffering. That's not the point. I guess I don't know what I expected from her."

I sat beside Zai on the bed, held her cold, limp hand, brushed her hair from her cheek. Her hair is black, straight, and bobbed; sometimes she tucks it behind her ears, but more often it falls into her eyes.

"It's good not to be in tune with anything," I said, as if I were initiating her into a precious secret. "When life is hard and lonely, when someone doesn't know his place in the world, everything is revealed: everything terrible and everything hard. He doesn't shield himself, he's prepared for anything, he pays in full and lives as if he were flirting with his own undoing. Someone like that doesn't yield, he's his own master. He doesn't need anyone. The more unbearable and hopeless his life is, the better for him."

I was lying, but Zai believed me. She looked at me with her slightly slanted eyes. This look, I don't know why, gave me a piercing pleasure. I felt that now, for the first time in our life together, I had mastery over her soul, and this thought gave me an utterly new happiness I'd never experienced before.

"If you always thought Dasha was in tune with the world— well, you were wrong, because no one can be. What happened today happened because of her harmony. If at twenty someone loves her equilibrium, then at thirty she stands still and at forty she petrifies from the well-being she's found. These harmonious natures are so predictable. They don't allow disruptions. Dasha's going to be happy. Let me kiss you, my sweet little Zai! How could I be angry at you for saying I have a deaf soul? You have a right to your own opinion about me."

She hugged me around the neck.

"Forgive me, Sonia. I was unfair to you. And very stupid. Forget I ever said it. I've been so caught up in my own happiness lately—but you're right, you have to see things as they really are. No one walks on water or heals the sick."

After a bit, Zai stood up and walked slowly out of the room.

Through the door she had opened when she left, raucous laughter rushed up from the dining room—evidently the merry-making was still in progress and they were all talking at once. I walked over to my desk, looked at the piece of paper lying under the lamp, completely covered with my drawings, and I wanted to tear it up, but suddenly I felt my arms drop. I couldn't lift them. They hung at either side of my body, and I was filled with a heavy, plaintive bitterness. I felt as if I had deceived someone close to me, someone who had believed in me up until now, as if someone I had trusted had wished me dead. I know it's going to happen and it won't be long! Because in the world everything flows logically out of everything else, because everything tends to flow down, a miracle flows into the everyday, despair flows into suicide. It's going to happen!

I couldn't endure that state for very long. My hands were hanging, I looked at the circle of lamplight on the table, not breathing, feeling all my terrible immobility. And then there was a long harsh ring at the door, someone ran down the hall, and Dasha's voice cried out: "Sonia, someone to see you!" And I went out to meet Volodia Smirnov, Madeleine, and someone else. They'd stopped by to invite me to hear Volodia's brother, who had arrived yesterday from Prague. So I went out with them, like an automaton, and returned late, when everyone else was fast asleep.

CHAPTER TEN

Seven of them were putting on a comedy. Actually, it was more like clowning for the stage. It was very fast-paced, so that by the end sweat was pouring from all seven and dripping on the parquet, covering it with dark spots. Sweat spots on the floor—Zai never would have believed such a thing could happen, but now, as she wrung out her shirt in the kitchen, she knew that anything can happen. The lavatory served as a dressing room for the performers, and their toilet articles were laid out on the steps of the steep staircase—powder, a mirror, one lone half toothless comb which everybody used. A corner of the parlor had been transformed into a stage, the rugs and bearskins had been put away, the furniture pushed to one side, the bric-a-brac dumped into a carton. Scraps of fabric tossed here and there on armchairs and end tables were hung on walls to provide the backdrop for their acting. There was such an uproar, Jean-Guy's mother and her friends, with their liqueur and *belote,* were forced to decamp from the dining room and go upstairs to the bedroom. There were rehearsals four times a week in the evening, and in the daytime, in the chaos of the disorder, they continued to see certain "clients." But Zai wasn't around during the day.

"Countess! Your son is turning into a jaguar!" This is how the first act opens. The doctor is reporting this and the countess lets out a scream. The young count's fiancée (played by Zai) throws herself on the doctor, pleading that he turn her too into a beast of prey. But the doctor spreads his hands, he is powerless, and Zai, forced to link her fate with a being like herself, gradually turns into a large green grasshopper while the jaguar chooses a girlfriend for himself from among the audience. A dozen different stories were played in succession and each of the participants acted three or four parts; in the last act the improvisation started, as the author (Jean-Guy's cousin) had noted in the text: "actor improvisation seven minutes, actor improvisation eleven minutes." The author himself, wearing a camel's hair coat and clenching a pipe in his teeth, stood from beginning to end of this noisy silliness, leaning against the door jamb, observing his progeny come to life. He was getting ready to rent a small theater for the troupe and to sign an engagement contract with the actors. He was bored; he had a lot of money.

After rehearsing, everyone went to wash up at the sink in the big, empty kitchen, where on every table and stool there were stacks of dirty dishes intermingled with clean ones—when anyone felt like a drink of water, he had to choose the least sticky of the glasses. Anyone who was hungry took three or four apples from the basket or found bread and butter, or eggs which were sucked raw through a hole in the shell. The gang filed upstairs and plopped down together on Jean-Guy's bed, lit cigarettes, and discussed their future. Only when it got very late did they go over to the Left Bank, to a café where they were already known and where they were regarded with curiosity.

Zai would start back after all the buses and the Metro had shut down, so Jean-Guy would see her home, walking all the way across town. She no longer ran away from him into the entry. Quite the opposite, she stood and watched him walk away, from street lamp to street lamp, disappearing and reappearing as he walked down the empty sidewalk. Then, when the sound of his footsteps faded away and his silhouette had dropped from view, she cut across the alley to her own entry, carefully shut the door, went up the stairs without making a sound, took the key out from under the mat, and turned it in the lock, having removed her shoes so as not to make any noise in the hall. But Liubov Ivanovna was standing on the other side of the door and Zai had to endure five minutes of reproaches and threats.

"You listen to me," Liubov Ivanovna said in an angry whisper. "This can't go on. Your papa and I have decided that you're going to study stenography. Enough of this frittering away your time. It's Dasha who puts that key under the mat for you! You're a capable girl. In three months you'll have a job. You can always keep on writing poetry."

"Auntie Liuba, you've been talking for five minutes, look— by the clock! And I don't in the least want to write poetry. I haven't been writing it for a long time, more than a month. Now I'm acting and I'm going to start getting a salary soon. I'll give it all to you, wait and see."

Liubov Ivanovna recoiled from her.

"You reek of wine and tobacco. In order to act, you first have to study, darling. Otherwise anyone could act. You have to work hard in school. And what theater is this, may I ask?"

"Really Auntie, you'll see. I am studying a lot. There's no point going to school, though, because the theater is temporary, too, just like the poetry. I don't plan to be an actress for very long. What will come next, I still don't know. These are the stages of my liberation."

"Queen of Heaven! Stages!" Liubov Ivanovna clutched her broad face with both hands. "What have you dreamed up now? First it was poetry. That's natural, so to speak: it's your heritage. From your mother. And now it's stages? Have you lost your mind or something? If something happened to your papa tomorrow, you'd be out on the street. Do you think the whole family can hang on Dasha's neck?"

Zai took a melancholy look around but she saw there was no place offering salvation.

"You're going to enroll in a typing class," whispered Liubov Ivanovna, pressing her entire body against Zai, as was her habit. "And that will be a stage, too, and then Moreau will take you into the bank, not his own, of course, but some other bank, and not as a secretary but somewhere in the back to start. And this will involve more stages. And then you can go finish bookkeeping school. That will be a real stage! It is a trade—it will feed you anywhere."

At this she let Zai go. It was after one in the morning. The moment Zai found herself alone, all her sadness fell away; dizzy from the happiness that life and youth had bestowed upon her, she pressed her hands to her chest and closed her eyes.

What would Boiko have said to all this? How pleased he would have been to see her so happy. If he were still alive (was that possible?) he might dream about her sometimes, right? She hoped he could see her the way she was now, but he probably saw her as a little child, the way she had been, when Grandmother had diapered her, with a prayer, as she did everything. Or the way she was just before her departure, when she trembled at everything. "Our Father," said Grandmother. Such an amazing whisper, the "ourfather" rustling on her lips. But Zai stood next to her in front of the holy image (which they ought to have replaced long ago with a portrait of Lenin, as all the neighbors had done) and was afraid: afraid of someone coming into the room at that moment and hearing the unpermitted prayer, insulting them; afraid of whoever lived on the other side of the wall and could hear their whispers; afraid in general of everyone who made it so that you had to laugh very quietly and say things in a low voice, too. Her entire life had been one long rustle, one long "ourfather," that is, a rustling in the half-dark of frightened, tormented people. Could liberation from all this ever really come? "Yes," Boiko had said then. "It will come, of course. This can't go on for a thousand years. But for you it will come when you set foot on the foreign—foreign to me—land where your mother was born and to which you have to return. It's a special land. In it live people who first told the world about human dignity and freedom."

Only now, for the first time in all these years, did she recall that time, as if it had been dozing deep in her memory, between different levels of memory, and now emerged quite easily and simply. Back then she'd felt like sleeping; it had been late and she'd tried to keep from nodding off, so as not to offend Boiko. At the time, though, she hadn't understood him. Every day they had sung about freedom in a chorus, and so had she. "Human dignity" was hard to figure out. Both words were familiar taken separately, but together their meaning was obscure. The fact that she read French did not yield an explanation. With Grandmother she had read *L'homme qui rire,* and sometimes out of boredom she would skip pages, undetected, doing it so deftly that Grandmother didn't notice. "After Hugo we're going to read *Peau de chagrin,*" Grandmother said once, and this didn't sound like much fun either. If only it had been about morocco leather or kid, but *chagrin* was probably something dreary again. She was afraid of Grandmother, though, and did not say anything. Yes, she was even afraid of Grandmother. That was what she was like then.

She had realized long ago that she would never resemble a marvelous book or a crisply tied sailor's knot. To say nothing of a carnation, which lived and flourished while books and sailor's knots disappeared, died, perished, left life without a trace. She could face becoming an insect, like her contemporary, Alyosha, who hid in cracks quaking and suffering, to keep from being blown away by the whirlwind. But no: now it turned out there was a place in the world where you could live freely and proudly. Uncle Lyosha, Boiko, had told her about it. There, you could walk free and proud, shedding this terrible shell, no longer needing it to protect you from savagery, grief, and humiliation.

Boiko also told her about the climate of this country's people, not the climate of the country but of its people—about the special air that envelops a person. It's not just a country's history and art, its cities and landscape—each individual person has the ability to carry this climate to others, to pass it on to other people. The person *is* the climate. She'd asked then: How can that be, Uncle Lyosha—can that really be so? "Yes, it can, and you will see it one day and you'll understand. Man can create the world around himself and let others live in this world. The foundation of it is set: freedom and human dignity."

These words stayed in her memory and though incomprehensible to her at first, like a kind of incomprehensible "our-father," began to fill with meaning as slowly and tortuously she began freeing herself from the fears she had brought with her. The words rang out and came to life—not bloodless and abstract but in her inner being. Without flagging, Zai was freeing herself from the gloomy shadows, loosening invisible chains, shining more and more brightly with every step, inhaling the special oxygen which had no equal in the world—the oxygen of freedom and human dignity. Gradually she was becoming herself a bearer of this mysterious, universal human climate, which unbinds everything man, free and proud, had brought with him to freedom.

Poetry was just a pretext. And the theater would probably be another. And love? Maybe. *But I don't love you any less because of it, Jean-Guy. I love you even more because you're not the goal but a means to the goal, which is my freedom, my affirmation in the universe. You show me who I am, and through you I gain my own humanity. I love you because you've taught me not to be afraid of myself alone or together with you, and that means not to be afraid of anyone. Thank you! When I leave your embrace I*

don't feel lonely and when I return to it I don't feel shy or hurt.
I'm happy. I'm free. I'm a human being, not a trembling insect.

I don't have anyone to confide in about what's happened to
me. You wouldn't understand, Jean-Guy, and you'd be hurt to
find out what your love means to me. Others might shrug and
call me immoral, frivolous, or, on the contrary, permanently
damaged by my unhappy and painful Russian childhood. I don't
care whether or not we keep loving each other, whether or not
you and I stay together or find a different happiness or a differ-
ent suffering. I'm going to read lots of books and meet lots of
people. I don't care what I may discover about myself or what
kind of future I'll have. I do know one thing: my road, my one
hidden road, is liberation. Whether waking or sleeping—that's
my one task.

Zai's eyelids were heavy and she closed her eyes. Through
fog and strange somnolent silence, she envisioned the far distance and a somber city rising up in this distance. She saw herself in this city. Little Vasya was cooing in the arms of pale,
round-shouldered Alyosha, and Alyosha's wife was speaking in
a peremptory tone: "Liza must be shown the Kremlin!" They
had stopped at the foot of a high wall, and concern gripped her,
alarm—she couldn't see anything behind it. She ran her eyes
even higher, searching—and suddenly above this blind, dark red
wall appeared the two slender spires of Sainte-Clotilde, two silver needles in a silver sky. They were disappearing into the
heights, melting, filling her soul with intolerable bliss. But Jean-
Guy's voice suddenly spoke into her ear: "Countess! Your son is
hopeless."

She woke up. How merrily and stupidly she spent her days!
Of course they were right, this could not go on any longer, she
had to start earning money like everyone else in the world, study
bookkeeping or fabric cutting, or take a sales clerk position—to
decide something in a general way, so she could help her father
pay off his debts. She would buy Liubov Ivanovna a new hat, her

father a tie, Sonia a new dress because Sonia never bought herself dresses but went around in patched ones—out of stubborn-
ness, her bad character, and a distaste for doing anything sensible after studying for so many years. Zai would get on her feet;
she would live like everyone else, and this would be one more
step toward freedom, outward and inward, and her entire life
would be nothing but pride and freedom until death. . . . *But
it's still too soon to think about that, that's too far off. Let's think
about life, happiness, suffering, a trip around the world, about
how I might have some talent for the stage after all.*

*We'll start our trip with Africa. We'll take a look at Dasha's
life, at Eridan burning in the southern hemisphere over the an-
cient mariners' route. They sailed around some cape, in the end,
and rounded it. And I shall round my cape. But some won't. I
shall cross three oceans. Jean-Guy will be a doctor on an ocean
liner, a pirate ship, an oil tanker. . . .*

"How fine!" whispered Zai, lying on her stomach, extending
her crossed hands.

Dasha, in her bed against the other wall, was breathing
evenly, barely audibly. *I'll reconcile myself to her fate,* thought
Zai. *My demands on her were childish. I love her and I want her
to be happy. And I believe she will be happy. Sonia, though, will
be unhappy because . . . because why? That I don't know, but
I have a premonition. Today I told her they aren't actors at all.
One is a future doctor, another is studying photography; both
girls play in the student symphony orchestra. I told her I'd introduce her to them at the dress rehearsal, and she'd see how much
fun it is with them. Then she just smiled at me strangely and
didn't say a thing.*

In the distance, near Sainte-Clotilde, a clock chimed twice:
it was quiet in the house and quiet in the courtyard, and it occurred to Zai that, just to be naughty, she ought to get up right
now, get dressed, sneak out of the house and into the streets,

which were wet from two days' heavy rain, run as far as the square, run all the way around the square, survey the night world in its empty and stern nakedness, and then crawl back under her blanket. Smiling at the idea, she felt her eyes closing shut, at last. "Countess, your son . . ." Zai was already asleep.

For the first time in many years Sonia took part in a family council.

"She never wanted to study and barely passed her exams at the community school," said Tiagin. "True, her life had been wrecked. Not everything went right back to normal after she moved here."

Liubov Ivanovna had been searching for a silver strainer in the buffet for a whole hour; the buffet drawers were pulled out, a mug and gravy boat were standing on the floor, and she herself was crawling around. "I don't know where it rolled. Other people study and nothing comes of them either," she muttered. "They study for ten years at a go, they know everything, but they don't find any way to apply their talents and as far as getting any help from them goes—zero."

"I think someone needs to have a serious talk with her, to ask her seriously whether she wants to obtain some kind of diploma for the future at last? If so, then I think I could help her with that next autumn," said Dasha.

"She doesn't want anything. She wants to have fun. This, she says, is only a stage. Now it's flowers, and the berries are ahead. She doesn't care about the theater, Papa is wasting his time thinking that." (Liubov Ivanovna always called Tiagin "Papa" in front of the children.) "He's wasting his time thinking she loves the theater. Everything just slides over her, nothing sticks. It's some kind of insensitivity."

"Of course she's not interested in any kind of diploma,"

Sonia said then, mirthfully. "I'll take her down to see one of my acquaintances. He has a bookstore near the quay. Last year he offered me a job. Maybe he'll hire Zai."

Tiagin stared at her. What was behind that face of hers, so harsh, so alien? And at the same time, all her features resembled his, of all the three she was *his* daughter most of all. But she was a closed book to him. And she didn't love him. That he had sensed for some time.

"Why didn't you take the bookstore job yourself?" he asked, trying not to let her haughty gaze intimidate him. "Things were so hard for us last year."

Sonia lit up. "I have other ways to earn money. And I didn't want to tie myself to that man."

Liubov Ivanovna got up off her knees: "And is that how it's always going to be?"

"We're talking about Zai now," Dasha rushed in, sensing that one more minute and everything that had been so solid for so many months, their tested and true house of cards, was about to collapse and restoring it this time would be even harder than the last time. "Let's talk about Zai. Let's ask her. And if necessary, she can go with Sonia to find a job. It's a little early to be leaving it up to her to do what seems right, to be perfectly honest."

"She said"—Sonia began speaking slowly without looking at anyone—"that this isn't a theatrical troupe at all, that they're just doing it for fun, putting on a bit of fluff. As for me, Mama, I was planning to tell you yesterday: I'll probably be going to the provinces. I sent in my application a few days ago. Dasha is going to leave and so am I. Zai will start working, and everything here will be different."

There was silence; no one felt like saying what he was thinking, but everyone was feeling a certain relief from Sonia's words. She herself, eyes lowered, was flicking cigarette ashes onto her saucer. She had lied: yesterday she had had no idea what she was going to do. The decision about herself had come to her during the course of this discussion. Decisions of this kind always come like this, actually—in the middle of a peaceful discussion, in the middle of a business transaction, in passing, on the step of a bus. They come haphazardly and later gather a person's entire life under their enormous wings.

When Feltman came, in the evening, he and Tiagin would now sit behind closed doors in the dining room, conversing in low voices. They didn't want anyone in the house to hear how pleased they were about Dasha's marriage. They pictured, somewhere on another continent, the same kind of apartment as this, only a little better, with the same kind of lamp on the table, only a little more expensive, and Dasha's life with Moreau was copied straight from their lives, so amiable and so sensible. Sometimes when Feltman came before dinner, he would sit alone in the room for a while, having put either a pickle or a turnover purchased in the Russian store by each person's place. Then Tiagin would appear, tired, and paler all the time, on his way to wash up and take his medicines before eating. Liubov Ivanovna would bring the tureen in from the kitchen. "To you the cooking pot is dearer still," Feltman would quote while he was waiting for his hosts to sit down and Sonia to come out to the dining room. And when the soup had been ladled into the plates, the key would turn in the lock and a very gay, although businesslike as ever, Dasha, already a little alien to the household but still belonging to it, would be home for dinner. In recent weeks Zai had been having dinner at home less and less often.

She was spending long hours sitting Turkish fashion in an armchair draped with a piece of old silk, or in the same pose in the middle of a long, narrow bed, which had been made specially for Jean-Guy. The springs sang so melodiously when he threw himself down on it crossways, his head at Zai's knees, and they would laugh, hugging each other, or they would sit formally side by side, discussing something serious. The street outside was somewhat reminiscent of the one on which Zai's childhood had been spent: it too had been provincial and quiet, with two-story houses, lilacs and acacia in spring, a thick blanket of leaves in autumn, and snowdrifts in winter. But there weren't any snowdrifts and Zai had still not seen the lilacs and acacia in bloom on this street or the frenzied October leaves falling in a warm thunderstorm. There had been only the sparrows and at first they had seemed to be the same, but thank God, they were different and chirped in French.

"In France the roosters sing in French, too," said Zai, craning her skinny neck toward the window. "And naturally I understand them perfectly."

A dusty clock was ticking away on a dusty shelf, and through the dirty tulle on the window you could see one more long, blissful day going behind the buildings, behind the clouds. The little iron stove was red-hot. They had opened the door, and downstairs people were coming and going. In the parlor, which had not been cleaned up since the day before, where everything was pushed aside, piled up, and sprinkled with cigarette ashes, there were "clients" sitting—either Jean-Guy's mother read fortunes from the cards or she was selling them a hair tonic she had concocted herself. She did this less out of need than for her own amusement, since she received a decent pension from her deceased husband's estate.

When it began to get dark, the same chatterbox girlfriends, who loved to gossip and lay out the cards, would arrive. One brought a mandolin along. Jean-Guy ran downstairs with a deafening rumble but came back up on tiptoe, carefully, carrying sandwiches, oranges, and a bottle of wine. Zai and he ate and drank at his desk, but sometimes they went down and had dinner with the ladies, who paid no attention to either one of them. Each lady was self-absorbed, and everyone was talking and laughing at once. Men sometimes came as well, but they didn't stay long and it was always on some kind of business. Not only were they not invited to stay and sit, they were seen out as quickly as possible.

The clock—old and ugly, with broken-off bronze filigree and very sooty from the smoking stove—was ticking, but for Zai there was no time, the outside world had moved off, and between her and it there was a no-man's-land, where all the sounds hid away in the emptiness and all the colors flowed together into one fuzzy distant hum, into one dull color. Day-to-day affairs, human relationships, all that remained intact, but all of it was seen from afar, across the distant no-man's-land that protected Zai with its emptiness.

"Why you, specifically you, and not someone else?" she asked, knowing he had nothing to reply to that, nor did she. "What a sweet face you have, Jean-Guy. You know that you are the most beautiful person on earth? You can't imagine what I feel when I say this to you, when I kiss you, when I touch you. All this is such a joy for me! This afternoon, when I was waiting for you by the university gates, I was so happy. You know, I'm going to go to those gates at that hour my whole life. You'll be a famous psychiatrist by then, and I'll still be waiting for you there. It's so nice. And no one, no one can stop me! I was standing there and waiting and suddenly your face, this face, with these eyes, out of the rowdy crowd that had nearly knocked me off my feet . . . I love you, Jean-Guy."

He kissed her eyes and lips and smiled at her talkativeness and said that there was something Chinese about her stiff, straight black hair, that she had a child's hands, a child's fingers, and a touching birthmark deep in her narrow clavicle. He played with her for a long time, examining her and kissing her, and then he got serious, sat up straight on the bed with a cigarette between his lips, furrowed his brow, and said that he was certain to fail his exam this spring because of the theater and demanded that she go over both their roles with him.

For some reason, when they were rehearsing in the parlor,

the verbal nonsense seemed terribly witty and brilliant to Zai, and she did and said what she was supposed to with pleasure, but here, when they rehearsed together, aware of each other's breathing, it was completely different, and she had to make an effort to keep Jean-Guy from noticing that she did not really find it all that interesting. She began to dance around the room on her toes, humming songs to him that he said were Chinese, too, until everything in the house and city had become quiet and the time came when the door downstairs slammed and the troupe gathered with much laughter for their evening rehearsal.

The ladies moved their things upstairs, and from the bedroom now you could hear their conversations, which were always the same, as if some invisible pedal had been pressed or put in italics in a book. Not: "I like" or "I don't like," not "bad" or "good," but invariably "I spat in his face," "a scoundrel the likes of which the world has never seen," or "she is an angel of goodness, you should get down on your knees and pray." But usually the door would slam shut and there would be nothing to hear. Downstairs the ladies were forgotten. The main task was the scenery, which a fragile, unattractive, acned boy with a thick checkered scarf he never took off was laboring over.

At half past ten, Zai announced she had to go home. "If I get home two or three times by eleven, then I can go back to the way it was." As had been their practice from the very first day, she kissed everyone in turn, saying goodbye to both girls and boys, cinched the belt around her coat and left.

Again the nighttime world, mysterious and magical; a green bus floated by, a truck with firemen raced past, pedestrians walked along. A pearl was returning to its shell, crawling across the green velvet into oblivion, Zai was going home. Sonia met her in the entryway and followed her into her room. Dasha, of course, was not home. An open carton stood in the middle of the room: a new evening dress had been sent that day from the store and Dasha had put it on immediately.

Sonia said, "Tomorrow you and I are going to see B. at his store. Do you know B.? Remember, he came to see me once last year; you still had a cold and took him for a doctor. Don't you remember? . . . Well then it doesn't matter. He has a large book business, and I think he will take you on. Do you want to get a job? To get paid the first of every month?"

"Yes," said Zai very quietly.

Sonia stood in the middle of the room, watching Zai slowly undress. *It's time, of course,* thought Zai, taking her dress off over her head. *Here it is. Life. It's starting for real.*

Sonia did not leave. "Didn't you promise to take me to some rehearsal?"

"Yes."

"Change your mind?"

"No."

"What's wrong with you today? Bad mood?"

Zai fished her slipper out from under the bed with her bare foot. "I've thought it over," she said, picking up her hairbrush. "I was wrong then. Remember? When I was so upset over Dasha. Now I'm certain she did a good thing in agreeing, that she acted correctly. She's going to be happy. And everything you told me then is totally wrong. I've thought a lot about this. There's not one word of truth in anything you told me."

Sonia turned toward the door and left without saying a word.

CHAPTER ELEVEN

On the street corners, along the fences, pasted to kiosks and Metro walls, were big yellow posters. Coming out as evening fell, Dasha saw one of them directly in front of her and chuckled to herself. In capital letters in a sea of small type, it said: DON'T THINK! She hurried to the corner, where Moreau the younger was waiting for her in his car (to cut down on gossip, he no longer waited for her at the entrance). On the corner, in the twilight, it flashed by once again: Don't think! She got in the car, and an hour later, in front of the restaurant door where they had dined and across from the Comédie Française, which they had tickets for, it caught her eye again: Don't think! Don't think!

But Dasha was thinking: *I'm thirty-three years old, and who knows, this may be my only chance. I despise myself for looking at it in just this way. Yes, today I despise myself, but in three years I won't even understand my hesitations—I'll be sailing happily along and maybe even gaily toward the life I make for myself. I'm drowning. There's no rescue. Don't think. Don't think. Only someone who dares think things all the way through can lay bare everything without taking fright at anything, draw conclusions, and on the basis of these conclusions say No! But I can't do that, I won't lay anything bare or say no to anything. I don't think things through, I won't understand what happened to me, so why start these reflections? I'm incapable of them. What are these posters for? What is this, a new play called that or an advertisement for toothpaste? Don't think. Don't start something you can't finish. Skim across life. Don't think. Don't think.*

(A few days later she found out it was an advertisement for refrigerators.)

The night before, Liubov Ivanovna had had Dasha sit down in the easy chair by the bedroom window and closed the door firmly, although there was no one else in the apartment. The chair had been the first purchase made for the apartment: they hadn't even had a cooking pot then or mattresses, but they already had this chair because it had been left by the former owners, who had sold it with the apartment. It hadn't been new then, but it was comfortable, upholstered in red plush, and Tiagin had made it his. He sat in it in the evenings, occasionally moved it into the dining room. He had grown old in it, and skinny, altered in face and body—and soul, of course—in some strange, sad way. The springs were poking out of the chair now. Dasha thought it might not be a bad idea to get a new one.

Liubov Ivanovna talked about how she understood everything and that Dasha had a lofty spirit, that she was making a sacrifice for her papa, who in the sunset of his days would be at peace. Liubov Ivanovna wanted very much for this to be so. It had come to her in a flash, the first time she had seen Moreau.

"It would be good if Papa left that exhausting, badly paid work," said Dasha. "But there is no sacrifice whatsoever involved on my part. There you're wrong."

"I know, I know! That's in novels—sacrifice—though not modern ones, the old ones we read in our youth. It's when a young girl is compelled to marry an old man, but you are getting married of your own free will and not to an old man."

"I'm not so young myself." Dasha laughed. "And really, all this is nothing like that. But you know, if Zai takes that job and Sonia finally comes to her senses, and with my help, Papa won't have to work."

Liubov Ivanovna brought in two tiny glasses from the buffet and both of them drank the currant liqueur Liubov Ivanovna had received recently as a gift.

"Dasha," and she focused her tender gaze on her, "That was awfully stupid what I said about a sacrifice. You're going to be happy, after all, and you're going to make him happy. There's not the slightest doubt of that, darling. Right?"

"And why not?" And Dasha laughed again. "It certainly looks like it. In any case, out of all the worldly combinations there are I find this one most suitable for me."

"Combinations?" Liubov Ivanovna repeated distractedly.

"Well, yes. Possibilities, if you like. To live the way I've been living until I'm seventy years old is really too sad. I don't much like the idea of being nanny to Zai's children when she marries, either. Sonia's—illegitimate—children even less."

"Illegitimate! What are you saying!" Liubov Ivanovna had developed the habit a while ago of repeating the last word she had just heard. She had picked it up from Mrs. Sipovskaya.

"I tried marriage once, but nothing came of it. I think I still had that skittishness in me then. You know the kind. Now it's gone, so many years have passed. And the man this time is completely different."

"What kind of man is he, Dasha?"

"He's a marvelous man, really. He has character, I think, and he's calm, balanced, educated. He knows what he wants. He's searched for stability all his life—in his position, in his personal life, in everything. But he didn't have it in his personal life: his wife died and he missed her a lot. He had no love of casual liaisons, he was afraid of the storms and disruption, he was afraid for his sons, whom he loves very much. The wound left a very heavy mark on him. Once he said to me: 'I know you are just the woman I need.'"

"And what about you?"

"Me? Nothing. He hasn't asked me about anything. But he knows that I have very amicable feelings toward him."

Liubov Ivanovna stood up, walked over to Dasha, and kissed her on the head. There was concern in her face when she asked:

"Dasha, if this is friendship, just friendship, then how can it all work out?"

She had said it and then regretted it. She wished Dasha hadn't heard, hadn't understood her words, and if that was impossible, that she wouldn't answer her. Which she didn't. She continued to sit there for a while in the old armchair, examining the worn plush drapery, which had torn off one of its rings. Shifting her eyes to the corner of the room she thought that the pattern on the wallpaper was dulled and faded, that the old color lithograph, a copy of some Madonna and child, had faded as well, that everything here in the apartment was old, drained of color after long, hard years, and that Liubov Ivanovna too was old, and in just a little while she herself, Dasha, would begin to grow dull and to fade. Somewhere the same Madonna and chubby-cheeked child were hanging, vivid, smiling. Actually, maybe they were as faded as their copy. Who knew!

This had happened the previous night, and today Dasha went to work for the last time, not the very last time, actually, because she would still stop in, but she would no longer be sitting there from nine to six, she would not be clocking in. Old Moreau was ill again, gravely this time, so his son was in a hurry to get married, because his father might die, and then there would be the mourning period when they couldn't get married and he would have to go back to Oran alone. The little boys were doing badly in school, the governess was threatening to quit, the cook was drinking, and really, one couldn't leave one's home like that for so long.

The pleasure he experienced sitting next to Dasha in the theater was of quite a special kind. He knew that a period of ease would now begin. He had been battling for a dozen years, and now suddenly there was peace: as if a permanent truce had been declared from on high throughout the universe. All around the talk was of war, which was fast approaching, but to him it seemed just the opposite: the war was over. At first the war had been with his own mother, then with his father, then he had gone to a real war and had his arm torn off, then he had fought with women, and when he married, with his wife. She used to say he had a difficult personality, and she was probably right. When she died, he fought with the servants, his sons' governess, his sons. Now the end to all this was at hand.

Now, especially in her presence, there was peace, and above all, peace with himself, a harmony Moreau had never felt before; this is why he treasured her so much. "People have always told me I have an unbearable personality," he warned Dasha at the very beginning. "What will you say when you know me better?" "Well, I have a good one," she said simply, "and I think it will all work out." Ever since that conversation he had acquired the habit every time he saw her of looking closely at her face, neck, and coiffure, as if to make sure it was she, the same she as yesterday, the she who would be his wife tomorrow.

Don't think! flashed by once again on some pillar, under a street lamp, and when Dasha went home, she mechanically repeated it silently to herself again. It was late. She turned on the table lamp. Zai was sound asleep, a book lay on her pillow, right by her cheek. Dasha sat down at her small desk covered with old blotting paper, shaded the lamp with a piece of cardboard, and began thinking.

She thought that alone in this room, in the dead of night under this lamp, she might find the answer to all her questions and doubts, which had lain heavily on her these last few months. She felt a faint presentiment, and at this a strange feeling of relief passed through her. Although questions and doubts had weighed on her, not once, really, had the ground slipped out from under her feet. She was firmly anchored. Was the world repaying her for her long trust with its support or was she by herself strong enough, even stronger than she had supposed? She didn't know. *No, I won't drown in water or burn in fire,* she thought, *and if I drown or burn then I might not perish. How could that be: not perish? What if I die? Something will be left all the same. What exactly?* And suddenly she felt a jolt in her heart, and all at once she knew: everything in the world is ambiguous.

Yes, if there is no God, then everything is ambiguous, she thought. *And there isn't and never was a God, even if sometimes I wish there were. Everything has two meanings: every action, every decision—no matter how you act, no matter how people act toward you—yes or no, for or against—there are two meanings, and you are free to choose. After all, the world was carved up a long time ago, not length-wise, between good and evil, but cross-wise, between happiness and unhappiness. So follow your instinct, because that's your only criterion and you are the only judge. I suffered when Ladd spurned me, and in that suffering I wished Sonia dead and saw that my desire was as small and impotent as everyone else's, that I can't change the course of things, so Ladd was right to spurn me. Now I'm starting a new life, and this new life, like everything else, will have two meanings: one about marriage and everything it involves—self-sacrifice, submission, separation from home, agreement to everything marriage involves—and the other will be my own fear of future solitude and my weariness from working, my retreat into certain prejudices and responsibility, and my desire for well-being. There's nothing in the world that doesn't have two meanings, not even the love of the chubby-cheeked Madonna for her infant, or selfless devotion, because even that has its reverse side; not even sacrifice. Open it up all the way and you'll see that it too has two essences. Choose whichever you prefer at the moment.*

I guessed long ago what Sonia thinks of me, Dasha mused on, resting her face in her hand and watching the blue vein in her left wrist pulsating. *She thinks this is what being unruffled and balanced leads to—insurance against suffering and passion. But someday I'll say to her: What does constant anxiety, discord, and struggle lead to? Suicide? Crime? Insanity? And what will Zai's perpetual ecstasy, her poetry, which will never come to anything, her dreams—awake and sleeping—lead her to? An enthusiastic old age, foolish exaltation? Or stupidity? What did Papa's hatred for our era lead him to? Or Auntie Liuba, her sensitivity and virtue? Sipovsky, his love for fine words? Feltman, his incoherence and dilettantism? Everything is ambiguous; there are two answers to everything. It's just that the one you crawl into is like a broken-in shoe and the other is still tight and uncomfortable.*

The vein throbbed, not too fast and not too slow; with her finger she drew the route across the table, over the sea, to another continent, a strange but not frightening continent. "The flora and fauna," Moreau the younger once said, "and the constellations." *But I was never a guest in time or space. I feel at home under any constellation. There's even ambiguity in constellations. Because they're not just overhead, above me, but in me, inside me, at the very bottom, where my thoughts are anchored.*

And the veil that had fallen over Dasha of late slowly began to dissipate, shot through with light. Something lifted from her soul, the way fog sometimes lifts from the earth, and her thoughts became purer and clearer; and taking a deep look inside herself, Dasha saw in its usual magnificent calm the still sky, dispassionate and tranquil.

Eridan, she remembered, and she smiled. *That too will be reflected someday, when the Great Bear is led willy nilly over the horizon, a ring stuck through its nose.*

In the days that followed, everything changed in Dasha's life. The date for their very modest wedding—a secret to most people—was set for the middle of February. The deserted and quiet back street, where the hulking five-story apartment house had been built at the end of the last century and where the Tiagins lived, threatened from time to time to be transformed into that ballroom with chandelier it had always called to mind. Meanwhile that was nothing but a trick of the imagination, since in reality nothing was supposed to happen here and nothing had changed, if you didn't count the automobile that arrived once a day. There was no celebration, nor was there supposed to be. Everything was supposed to happen in the most discreet fashion possible. The preparations were more for the departure than for the ceremony itself, and even that word was not altogether appropriate for what was supposed to take place. The morning came when Dasha told herself: it's today. At two o'clock she was supposed to be at City Hall and at five fly from Le Bourget. Blocking up the room were two new suitcases, open and half filled with her things. Zai was singing loud, merry songs and hopping around.

Of course, Tiagin did not go to work that day. He stayed home, cautiously trying to guess what was happening on the other side of the wall, where Dasha was walking back and forth deciding what to take. It was like a Sunday: Liubov Ivanovna, red-eyed, in total and unaccustomed inactivity, was sitting by the window. Domestic occasions, even happy ones, made her cry. She could not take good-byes at all.

"Sonia, may I come in?" Dasha asked, and she went in. Sonia was lying in bed, covered up to her chin with her blanket, on which some thick books and a great number of newspapers were heaped. "Are you sick?"

"No, I'm fine."

"Why aren't you getting up? It's after nine."

"I'm just about to."

Dasha sat down at her feet; Sonia pulled her hand out from under her covers and threw the newspapers on the floor. There was a flash of bare shoulder.

"What, are you sleeping without a nightgown? Aren't you cold?"

"No."

"Don't you have a nightgown?"

"No."

Dasha raised her eyebrows and dropped them immediately. "I'll leave you my two. They're well worn, but they might still be some use. Actually, I came to ask whether you wanted my old fur coat. I have another one now. If not, I'll give it to Auntie Liuba."

"Why don't you give it to Zai?" said Sonia very calmly. "It will console her in her grief."

"Is she really grieving? Somehow I can't see it. She's been singing all day long. And in the fall, she may come visit me, so that the parting—"

"I'm not talking about the parting. She's grieving about you—how can I put it?—metaphysically. Once she even cried. I think she wanted 'love that would move mountains' for you."

Dasha raised her eyebrows again and looked long into Sonia's face.

"She kept thinking you would figure out something special. Why, I don't know. That you would raise someone from the dead and then marry him. She believed in you. She used to say you weren't like everyone else, and she probably assumed you wouldn't make any compromises. In short, she had all kinds of illusions on your score."

"Is that so," said Dasha, making a mighty effort to maintain her composure. "And what is your opinion on this subject?"

This question was somewhat of a surprise even to her. Never, at least not for a long time, had she asked for Sonia's opinion about her actions, but now it was easy. First of all,

Sonia's opinion wasn't going to change anything, and secondly, in a few hours she would be so far away from her that none of this would matter any more.

Sonia put her hand behind her head and ran her long slender fingers through her hair. "I think," she began, quietly sorting through her dark curling locks, looking up into Dasha's face, "I think that if I did this, that is, decided to marry the way you are, that would be just a caprice, a whim, a crazy action, and for my mate it would be a catastrophe. Or it wouldn't mean anything. But since it's you who's doing it, it means something completely different."

"What does it mean?" asked Dasha, holding her breath. "How am I marrying?"

"You know yourself how. Why do you ask? When Zai told me about it I thought, Of course! It's perfectly natural. It could have been predicted. The kind of person you are—"

"What kind am I?"

"You have to ask? Don't you know? Good, sweet, and most important, guaranteed, insured against everyday storms, prizing your equilibrium above all else, as well you should! Serene, and living this serenity of yours, which is primordial, organic—you could not have chosen otherwise. That is, there wasn't really even a choice, it just happened and you accepted what happened. And when I say you're in balance, that doesn't mean you have a phlegmatic nature, not by any means. It's much deeper in you, it's like a world view. And don't think I condemn this in you, but I can't admire it either." Sonia, with bare shoulders, disheveled, suddenly sat up in bed. "And here you are mooring at a quiet harbor, a prosperous life, acting the same way anyone would in your place. And we both thought you weren't like anyone else. That's all.

"No, that's not all. That's only the outward aspect of the matter. The other has to do with the inward aspect. Zai was expecting a miracle from you, God knows what. I don't know anything about it, but I always thought that you had something special inside, a kind of consolation for other people who don't have what you have. What is it? As if I could say! If I knew, everything would be different for me!

"And so we thought—Zai and I separately, notice—that you wouldn't give up something strong and beautiful for a feather bed and a sweet tidbit, that there was this calm inside you, this kindness, this mysterious possibility of fixing something in the world. You always had that in you. I noticed it in the first days after we met, and I wasn't even ten years old! Remember when you arrived, after everything that had happened to you, wrapped up in a bast mat, in a peasant's sleigh, alone, in the rain, with this wound in your heart that I thought would never heal, and then just think what you had come to! Not only to strange people but to your stepmother!"

"I've never thought of Auntie Liuba as a stepmother."

"But you didn't know that then. You didn't know how it would all turn out. That day you arrived at your stepmother's house, where they already had their own child, and your father, the only person you had, was lying in a field hospital awaiting evacuation. And from the very first days you amazed me."

"How did I amaze you?"

"With your clarity. Your balance. Of course, I didn't understand any of this at the time. It's astonishing how backward I am in my development compared to you and Zai. I was a complete child until I was seventeen."

Dasha pulled out a cigarette from the package lying on the table and lit up.

"Smoke, please. I'm trying to cut back, I have very little money and I want to test myself. One shouldn't fall slave to smoking!" said Sonia, and suddenly she was embarrassed. She didn't think she would ever be able to talk to Dasha about her own poverty now.

"So," she continued, inhaling with pleasure the smoke from

Dasha's cigarette, "to be perfectly blunt, what you're doing em-
barrasses me. And at the same time, it proves to me that there is
a certain logic in life, and the one who was A, B, C will inevitably become D, E, F and then—don't try to stop it!—inexorably, G, H, I! And when it becomes Y, those of us taking a different road will be a little frightened. But there is also the
reverse of the matter after all. You're marrying someone who
won't be any fun and who knows, of course, that you don't love
him. Every day you'll face the question of duty, and you'll be a
stepmother, too. You'll have problems, which you'll overcome,
and you'll undoubtedly bring joy to everyone you live with. That
is, you'll get your sweet tidbit and featherbed for a price—you'll
earn them morally. That's the other side of the coin. So why
grieve? You should celebrate, like everyone else. Zai only
grieved for one day, and now she's celebrating, too. I was just
joking."

"You mean, every decision is ambiguous?" asked Dasha.

"I won't answer that"—and Sonia suddenly gave a chuckle
that was not very nice yet was also sad; suddenly her previous
tone of voice lapsed. "Because if I tell you that any decision is
ambiguous, you'll be terribly pleased and go to dress with a light
heart, consoled. You'll say: I'm surrendering wholly to this tasty,
gay, and empty life because this decision of mine has a second
meaning that justifies everything. If I said there is no ambiguity,
there's just the same terrible, disastrous meaning to everything,
then you'd probably be unhappy. What do you think?"

"I've thought for some time that there are two answers to
just about everything, and that's what puts the world in harmony—it's balanced by two weights. It's complex and whole,
inflexible and fluid at the same time. For the longest time I
thought there were many truths. That was when I felt that there
was no more Christianity. And if that were true, there could be
many truths. And I felt—"

"Comfortable?" Sonia interrupted Dasha. "But in the first

place, why do you think there's no more Christianity? And secondly, where did you get it that the world is in harmony?"

Dasha crushed out her cigarette butt. She sensed that in this conversation they had both approached something vast that she had accepted once and for all and had no desire to stir up.

"I'm of the opinion," said Sonia after a pause, "that some human decisions don't and can't have any ambiguity. When a choice is made and there's no going back. When you accept this choice, this decision, wholly, without reservation, and you pay for this meaning with your life. And there's no more changing your mind, even a little, no compromising, and there's no advantage (even spiritual) to be gained. Basically, when you feel like you're turning into a crystal in doing it, that you're nothing but will and faith."

"What decision is that?" asked Dasha, her heart sinking.

"Suicide."

"Only?"

"I don't know of any others. All the others still have a loophole."

How alien all this is to me, really, these thoughts of death, suicide, choices. Should I tell her about the stars? No, she wouldn't understand, thought Dasha. *She can't understand; her mind works differently. A different rhythm. Yes, rhythm. Death? It has to come of its own accord, there can be no question of will here! There mustn't be!*

Sonia's eyes were lowered. "Where did you get the idea that the world is in harmony?" she repeated suddenly, ridicule in her voice.

Dasha shifted her gaze and they looked at each other for a minute.

"The world is in harmony because you're in harmony," said Sonia, "and you're in harmony because the world is in harmony. Is that how it goes?"

Dasha looked down. All of a sudden she thought she heard a

clock chiming somewhere. She snapped out of her reverie and thought it must be late. What time was it? How long had she been here?

"I'm asking you . . ." Sonia went on. "Actually, you won't answer that question, you can't answer it. That's it, really—you couldn't even if you wanted to. The world, I'm telling you, is not in harmony at all. The world is split, torn, smashed. There's no way out for the world. Can't you see that people have nothing to live by, that all is lost, dead? That there's nothing to believe in, that everything's gone to hell in a handbasket? That there's going to be a war and it will last ten, twenty years—fifty maybe. And no one can do anything about it, no one can do anything to help, or reconcile, or justify it. Everything is rolling away, everything is going to be wrecked. Can't you sense that?"

People have said this in every era, thought Dasha, but she remained silent.

"And you say the world is in harmony! Look around you at what's happening. And Russia? Can you still sense it? What that is? That silence of the grave? What will Russia have to say in all this?"

"You shouldn't read so many newspapers," said Dasha coldly. "It's an absolutely fruitless activity."

"Russia is going to have to have her say one day! I'm not talking about the government but about the people. Ten thousand versts of silence, twenty years of silence . . . You're right, actually, there's no need to read newspapers, because newspapers give hope and there is no hope. There's no point discussing it."

She glowered in the direction of the window and then looked at her desk, at her books and papers, at her striped skirt hanging from a nail, and suddenly she was ashamed of all these poor and unattractive objects, the dusty books, the window so long unwashed.

Dasha stood up.

"Sonia," she said. "I'm leaving you my fur coat and two

dresses, which Zai will make over for you; she'll do a good job. And my white shoes for the summer, take those, too. There are all kinds of small items in my dresser that might come in handy."

Sonia stood up as well, hooking her brassiere as she walked, searching for her stockings, and no longer looking at Dasha.

"I'm very grateful to you. But I don't need much. I don't really like things. Anyway, I'm going to be changing my life very soon, I think I'm going to get an assignment in the provinces. At a private lycée, teaching Greek and history."

"When?" asked Dasha.

"I suppose starting in the autumn."

"And until then, Sonia, how are you going to survive?"

"I've made it this far," said Sonia, irritation in her voice, and shuffling her old slippers, she walked out of the room.

CHAPTER TWELVE

I t was all like a happy family photograph. All that was missing was a little boy to sit in front, his long skinny legs crossed. Tiagin and Liubov Ivanovna side by side, on chairs, exhausted by the day and the sad parting they faced; Zai and Sonia there too in the room, their expressions somehow special; in the doorway, in an expectant pose, Moreau (their bags had already been put in the car), and at the center of everything, Dasha, merry, elegant, and festive, with a white camellia in her lapel held in place by a large diamond pin.

Tiagin said, "So you see how it is. I can say that up until now, for centuries, we had secrets from each other" (he was addressing Moreau, who was listening to him with a polite smile), "we Russians had secrets, and what did we know about one another? Nothing but all kinds of silly things: you French knew that we ate candles and lived with bears, and we knew that you danced in the streets and every year dreamed up new ladies' hats. And that was all, or nearly. And that was how things were. Meanwhile, there was some truth to it, because you really do dream up new hats, sometimes several times a year even, and on the fourteenth of July you do dance, and we are friends with the bears and, of course, they seem like much closer forebears to us than the apes. There's just the matter of the candles. . . . There were all kinds of things we wanted to be known about us. The rest we concealed, hid neatly away—things we were ashamed to admit, things we ourselves wanted to forget. And then in short order . . . would you look at that! No more secrets. We've been living together for twenty years and now we know everything about each other: your food, your politics, your personality, your passions. . . . And you know everything there is to know about us: the fullness of our disgrace, our valor, our nasty side, and our perfectly decent conduct sometimes, and our perfectly indecent conduct, too. So now we understand each other completely and are well acquainted. And now it turns out that all in all we like each other."

Moreau laughed, "A lot sometimes."

"And sometimes not at all. But on the whole, we do. The main thing that's interesting is that we found out about each other in such an original way: usually people learn about each other through conquest. But here we had a peaceful way."

"My dear nations!" said Dasha, addressing her husband. "If you would, please sit down."

Then began the farewell, the kisses, the search for gloves, a few words from Zai, separately from the rest, two tears in her slanted eyes (one tear was suspended from an eyelash and then fell on her cheek), the soft and perfumed embrace of Liubov Ivanovna, Tiagin's rough, tobaccoey embrace, his skinny moist cheekbone under her lips, and finally, Sonia's quick light kiss, and Dasha was already going down the stairs. The staircase seemed broad and marble to her, and white. It was leading her to a ballroom where, catching up her muslin veil, with orange blossoms fluttering over her forehead, she was just about to join the circle of dancers. . . . This was a fleeting dream, though, a dream she dreamed at the door. On the other side of the door, in the silence of the twilight street, stood a large automobile she knew well.

"I'll be back this summer," she said, slightly agitated by the farewell and the whole day. "Dear Auntie Liuba, Zai, and Papa, don't forget me."

The smell of gasoline, the scent of perfume—that's how Paris always smells in the twilight; it is the aroma of partings. Gas and perfume mix into one and linger in the air briefly.

Tiagin locked himself in his bedroom. Liubov Ivanovna cried for a long time—from happiness, she said, and she thought that was true. There was happiness, of course, but there was also sorrow, and the grief of parting, and concern for Tiagin, gray and old, looking at her sadly, silently, and acute worry about Sonia's fate, and the vague but lately constant alarm over Zai.

Zai, her feet on Dasha's bed, her arms hugging her sharp knees, looked at Sonia, who was pacing around the room. Zai thought there were only two possibilities for spending this evening, which had only just begun and would be so long: either ask Sonia to leave, close the door, and turn out the lamp, lie down with her face to the wall, and think without anyone bothering her, think about Dasha, herself, these years spent together, when she, Zai, had grown up, recall their life together, dream of summer or autumn. Or, the other possibility: have Sonia sit down next to her, close, so she could feel her, maybe hug her, and talk to her about Dasha, about both of them, about the past, the future, happiness, life. But this pacing of Sonia's from corner to corner was getting unbearable. *Either sit down or leave,* she felt like saying, but she didn't have the nerve.

The room was in disarray, but Zai didn't notice it; it would all have to be tidied up tomorrow morning and then the question of Sonia moving into the room decided, so that they could rent out the room on the courtyard which had been hers until now. Liubov Ivanovna had already spoken to her about this.

"Sonia, do you think you'll move in with me?"

"No, I don't think so."

"How come? After all, Auntie Liuba said—"

"I can't live without a room of my own, I already told you."

"But Sonia, I'm gone all day, and in the evening I'm at the theater."

Sonia sat down at last, but far away from Zai, in the corner, by the window, on a chair, sweeping an empty shoe box off it and onto the floor.

"Share a room with you? I don't know. . . . It would be hard. . . . Maybe, though. What's going on with your theater?"

Zai was always embarrassed when other people said that word. She felt a little guilty for being involved in the theater when maybe she ought to have been sweeping streets.

"Oh, it's not really a theater! It's just us, an experiment, a crazy idea. Some of the group are taking it all terribly seriously, and so did I, of course, at first. There's going to be a dress rehearsal, finally, next week. It kept getting postponed, the costumes weren't ready. . . . Now I'm much more interested in selling and reading books. I've lost so much time, I haven't read anything, I don't know anything. . . . If it weren't for Jean-Guy . . ."

"You mean there's already a Jean-Guy?"

But Zai didn't answer. Suddenly she felt that Jean-Guy might not be quite what he was a month ago, when nothing could have made her say his name. What was most important now was to be independent, to work for B., to spend all her free time reading, growing, keeping going. Dasha would probably have said: smartening up.

"Listen, Zai," Sonia said suddenly. "Why should you read books?"

Zai looked at her, astonished.

"That was a stupid thing to say. Don't listen to me, go ahead and read what you want. Remember how you and I once talked about Dasha and I told you that no one could be in tune with the world? Remember? I told you a lie then, on purpose, to have my fun, so that you would doubt life itself. But it didn't work."

Zai froze, her chin pressed to her knees.

"But I'm the one who began doubting everything: the harmony, the world, and myself. I'm hurt—can't you see that?—that everything always works out so well for Dasha. I hope everything is like that for you, too. I was lying to beat the band then. Just forget it."

Sonia stood up and crossed on the diagonal straight toward Zai; there was some purpose, some calculation in her movements. She sat down next to Zai.

"Forget it and be happy. Be happy, don't think, don't read any books, stroll arm in arm with your Jean-Guy, and put on all kinds of silly plays to amuse eccentrics. Do you know what being ecstatic, putting on all kinds of little plays, falling in love, and writing poetry leads to? It leads to your being fifty years old and your voice ringing when you utter complicated words and your face showing constant delight at all the things you don't know. . . . And you'll be in tune with yourself, always in tune, as are most people, actually, without ever asking themselves, What is it really, this world? And what am I in it? Am I at one with it? Does it agree with me the way I am? Or could it be that only by perishing can I merge with it? The world is moving toward disaster. I'll tell you this, but don't you tell anyone, not even Jean-Guy: everything is coming to an end, and all you can do is mourn the world as if it had been sentenced to death."

Zai stared at Sonia. How horrible if this were a lie too, if in a week Sonia repeated what she had just said: "Remember, I was bemoaning the universe and making you bemoan it with me? I did that on purpose. Love it, it will always be with you."

Zai started having difficulty breathing in Sonia's proximity. *Sit down or leave. No, leave, leave me!* But Sonia took Zai's hand.

"I'll move into your room," she said, and something tender flashed across her face and adorned it. "You and I are going to live together. Jean-Guy will pass. Those things always pass. Remember Ladd? Remember how quickly Dasha got over that? You and I are going to be together. I love it when you listen to me, Zai, with your face so full of rapt attention and so much dear submissiveness, and your eyes look perfectly Japanese. Do you like it better when people say 'Chinese'? I'll say it that way. Where are you going?"

Zai slipped off Dasha's bed. She felt deeply uncomfortable. "Please, Sonia, do me a favor," she said. She felt her palms sweating from agitation and a shiver run down her spine. "Leave me now. I feel like being alone."

But Sonia didn't budge. A slow smile stuck to her face. Zai sat down again next to her.

"Now you're driving me out, and you were the one who suggested we live together!" Sonia said, suddenly gay. *When did I suggest that?* thought Zai. *I only asked.* "You were Dasha's, and now you don't want to be mine? Zai, are you capable of friendship at all? There are people who aren't. Friendship is such a special, such a marvelous thing between people."

Zai searched for something to say in reply but could not find the words. Never in her life had she felt so awkward.

"B. and I got to be friends last year. He'll tell you about it. It was nice. We spent so much time strolling up and down the quays together. Do you like to stroll, Zai? You used to wander up and down the streets a lot."

"I like looking in windows," said Zai, "at strangers. To know them and not be afraid."

"What are you saying! What do you need strangers for? What do they have to do with you?"

"I don't know, maybe I felt like learning about their *douceur de vivre,* their sweetness of life. There's no such expression in Russian."

"Douceur de vivre," Sonia repeated, stunned. "Not only that, but a stranger's!"

"No, not a stranger's. Little by little it became mine, too, like a lot of other things."

"I find all this terribly surprising. Does *douceur de vivre* exist all by itself?"

"Of course it does. It didn't exist *there* in Russia. For a long time I didn't know what it was."

"Forgive me, but what kind of *douceur* can there be when there are so many horrors in the world—hungry, cold, desperate people, murderers. . . ."

"I don't know. But there is."

"What can you do with it?" exclaimed Sonia, upset. "After all, it's just one step from there to that same soft featherbed, that same sweet tidbit!"

"I don't know," Zai repeated, "maybe. I'm not as smart as you and I can't explain it, but it is a great happiness just learning that it exists. I even think that desperate people, even murderers, love the idea. Because without it people become completely different, the way they are *there:* like insects or nails."

"Like nails? People like nails? And thank God if that's so!" Sonia exclaimed again. "A thinking nail. Isn't that better than a thinking reed? That is simply marvelous! My last hope after all might be for a thinking nail!"

And my last hope, thought Zai, *is for you to leave me alone and go to your room and for me to stay here and think about them flying over the clouds now, drinking orange juice, looking at stars we can't see, talking very quietly about the life that lies ahead of them. And maybe suddenly Dasha will think of me, this room, all of us. And still love all of it.*

"Listen, Zai," Sonia started in again, but calmly, even dryly, now. "I can tell you don't want me to stick around, so I'm leaving. I can tell you don't need me at all." She waited a second to see whether Zai would object, but she didn't. "Thank you for telling me openly that you have a Jean-Guy or a Jean-Paul. I hope you're happy with him."

And she got up, distraught, looked around for a few moments and seeing that Zai was not going to say or do anything, went to her room. It was eight o'clock in the evening.

They could hear Tiagin going to the kitchen and putting the kettle on the fire. Zai no longer felt like lying with her face to the wall. She felt a vague anxiety and a restless sadness about Sonia's leaving. She tiptoed through the half-opened door of Liubov Ivanovna's room.

The radio was playing softly; Liubov Ivanovna, all cried out and wearing her old shapeless housecoat, was lying on her bed with a raging migraine. Tiagin was sitting in his easy chair and smoking. Zai sat down, too.

On the radio the music stopped. A voice began speaking.

"Shut it off!" said Tiagin.

"No, leave it." The voice continued speaking. Zai listened and her thoughts carried her far away.

It was amazing that through this machine, at one specific moment, hundreds of thousands of people, and sometimes millions, were listening to the same thing all over the world. This had always amazed her. Hundreds of thousands, maybe, were listening right now, as she was, to this voice telling some straightforward story. When Menuhin or Gieseking played somewhere on the planet, tens of millions of people listened at the same time— these concerts were probably even broadcast in America and Africa. The world listened together, as if with one ear. If there were a war, millions would listen to the same dispatches from the theater of war. One big, one huge world ear. Today that ear is listening to a Beethoven quartet, but tomorrow a savage may come and cut it off, string it with others on a thread, and hang it around his neck like a necklace. There's going to be a war, and Jean-Guy, carrying a suitcase and with a rucksack on his back, will hug her and say goodbye to her, just like in a painting, at the Gare de l'Est, which once seemed so beautiful to her. Now she preferred the curl of hair and comic face that Volodia Smirnov had drawn and that hung over her bed: he was predicted a great future. He hadn't been trying to draw any kind of face at all, just abstractly manifest his response to . . . but she forgot what. It came out looking comic and also a little like Sipovsky.

The radio voice was still talking. It was telling an astounding story: about a month ago it had spoken one evening about the old children's books that everyone used to read and love— twenty, forty, sixty years ago. There was one that three generations had read. It was the story about two little boys who sailed away on a homemade raft to the Fiery Earth, but there was a mistake and they wound up in Capetown. And now it turned out that both of those heroes were alive, one was eighty-eight years old and the other eighty-two, and that this story had been written about them. All life was basically like a marvelous story. The main thing was to be free—from everyone and from yourself.

I always thought they were bored together, thought Zai, looking at her father and stepmother. *But they aren't bored in the least. On the contrary, it's very nice for them. I'm the one who's bored with them.* And she stood up to leave. "I'm going out for half an hour."

"Again—will you be late?" Tiagin asked in a dissatisfied voice.

"No, just for half an hour."

She put on her coat and went out. And the first thing that struck her was the new, timid, springlike breeze that flew toward her.

She had warned Jean-Guy and the others several days before that she wouldn't be able to come on her sister's wedding day. They weren't expecting her and she didn't even feel like going there now. She walked down the street and a soft wind brushed her face. Skirting the fence around the little square, she plunged down the poorly lit back streets, which were quiet and deserted. With her hands stuck in her pockets, she walked, breathing deeply this first spring air, which promised, perhaps deceptively still, but nonetheless promised spring. There were occasional passers-by, the café window on the corner cast an orange glow, and after that there was some garage lit up. The big buildings were dark. Maybe people lived in them. Or maybe these were just institutions, ministries, shut up tight until morning. She walked around a few blocks and turned back toward the church with its two tall, pale, pointed spires receding into the pinkish-gray sky. Walking back along the fence, Zai caught sight of a dog lying on the sidewalk.

She shuddered and stopped. Had she really failed to notice it when she walked by here the first time? Or hadn't it been here? The dog was lying in an odd position, on its side a little more than was natural, its legs bent; the closest street lamp was reflected like a drop of strange, lifeless light in its large open eye. It was a big, dark brown German shepherd with sharp upstanding ears. There was a puddle beneath its sinewy belly and its tail was tucked under. The dog was dead.

Zai shuddered. She ran along the fence, toward her home. Did the dog die by the garden or did someone bring it there, dead, from his apartment, unwilling to deal with it? Or had an automobile run over it? How awful that it lay there in its petrified fur. It could have been a person, run over or dead or killed. . . . It was death, in the living world, in the living city, and it made her feel terribly alone.

She walked into the apartment. It would be nice to find Sonia in her room, by her lamp with a book, wearing Dasha's cozy robe, and to talk with her about how the airplane would soon begin to descend through the clouds and the lights of an unfamiliar city would be visible. It would be good to find someone's living presence in the room which had become so empty today. But Sonia wasn't there and Zai couldn't even tell whether she was home. Zai drank a cup of tea in the dining room with her father. Liubov Ivanovna never did get up.

So here she was alone in her room. Hadn't Sonia been try-

ing to replace Dasha for her this evening, and hadn't she rejected
her? How did that happen, Zai rejecting her? Why? What was
there about her in those moments when she was talking about
friendship? She'd offered Zai friendship. Sonia, proud, intelligent, solitary, and special, had offered her, cowardly, stupid, and
frivolous Zai, her friendship, and Zai had wanted her to leave as
quickly as possible. Everything Sonia had said just hadn't
seemed real. It was so hard to understand, so distant, and probably so painful for her. But most of all, Zai saw that this was the
real Sonia offering her friendship, the Sonia who loved no one,
who called Jean-Guy Jean-Paul, such a stranger. . . . Zai was
struck by the feeling that she didn't want to think about this any
more, just as she didn't want to think about the dead dog, though
her thoughts kept returning to the iron fence on the stone foundation along the nighttime sidewalk: the ear jutting out, the petrified tail tucked in between the paws, the dark spot under the
belly on the sidewalk.

    She, Sonia, did not love Dasha, she never had. She'd
laughed at her often over little things and her laugh had been
anything but merry. What a pity, she was so beautiful! She
laughed at Zai sometimes, too. At first Zai was insulted, but then
she got used to it. How did Sonia know about Ladd? How odd it
all was. Had that German shepherd really been lying there when
she'd walked by the first time? Of course, it hadn't been run
over, you could have seen, there would have been blood. It had
been carried out dead from the building across the way, from
one of those buildings she had once looked into, where happy
people lived so pleasantly. The dog had died of old age. It was a
loyal dog, but those nice people had no time to bury it or bother
with it. How strange it all was, and sad, and awful. Yes, it was
getting awful again, the way it used to be. *I don't want to think
about that.*

    Zai made an effort not to, and in the rosy gloom, in her half-
sleep, finally, she pictured Jean-Guy the way he was last evening,

when, after her job in the bookstore—where so far she had man-
aged to read several hundred spines but not a single page—she
had shown up at Passy, tugged on the copper bell handle, the kind
they don't make anymore, and he had opened the door. He was
upset that the costumes were fading. It was horrible! Terrible!
Disgraceful! It was a swinish trick plain and simple! If it were
only under the arms, but his back was lilac, and at the waist there
was a band of navy. "They don't make them like they used to!"
said Zai, gently examining the bell that was still ringing over the
front door. "No, they don't," said Jean-Guy angrily, "but they
make thousands like you every day, especially if they're Sta-
khanovites."* As was the troupe's habit, Zai kissed everyone in
turn and suddenly remembered she hadn't kissed Jean-Guy. She
stole a peek at him to see whether she'd made him angry. But he
hadn't noticed her inattention and was nearly in tears at the sight
of his sweat-stained purple cloak with the raspberry coat of arms
painted on it. *Oh, Lord, I wish he'd just get angry! Does it really
matter?*

Evidently the young photographer with his long, ginger
beard thought the same, because he said: "You can't go crying
over spilt milk!"

Jean-Guy immediately raised his voice: "If you think it's
spilt milk, then I'm amazed you ever come here. Either you take
this seriously or you should give it up."

"Not at all. But you can't sob over a costume as if it were a
dead man."

"For me a costume is more precious than a dead man. How
dare that scoundrel use a dye that bleeds!"

"Go pierce him with your sword."

"Fool!"

Zai laughed, walked over to Jean-Guy, and stroked his head.

---

* A movement begun in 1935 in the Soviet Union aimed at increasing industrial production by
use of efficient work techniques.

"You're making an elephant out of a fly," she said.

"What elephant?" asked Jean-Guy, suspiciously.

"An elephant out of a fly. It's a Russian expression."

"You're in France here."

"I know. But it's a Russian saying. It means, if you make an elephant out of a fly it's . . ."

Then Jean-Guy became truly angry: "Leave me alone with your Russian elephants. We're not a zoo. What an uncultured attitude toward art!"

Everyone started shouting at once: about his sense of irony, which he'd lost; about his nerves, which were overwrought; about the point of arguments; about the time that was being wasted. Five minutes later all was forgotten and forgiven and it had been decided to make "that scoundrel" redye the cloaks. As the evening drew to its close, Zai remembered she couldn't come the next day. Once again Jean-Guy made a dissatisfied face.

"I warned you about this on Tuesday," Zai said timidly.

"Then I would suggest you give it up altogether. You can't work like this." But she tenderly brought her face close to his face and her eyes, long and narrow, looked into his. He laughed, drew her close, and she felt that in that minute everything was back to the way it had been before.

But there was a moment when it hadn't been the way it was before, she thought now, envisioning Jean-Guy through her eyelids, in a haze that made everything darker. She envisioned him walking toward her, his head thrown back, the collar of his white shirt unbuttoned, his eyes flashing. *Something was not at all the way it always is. We quarreled for the first time, not even really quarreled, but I could see how he might be if he did get angry. And if he flares up again and again, who knows how it might all end? Because, of course, I know now that this will pass, the way the theater will pass, the way poetry passed.*

She started thinking about her new job; she wasn't sleepy and she didn't put out the light. Thousands of book spines, running up and down the stairs to the cellar, where two painters were painting the shelves, and on top, the fat book in which she was supposed to record something. Workers were putting in wiring and repairs were ongoing in B.'s office. He had decided to expand the business, renovate the building. She had come to him at just the right time. *Lord, help me make everything all right, so I don't get fired, so Papa and Auntie Liuba live, so that I'm not left on the sidewalk like that dog, so that Dasha is happy and we get to see each other.*

Like the dog on the sidewalk. She shuddered and opened her eyes. The empty bed by the opposite wall. She trembled under her blanket. What was she afraid of now? It was warm here and the light was on. The airplane was landing at this hour at the Oran airport; the Tiagins were on the other side of the wall. What was so frightening? What was the dog to her and she to it? Plenty of dogs die in Paris, plenty of people, too. You can't be afraid of them all. Plenty of dead, killed, drunk, sick, and homeless people lying in Europe's cities right now. Was that terror, that trembling, really going to start in again, the way it used to be, when she took fright at the shadow that crossed her face when the pigeon took wing at her feet, on the Place de l'Etoile? She had been frightened by the pigeon's shadow, and she'd been frightened by the dead dog. Might she lapse back into that familiar state of feeling just how pathetic, defenseless, and transparent a person is?

The empty bed saddened Zai and she put out the light so she couldn't see it. She forgot to draw the blinds, and a white ray from a nearby street lamp fell into the room. She noticed that the silence held a whisper: there was rain outside, not a noisy winter rain but a whispering, rustling, spring-like rain. It was whispering, it was hinting, it was saying something, running down the glass of the window, sighing along the ledges. And it sounded like a rustle, a muffled rustling, like the "ourfather" in the dead of night, in a house where everyone was already sleeping. Zai pulled the blanket over her head so she couldn't hear it.

CHAPTER THIRTEEN

Sonia Tiagina's Notebook

Off and on for years I had the same dream—starting maybe ten years or so ago. Once or twice a year I dreamed I was on train tracks, hands and feet bound—tied to some kind of a board rocking evenly along with a soft whirring—in a thick, yellow-gray fog. The tracks are straight, infinite. Out of the fog, dolls that look exactly like me, bound up the same way on the tracks, start coming toward me, diving out of the fog. The whirring is incessant and the fog colors everything a yellowy gray. I get tenser and tenser, and space and time seem to merge. When I can't bear the train tracks, the whirring, any longer, I wake up. And for a while that feeling of space and time fusing lingers.

In the last few years I haven't had this dream as often. If I went too long without it, I began wishing I would have it, even though the solitude, death, and horror it brought were so hard to take. Space and time fusing is too much for me. I know that the most powerful elements of my own destruction are rushing toward me. But the fear that I might never dream this dream again bothers me more than the dream itself.

I hate contradictions—everything around me is one great

contradiction. I'm a contradiction, and my life—both physical and metaphysical—is nothing but a contradiction, so it's not really a life. But people are deaf to anything that doesn't affect them personally—love, faith, death, will, freedom. People are deaf to themselves most of all, and they stay that way until that "moment of horror" which turns their consciousness around—though not everyone experiences that moment. When horror does strike, out of the blue, it pushes a person to the brink, where he sees the void. If you haven't been there, you can't understand what I'm talking about. The fact that so many people never experience a moment of horror is one of the many stupidities of existence and underscores that very void. That moment should be as much a part of everyone's experience as birth and death.

I can't bear it—all the different inward and outward manifestations of the meaning of life. . . . I get lost in them. Unattached to the cosmos, disconnected from the world, I'd gladly give up all this diversity for the power and simplicity of one simple truth free of contradiction. Without it, I'll never find my way to the universe and vice versa. If I exist without any connection to anything, then how can there be an all-encompassing truth? There is no capital T Truth. Our whole lives are spent anticipating—and surviving—the "moment of horror."

I have no connection with the past, just an artificial understanding of it that I invented. I have no connection with the present because family, state, religion, and nature have lost any grip they ever had on me. I have no connection with the future because I can't figure out my place in it and have chosen as my cause what is advancing upon us inexorably, which only a blind man could fail to see. I sought meaning in beauty and wanted to find it in friendship, but there was always some worm eating away at things, and what I hated wasn't that they were eaten away but that I had known from the beginning they would be. Whenever I rushed headlong into love, it would turn out that loneliness starts not "two steps away from you," as someone somewhere once put it, but "in your arms." The loneliness and randomness of what goes on, the physical rather than meta-physical fusion.

I don't know who destroyed the world or when. It might have been a hundred years ago. Remnants of integrity still exist, but it's dying for many people, dying like Rome, and like Rome may go on dying for the next five centuries. But does it really matter? Some will see it as a natural consequence of some kind of evolution; it will please them because supposedly this makes people freer. Others won't give it a thought because they think they're in balance with the universe so the rest doesn't affect them. Still others believe there's still time to fix things. Others put a bullet in their heads—literally or figuratively. "Byron, where is your Missolonghi?"

I envy the first group, they're on a comforting, utterly false path; I'm afraid of choosing the path of the next group, who have fenced off the world with art, family, and politics without ever realizing why. I do listen closely to those who dream of fix-ing or finding something, but what is there to fix when the spirit of destruction has settled in, smashing and scattering everything, and this destruction seems so natural while creation and har-mony don't?

At one time a clearly defined person was released into the world like a planet, circling around its sun. Everything was pre-cise and strong: the desire to struggle, to continue the line, to ob-tain food, the desire for beauty to become art, for knowledge to help people find the truth. Good was here and evil was there. The good people gathered together and so did the evil people. The heroes loved glory and the women loved heroes; the execu-tioners executed; the dead were supposed to rise up. What's left of this? Does anyone long for selfless struggle? Half the people don't even want to continue the race any more. Do we need to obtain food? Wouldn't it be simpler to reduce our needs to a minimum? Art wants no part of beauty, which is only good for postcards. Knowledge doesn't yield truth, which is ephemeral. Good people don't gather together, they're bored; they scatter and mix with evil people, to learn from them or help them or talk with them or study them. Heroes love money more than fame and there are women who don't give them a second glance. Poets have lost the gift of prophecy, not that anyone would be able to hear them anyway. We find criminal and executioner identically repugnant or identically attractive now. The dead will never be resurrected—they've been tossed onto the garbage heap. As in peacetime a rival often attracts us more than a friend, so in wartime an enemy is sometimes more interesting than an ally. And if all this is so, then there is nothing absolute and indisputable anymore, there is only ambiguity, two answers to every question, and there isn't a stone in the universe that won't wobble.

Just as I await the nightmare's return, though, so I plunge over and over again into the very thick of these contradictions, I can't imagine my life apart from them, I live and breathe them, and never for a second do I think I could be rid of them. I race along on them down black tracks, to a soft whirring, and around me is a thick, yellowy-gray fog in which, no matter who I meet, I'm always alone.

"It's good that you're alone," B. once told me. "What kind of savagery is this herd mentality, all for one and one for all? Why does everything have to be lived through and resolved as one world? Why should I have to answer for all the fools and scoundrels in the universe? As Europeans it's time we forgot those sheep's laws. You answer for yourself, you're worth yourself. Dependency on your peers is demeaning and pointless."

B. and I were walking down the long staircase from his dark and dusty office and across the entire first floor, which is full of employees about whom B. knows and wants to know nothing and who know and want to know nothing about each other. Out on the street people were strolling who were complete strangers to us and to each other. I realized that no one will ever understand me. Merge. Is my union with the world really possible for me only in death? Or is death ambiguous too? Is death strong and weak simultaneously? Suicide, both an indisputable act of will and nothing at all?

Zai didn't let B. know about her theatrical performances, and I didn't give her away—I'd promised. On the day of the dress rehearsal a group of us came to the store to go with her to the theater, but she started hemming and hawing and saying she had to wait for someone she'd promised to go out with for a quick bite. Volodia Smirnov, in his usual manner that Madeleine likes so well, said in French: "Zai, do you know what *la mère de Couzka* means? That's where you can go!" Zai blushed and declared that if we made a scene she would be fired from her job. "You're not doing anything, just loafing about, while I'm earning our give-unto-us-our-daily-bread!" She obviously didn't want anyone in the office to notice us. She may very well have pressed her goods on customers with expressions like "Monsieur Hugo," "Monsieur Simenon," and "Monsieur Mauriac." Or at least, there was that look about it.

Poor kids! What a disaster! Actually there was some applause, not just whistles. The applause came mostly from friends of the author and director. Two or three theater critics dozed despondently in the front row. We whistled and clapped all at once; an awful din. Zai was very sweet, all made up and wearing a strange wig, but they all sounded as if their mouths were full of mush—nerves and inexperience. By the end we were getting very bored. "Author! Author!" certain elderly persons in rather vivid dress began shouting. The author came out followed by the lead, a handsome boy whose acting was *the* worst. Shouts of "Bravo, Jean-Guy!" from the back of the hall. Someone let go with a piercing whistle from our side. The audience jumped up from their seats. The show was over.

I never knew gloomy people could make so much noise!

Because you can cut my head off but there weren't any cheerful
ones in the hall.

Volodia Smirnov, the marshal of the whole honest band I'm
rarely a part of, is an unusual mixture of the Franco-Russian
spirit that marks our generation. Of course, as almost always
happens among us, his father and mother divorced long ago. His
father's a colorful figure who knows five languages perfectly,
started out the life of an émigré as a paid dancer—and now he's
a doorman at a big hotel in the south of France. Volodia's mother
embroiders sofa pillows. Two old aunts and a nanny are living
out their days in the house. The sofa pillows feed everyone. By
some miracle, half-starving, Volodia lasted all the way to university, which he abandoned, taking a job as secretary to some
French writer. The writer is famous, lonely, capricious, and old,
and he is both extremely stingy and excessively tender with
Volodia. For some time now Volodia has been wearing an expression of constant aggravation and hatred for the world. He's
very noisy—the more restless, loquacious, and noisy he is, the
more distressing it is to be in his presence. But the pillows are
still being embroidered and the aunts are still not dying.

Madeleine is in love with Volodia. Where she came from no
one knows. She's totally alone in the world, says she's never received a single real letter in her life and has never been outside
Paris. What she does, no one knows. Sometimes she has money
and then she goes around for a few days all overexcited and
wound up. She cries a lot—over nothing at all, or at least we
think over nothing at all. Last year she took poison for some reason that was never made clear. Volodia says she likes to fight, but
he's lying, naturally.

Volodia's brother, recently arrived from Prague, is ten years
older than the rest of us. He never got an education and knocks
around from one trade to another. He never smiles. He left a wife
and child behind in Prague and likes to talk about how everything is coming to an end. No one argues with him, it's as if no

one cared. I still think that one fine day he'll disappear and leave no forwarding address. And no one will be surprised.

We call the little ballerina and her husband, the artist, the "Blues." Both of them have an identical bluish cast to their faces. She dances complicated acrobatic dances dressed in a colorful leotard, folding up in half and rolling like a wheel. She is always looking for a partner but never finds one and she's always either on her way to Monaco or gone missing for nights on end in various Parisian cabarets, sad, with her bluish face and large moist eyes. In the end she's going to run a cloakroom in some music hall and drop from sight. That might take quite a long time, though.

Her husband, Silvio, exhibited a few times at the Salon of Independents, but now he has no opportunity to paint. They live in a cramped hotel room and so he's taken a job: he has to write *"Oh, mon doux Jésus!"* 3500 times on 3500 cards (depicting an infant in the rays of the sun) in watercolor with a fine brush. The cards are going to be sold at Lisieux and Lourdes for Christmas. Blue Silvio does this for days at a stretch. I look at him and see him getting bluer and bluer and always grave. I think he has some disease.

Bringing up the rear this evening were two inseparable friends one rarely finds in Volodia and Silvio's company. One has a job in an insurance company, but about five years ago he tried to write for the newspapers: the change of profession has given him the look of a man buffeted by fate. He never talks about the past (which in retrospect must seem brilliant to him), but he often complains of being bored: "I'm bored, gentlemen, bored," or, "Oh, how boring it is to live in this city. And how boring you all are as well. Sonia, Sonia, why is everything so boring?"

His friend, who studied in the same department with me and is now a teacher at a lycée in Angers, has come with him. He and I are old pals; I've known that trembling gaze under slightly puffy lids, those waxy hands, the black locks falling on his thick black brows, for so many years! He took me by the arm. His breath was acrid from tobacco, and it felt like we were walking not down a boulevard fragrant with the scents of spring but along the stuffy corridor of a third-class train car. All of a sudden it struck me that none of us had any connection to this marvelous, pale green, gentle Parisian spring, the porcelain sky, the necklace of street lamps, the starry square—all of us might as well have been in some third-class train car or have just come out of one and be roving, untethered, through an unfamiliar train station, through the main hall, amid the spit and cigarette butts, the flies and old newspapers. "But why? Do you sense it, Frederic? Remember how five years ago it was completely different somehow?" I asked him.

"No, it's always been like this," he said calmly. "I don't notice any difference."

"Don't you think, Frederic, that once we were at least a small part of what went on around us, that it had some effect on us (like this spring, say), and we could have affected it, too, if we'd wanted, but now we're over here, and all this (I swept my arms around) is over there, and we're beside the point?"

He looked at me with his expressionless eyes and said after a pause: "I partly get what you're trying to say. But there's nothing you can do about it."

Walking next to me was the former journalist who was now working for an insurance company. He joined in the discussion: "You don't understand the times well enough, Sonia. You have to walk in step with them, you're lagging behind."

"What does that mean?" I asked. "Aren't I my own time?"

But he couldn't explain to me what "our time" was or how and why I, the way I was, was "lagging behind" it. He himself believed that everything as it stood was marvelous. Life was beautiful, France was a beautiful country, Paris was the premier city in the world, and there would never be a war because people were smart and far-sighted and loved their calm and comfortable life just as much as he did.

"That's all true"—I was laughing—"except that there will be a war and it's going to last fifty years."

He moved away from me, shrugging his shoulders. Maybe in that instant he felt a rush of acute dislike for me, but no, that's not in his nature.

I caught up with Silvio. "Blue, why are you even sadder than usual today?" I said, taking him by the arm. He was silent. "Silvio, it's spring!" I said again, and I tried to sing something.

He quietly freed his arm and slowed his step; so did I. He turned a face of such sadness toward me that for a second I stopped.

"Ruth is pregnant," he said, and I realized what a catastrophe this was for them both.

Oh, mon doux Jésus! She hadn't had an engagement for two months. She wasn't dancing any more and wasn't going to for at least a year, even if all went well, and after that—who knew!—would she be able to work again the way she had? They were living in a tiny hotel room, he was never going to have a studio, and she was never going to have a chance to become a real ballerina.

I just looked at him. There was my answer. I didn't need any other.

We went to the apartment of the elder Smirnov, or rather into a huge, half-empty room that looked like a storage space. There were no curtains in the window and there were posters from the Brazilian and Argentine performances of the singer who used to live here hanging on the walls. I examined them, then sat on a stool and lit up. Volodia walked over. "Sonia," he said, "what next?"

I didn't know what to reply. "Crank up the gramophone," I said at last, with an effort.

He gave me a good shove. "Oh my oh my oh my! What a

muttonhead! I asked her what next in general, what next in life? Should I marry Madeleine? After all, if they mobilize me and kill me, then at least she'd have my pension. Hey, why don't you marry me?"

"No."

"And you shouldn't. Like in that Armenian joke: we'll find someone else for their ugly mugs."

I caught him by the sleeve: "Volodia, it's like the joke: a short guy reaching for a straw. Tell me, why is there no solution for us?"

He looked at me and suddenly his face became a soft, sad, human face. He understood me. "Do you really think I know anything? That I know anything at all about that?"

"Don't you think it's because there's no Russia?"

"I do."

"Because God is dead?"

"I do."

"Because we're living between two eras?"

"I do."

"What are we going to do, Volodia? How can we go on?"

He stroked my head: "Don't you have any friends who are smarter than me you can ask about that?"

I couldn't tell him the truth, that I could only talk about these things with him, and I could precisely because he wasn't smart or educated, because he was a little cowardly and arrogant and, in the final analysis, dishonest.

He sat down beside me at the table, over me, kind of. I put my hands on his knees and felt how skinny they were. "For a thousand years they've been told: reconcile yourself! Have patience! And now—over that whole expanse—they're asleep, put to sleep by that thousand-year past, sleeping the sleep of the mammoths."

"They have industri-"—and Volodia suddenly yawns wide—"-rialization, very intensive . . . -tensive . . . -sive."

"Won't they wake up, rise up?"

He shrugged his shoulders. "You have to understand it in the human sense."

"I don't care about the 'human sense.' I want 'according to Roman law.'"

We were both silent. Suddenly I noticed that everyone else was silent, too, as if they were waiting for something. But there was nothing to wait for, it was all going to get even scarier and darker. We weren't in fact in a train station, sitting and waiting to change trains, we were living, we were alive, we existed.

When I was leaving Volodia told me: "You know, I think it's all on account of two things: the demands of the iron age and the awareness of our own abandonedness," and he turned on his heels, embarrassed that these words might sound banal to me. Especially "iron age."

Volodia and Madeleine flagged down a taxi. Silvio and Ruth slowly walked toward the Seine; they lived close by. The other two rushed to catch the late bus. I stood on the sidewalk with the elder Smirnov, who was going to walk me home. He took me by the arm and we fell silent, walking in step, not fast or slow, silent for a long time, silent as if we were both mute and it was too dark to sign. Once I saw two mutes hurrying to come to some agreement, in the twilight; night was falling very quickly and they were clearly afraid they wouldn't manage to finish saying what they had to say to each other in time. It was on a corner and passers-by kept turning to look at them.

The elder Smirnov and I were silent and walking—this silence utterly new, surprising, filled with some weighty significance. Did he know anything about me? Had he heard something, if only this evening? Had he observed me those five or six times we had seen each other, had he asked someone about me? I didn't know. But I sensed the silence was continuing not because he had nothing to say to me or because he was searching for a topic and couldn't find it and he was uncomfortable (and the next day he would remember he had seen me, Sonia Tiagina, home and couldn't find anything to talk to her about the whole way!). No, I knew that he and I both found our silence easy, that in this silence something was happening to both of us, some strange mutual recognition, an understanding, an accord was being established. Human speech developed and strengthened only to turn into silence and be consoled by it!

Can it be believed that two people who basically hardly knew each other were walking through the streets in silence without being weighed down by it, their muteness destroying the communication established between people and legitimized by nature? Could we have been silent not because there was nothing to say but because there was too much to talk about? For the very first time I felt tightly shut up not alone but together with someone. It was very strange—I was strangely happy in this negative contact with another person. In the half-dark of the street we couldn't see each other, we never looked at one another, we read nothing in each other's face or eyes, which always give so much away. The sound of our shared steps was even, unbroken, not too loud. Above the recently leafed-out trees there was a bright, sharp-edged spring moon, dead ahead, and we walked toward it for a long time before turning off. Peace and calm; a feeling of gratitude—an arm leading me, supporting me steadily, dispassionately.

I think we had already walked past my entry once because when we turned the corner I realized we had already been there. The moon was now hanging on the other side. We stopped. He let go of my arm and looked around. "That was nice," he said, "very nice." As if he were speaking of a journey, something complete, something unrepeatable. I came to and suddenly felt an immense weariness, as if I had walked across the entire city. Without saying anything, I held out my hand to him.

The most amazing part of our silence was the absence in it of anything mysterious. It was precise and meant just what it

meant. It corresponded exactly to the fullness of our solitude together. When it was going on, it was full of meaning not just for
the two of us but in and of itself. For me it was an unexpected
experience that enriched me. Today some of the meaning seems
gone, like a letter written in "heart's blood" that later seems
overdrawn and awkward, making reading it embarrassing. Or
else (to bring the comparison down a peg or two) like those ugly
faces I have a habit of drawing on the margins of this notebook.
While you're drawing them you see something funny, or scary,
or "Miss America," or a Mongol, or a clown, or a shepherd in
them, and a minute later they don't mean a thing. They're just
profiles, badly drawn, lifeless and flat.

But that time when we were silent together (why with him
and not Ladd, who always talked so much, or B., or Volodia?)
will stay with me no matter what. I know precisely what we
were both thinking about: the "iron age" and "our own abandonedness," about the mammoth's thousand-year dream, about
the end of a common God (who did not include man in his sepa-
rate circle), about the east of Europe from which Smirnov had so
recently arrived, and about the coming months, which might
crush us completely, or just a little, but during which, no matter
what, there was still one hope, one hope flickering, alive.
Maybe. That was what our silence was about.

CHAPTER FOURTEEN

Zai had lain ill for a week. She had a high temperature, a sore throat, and an earache, and she slept almost all the time. When she opened her eyes, she saw a big, empty room, but a few seconds later everything fell into place: the tables and chairs, the books, the window, and even Dasha's bed, which still stood by the opposite wall, everything popped up almost at once, the walls closed ranks, and she shut her eyes again, reassured.

The awfulest thing . . . She loved to play at what it was. The awfulest thing would be to lie here on this bed in the middle of the street. Not brought out on a stretcher and set down on the pavement to be lifted into an ambulance, the way people sometimes are—no, differently. She had seen a stretcher once, and no one had even been lying on it. It would be awful to lie in the middle of a noisy square, in the middle of the buses, trucks, and automobiles, under a blanket, and see a crowd gathering. People pointing and laughing. A cold drop of sweat ran down between Zai's eye and nose. Liubov Ivanovna, who had stopped in the room for a minute, said calmly: "Sweat, sweat. That's good."

It would be truly awful to wake up on a big white table in a

clinic. The doctor pulls back Zai's shirt and twenty people examine her. What if she isn't quite like everyone else? Again
sweat ran down her cheeks and her feet turned cold from fear.

Finally, Zai woke up and could tell that her temperature had
fallen a little. She picked up a hand mirror. What an uninteresting, insignificant face! No depth in the eyes, no trace of long and
deep reflection! Her father had said, laughing: "Think, think
more, and then your face will be intelligent." But did she really
know how to think? Actually, he was right. The smarter a person
got, the better it made his face, and in the end, in old age you
couldn't conceal whether you had ever thought during your lifetime or not. It was written all over your face. You could tell right
away—in some at forty, in others at fifty, in still others at sixty—
not only whether they had any thoughts but even precisely what
those thoughts were. Her father had a soft, tired face, and of
course he had had thoughts, many sad thoughts, but they were
approximate, and his face had become approximate. She decided to tell him about this as soon as the occasion arose: "Papa,
what an approximate face you have. But I love you for not thinking about anything, I love you the way you are."

B. had a special grave face. Every day he selected some
book for her, and she read it in the evening, sometimes late, and
in the morning while she was dressing, and at breakfast. B. had
an intelligent and stern face. Whereas Liubov Ivanovna's face
was two-sided; it was good, submissive, full of concern, and at
the same time you could tell this was not all there was to her
life—Tiagin and the three of them, and the laundry, the radio,
and the pharmacy. There were also other more complicated
things. Yes, passions and jealousy, the fight for the man who
tried to abandon her more than once, and fleeing behind him all
across Russia, Sonia's illegitimate birth, and in that old life all
the difficulty, all the burden of breaking with her own family,
who never forgave her for her liaison with a frivolous married
man who, as people used to say, was not serious. So now Liubov

Ivanovna had a two-sided face. And someday Zai would tell her about that: "Auntie Liuba, you have a two-sided face, but I love you so much, just as much as you love me."

Cautiously Zai opened the drawer of her nightstand and out of it took a small, bronze, round frame, the kind they used to make, all decorated with curlicues that snagged on everything. God forbid lace was nearby, or a veil or stocking; they would crawl over to the frame to snag and tear. The photograph in it had been given to her by Alexei Andreyevich Boiko (who had the best face in the world). The photograph was washed out and had ripped in two. It was Zai's mother, the actress Dumontelle. She didn't seem to have a face at all, just a big hat over a luxuriant coiffure. She couldn't have had a face: she was too young. Someday Zai would tell her, too, perfectly frankly, "What a pity, dear mama, that you didn't get to have a face."

All this would happen when she stopped being afraid once and for all. Then she would feel completely happy and free everywhere in the world; she could be everywhere simultaneously, stride back and forth, in the heat and the cold, up and down.

She snuggled under her three blankets and fell back to sleep.

At about nine in the evening. Tiagin cautiously opened the door to Zai's room. "Liza, wake up, a young man has come to see you," he said, approaching the bed. Of all of them, he alone called her by her real name. "Wake up, Liza, you can sleep tonight. There's a guest here to see you."

She opened her eyes. Her father was standing in an empty space. But the room quickly filled up with furniture and the walls grew back.

"Have him come in," she said, taking a comb out from under her pillow.

Tiagin turned toward the door, Jean-Guy was already standing on the threshold.

"Papa, this is Jean-Guy," said Zai.

"I know."

She ran the comb down the right and the left and her black locks fell along either side of her face. "Why are you walking so softly, just like a Malay?"

"I walk the way I walk."

"Hello, Jean-Guy."

"Hello, Zai."

He sat down beside her on the bed. Tiagin went out and closed the door behind him. Zai looked into Jean-Guy's face, his young, dark, regular face. There was something greedy in his expression that she had never noticed before. A few moments later, though, it was gone and his eyes and his smile were filled with tenderness.

After the evening of their failed performance, he had dropped out of sight for a week, then they had seen each other briefly at his house, with other people around, and then he had gone somewhere, to Brest, to see his uncle, as he later explained. Twice after this he had telephoned, but she was already sick in bed and couldn't come to the phone. The night before he had come by after nine and Liubov Ivanovna had said it was too late. So now here he was, with her. He held her hand and smiled.

How could I think I didn't love him anymore! I would give all the books in the world for this smile of his, I would give everyone and everything for him. When he's here I'm not afraid of anything, I'm not afraid of myself. Oh my happiness, stay with me!

"So you really are ill?" he asked. "Is it contagious?"

"Of course not. Are you afraid of catching it?"

"Not very."

"But still? . . . Oh you future psychiatrist! Tell me, Jean-Guy, what have you been doing all this time?"

"I've been studying for exams. I've passed two and I'll take two more this week. What do you think, why did all that happen then?"

"I think it was because the play was stupid, the actors were lousy, and also because I didn't love you enough."

"You didn't?" he broke in, frightened, and suddenly his changeable face was sad. "Why didn't you love me enough? And when did you notice that?"

She put her arms around his head and began kissing his eyes and cheeks and smoothing his hair. "It just happened. I noticed. Even at the dress rehearsal I felt it, and later it came to me that it was all over in general. But I can't go on without you, I'm not me without you."

"And I can't go on without you," he said quietly, hugging her, squeezing her shoulders, covering her face and neck with kisses.

"Tell me, Jean-Guy, do you think I talk too much?"

"No, you know, a little, sometimes. What have you got? It's not contagious?"

"I don't think so. I'm afraid you think I talk too much."

"No more than anyone else."

"Ah!" Zai drew it out softly. "Never talk to me like that. You hurt me."

He laid her cautiously back on her pillow.

"Hurt you? I hurt you? That's impossible."

"You consider yourself good?"

"Yes, I'm good."

"And intelligent?"

"And intelligent. You're making me say silly things."

"It doesn't matter. Do you love me?"

He nodded and put his face close to hers. How incredibly animal-like his breath smelled. Zai lay for a while completely still in his embrace.

"Do you love me?" she repeated.

"I love you."

This was amazing. It had two aspects: immediate happiness and the prospect of a very real, strong, larger life free of fear. Part of her very soul dwelled on this and melted at these words; the other part seemed to grow in spurts, sideways and up, powerful.

Finally, she pushed him away and without letting go of his hands said: "It's so good that you came."

"They wouldn't let me in yesterday."

"They will tomorrow. Come earlier."

"When will you get well? I want you to get well as soon as possible."

"You don't like sick people?"

"Not one tiny bit. Especially contagious ones."

"But you're still very good?"

"Yes, I'm good."

He repeated these words with obvious satisfaction and Zai laughed. There definitely was no one in the world better than Jean-Guy!

He took a cigarette out of his pocket and asked for a match. There weren't any, so he went to the kitchen, found the light switch, found the box, and returned.

"You've started to walk just like a Malay," she said through her laughter, and she felt like bouncing on the bed. "I can't even hear you."

He sat back down in his former spot. "Once," he said, closely examining the cigarette smoke, "you told me a terrible thing. Once, remember, you told me that everything would pass, including this. All this was just your liberation. What did that mean?"

Zai sat up on her pillow.

"Did I say that? Impossible. You must have misunderstood."

"It makes it sound as if I'm just a means and all this love of yours is just a path to some other end."

"You're out of your mind! I never could have said or thought that."

"Think back carefully. It was by the Metro, I think, one evening."

Zai frowned, looking straight ahead. "No, that can't be. I don't remember anything."

"But doesn't it seem to you now that all this between us is just a coincidence that will pass and tomorrow you and someone else—"

"Don't talk like that. How can you talk like that! I love you and you love me. Who else could there be?"

"Do you love me?"

"Well naturally I love you."

And they fell silent again, wrapped in a firm embrace.

After this long silence Jean-Guy stood up. "But why is it that you abandon everything you start? Why don't you write poetry any more? Why didn't you believe something worthwhile would come of our show? That was temporary, too, and you knew it would pass?"

"No, I didn't know that. And there was even a day when I thought something worthwhile would come of it. I swear to you there was a day like that."

"Just one?"

Zai silently drew him to her. What could she say? She didn't feel like talking at all, especially about the past, because it was not all that simple and honest. But Jean-Guy was silent for a couple of minutes.

"Now you've taken a job somewhere, and for the time being you're terribly fond of that, too."

"But why do you want me not to like it? Would it be better for me to work in the book business against my will?"

"I don't know. Maybe."

"Did you really take your exams against your will?"

"That's me."

"What, and you're special?"

"I'm special and you're special."

Zai gave a quiet laugh and lowered her eyes. "I'm special

and you're good and intelligent. We've told each other more nice things today than ever before."

Jean-Guy closed his eyes with their long, femininely curled lashes.

"If you only knew," he said quietly, "how much I want to be loved."

"What did you say? What do you want?"

"To be loved."

"By me or in general?"

He opened his eyes. "In general."

She dropped his hand, feeling him slipping away from her.

"In general," he repeated, "but right now—by you."

Once again he came nearer, from some human distance of his own. How mysterious it was! But even more mysterious was what was happening to her.

"Do you believe in miracles?" she asked shyly.

"Miracles? No."

She regretted her question. How tender and firm his embrace was and how ardent his kisses. And what he told her when he was kissing her was even sweeter and hotter than his kisses.

Then he covered her up and began stroking her hair. "Ever since I was a child I had an inexplicable fear that no one would love me," he said, as if he were starting some long tale, but there was no continuation and silence fell.

"You've had a fear since childhood? You've had a fear?"

"Since childhood. The terrible sensation that it might pass me by."

"And now?"

"No, now that's passed, or almost passed."

She looked at him with agitation. "I love you," she repeated twice, insistently. "Let's help each other."

"In what way?"

She was embarrassed. "In every way. And then we'll be very happy."

"You think it's possible to be very happy?"

"Oh yes! Of course! When all our fears are gone."

"They don't bother me. I'm used to them. They're mine."

"What are you saying! I hate them!"

"How can you hate yourself?"

"Do you really love yourself that much?"

He thought about it. "Yes, I love myself."

She was wistful for a second. "Listen to what you're saying, Jean-Guy: You love yourself and you want me to love you. What's left for me?"

He laughed: "You'll be a part of me."

Something seemed to snap and close in her. In the blink of an eye, she took her hands out from under the blanket and pressed Jean-Guy's head to her bosom: "Hush! Hush! Don't say another word! Let's love each other without words. We don't need words. I'm afraid of them. I'm afraid of life, Jean-Guy. It's a secret but I'm telling it to you. There are moments when it passes, and it ought to pass completely. . . . What do you think, how will it all end?"

"I think basically everything in life ends in some bit of nonsense."

She was stunned. She was expecting him to say something like "it's never going to end" or "there's no point asking about that." Of course it was never going to end in the amazing sense that even if they stopped loving each other and parted, and forgot one another, something would remain forever in her from what they had right now. Something would live on in her as long as she was alive, and maybe even a good deal longer, and not just a memory. No, not just that!

She shifted easily and simply from this thought to a conversation about nothing, about how it was in Brest and what the others—their whole unlucky troupe—were doing. He hadn't

seen anyone since the performance. The author had vanished.
They said he was writing some book now. Suddenly Zai said
cautiously: "I'm afraid it's getting late and it's time for you to
go."

She took his hand and, quietly removing her small gold ring
from her own hand, put it on his little finger. "What slender fingers you have, from my middle finger it fits your pinkie fine, it's
even a little too big. How I would like to give you this ring, Jean-
Guy, how I would like to give you something I love. But naturally you wouldn't wear the ring, would you?"

"No, I wouldn't," he laughed.

"I understand. Maybe you'll leave it on like that until
tomorrow?"

"Are you crazy?"

She put the ring back on her own finger, which made her
sad.

"How sweet you are, Zai, how sweet, and how unlike anyone else! I've never known anyone like you ever."

She smiled. "Have you known many?"

"Quite a few."

He pestered her in the end, demanding she recover as
quickly as possible, then he wanted to examine her, but she
wrapped herself up in her blanket and refused. "Doctors only
treat strangers."

"What idiocy!"

"Could you treat your own family?"

"Why on earth not?"

"Could you operate on them?"

"Well, certainly, what's so special about that?"

"Oh, what a wonderful man you are, Jean-Guy, you're
simply extraordinary!"

He pressed her close, wrapped up in the blanket.

"I always thought I was extraordinary, Zai. I've never met
anyone like me."

She looked at him with admiration. His face was so close she could see only a small part of it: an eye, a cheekbone, the edge of a temple, but that was enough.

"Tell me, Jean-Guy, why do painters paint such big pictures? All you need is a little square to understand everything: a bit of the face, or a bit of the dress, or a bit of the upholstery . . . Or in music: my God, five or six notes are enough. You don't need a symphony or an opera at all. You know, I think in the future that's how it will be. People will save so much time!"

"Then a single note would be even better. Why five or six?"

"And one single word. What's important is finding that word. Art would consist of one single word that man would find and speak at a specific moment. Everyone would find his own word and his own moment."

"And we would all get very bored," replied Jean-Guy.

She stopped talking, and there were a few seconds of silence that seemed infinite to her. "You don't think I talk too much?" she asked again.

"I already told you no."

"But do you think I'm very ugly?"

"How stupid you are! You aren't ugly at all, you're very pretty, and I love you."

"You really love me?"

She wished he would repeat the same thing ten times, and he wished she would do the same. And then the glint of happiness appeared on their faces and a silence full of meaning reigned all around them.

Beyond the walls there were no footsteps, no automobile horns. Zai felt like telling Jean-Guy about how Dasha often said that the windows of their apartment opened out not onto the street or the courtyard but onto some enclosed building, and all of this reminded her in a way of the Tiagin home there, in Russia (where they'd opened a cafeteria). There the windows of the vestibule also looked out on a covered gallery, or the gallery windows looked into the vestibule. The vestibule, as Dasha also said, had reminded her of a ballroom when she was a child, and she often imagined it full of music, lights, happiness, and beauty. But then something happened in the vestibule and that impression was lost. Zai herself had never seen the inside of the Tiagin house; there had never been any reason to stop in there, when it had become a cafeteria. She wished she could tell all this to Jean-Guy before he left, but she held back because it was true, she had already talked too much today. He might get bored and go away. He didn't know Dasha. There was no need to tell him about Sonia; he didn't know her either.

Just then there were steps in the hall and Sonia walked into the room.

"I beg your pardon, but it's time for you to go. It's late, and Zai needs to sleep. This is not coming from me; as far as I'm concerned you could sit here all night. It's *patria potestas."*

"I don't know Latin," Zai said coldly.

"Too bad. I advise you to read your Larousse. On the pink pages there's much that's instructive."

"For example?"

"For example, *Quio nominor leo,* or *Post mortem nihil est.* Actually it would be even more useful just to read Seneca or Phaedre."

"Why is she making fun of you?" Jean-Guy asked. "Who is she?"

"This is Sonia. It doesn't matter. What does *quio nominor leo* mean?"

"'I'm called the lion.'"

"I'm called the lion!" Zai exclaimed, excited. "Jean-Guy, I'm called the lion! And you?"

"You'd do better to introduce us to each other than to call yourself a lion."

"Forgive me, please. Sonia, this is Jean-Guy, who you saw in the play. This is my sister Sonia. Half-sister," Zai corrected herself.

Sonia was standing at the foot of the bed, her arms crossed. She did not bow or give Jean-Guy her hand.

"Ah," she said mockingly. "Are you the one who acted so badly?"

"Yes, that was me. Along with everyone else."

"That doesn't lessen your guilt one whit. The show was begun out of boredom and it failed."

"That happens to real actors, too."

"Really? I never go to the theater."

"It happens more often than you think. It was a joke—that didn't succeed."

"There's something terribly pathetic in that, when people decide to make a joke collectively."

"You're probably right."

Jean-Guy stood up, kissed Zai, and whispered something in her ear. Her face beaming, she answered, "See you tomorrow." He walked past Sonia, bowing to her. She went to the door, too.

"Would you like to smoke a cigarette in my room? It's not that late."

He nodded and thanked her.

"Jean-Guy!" cried Zai the moment they were in the hall. "I beg of you, don't go to her room, go home."

He paused in the doorway. "Have you gone out of your mind? I do what I want."

"I beg of you, don't go to her room. I don't want you to go to her room."

"Most definitely"—and he raised both arms to the heavens—"you are a child of nature."

"Sonia!" Zai cried, with what felt like all her might. "Don't you dare take Jean-Guy to your room. Don't you dare!" But no answer was forthcoming. The door to the hall shut, the steps

died down, and another door, not the front door, closed somewhere.

Ashamed of this outburst, of this whole brief, unexpected
scene, Zai covered her face with her hands. "Lord, forgive my
stupidity, my idiotic suspiciousness, my lack of control," she
whispered. "I'm called the lion. . . . No, I'm called the rabbit
and I'm burning with shame, or could that be my temperature
spiking? I'm burning with shame as if I were lying in the middle
of the Place de la Concorde, between the fountains and the quay,
and everyone could see me, all of me, right through me. Once I
saw right through myself—it was terrifying. Jean-Guy, protect
me. I'm afraid of life. I should pull the blanket up over my head,
squeeze myself into a ball, pretend I never existed."

Gradually this state began to pass, as if a window had been
closed that had been letting in an icy draft and she had found
herself back in her warm corner, not protected as much as a snail
or a tortoise, but protected nonetheless. She had known for a
long time where the draft came from, which direction the window faced: this was what she had brought from her childhood,
not individual events and impressions but the terrible spirit of
slavery and death, sadness and fear. Would this pass on its own,
as it sometimes seemed to her in moments of happiness and
serenity, or would it take her a long time to vanquish it? And
how could she do that? Where could she find what would make
her a person at last? Who did she know who was a person? Was
there an example near to hand? Or could one be found in books?
Or would the answer be revealed to her, her alone, some special
answer? And what would it be? Did she have the intelligence to
understand and accept it and be resurrected at last?

Her thought turned to the people she knew. She started
thinking about Dasha, whose choice now seemed a mistake. Zai
recalled her bitter disappointment in Dasha on the eve of her
wedding and saw that there had been a glimmer of truth in that
almost childish disappointment. Subsequently this truth was

clouded by the sense of ordinary satisfaction about Dasha's future, but now it had resurfaced even sharper, stronger, and more insistent than three months ago, and this time there was nothing childish about it. Dasha had left something undone: herself. She had gone off to live an easy life, to the joy of everyone who knew her, but was that good? No, that was not good. Zai could see this clearly now.

Now she had Sonia, who had probably never been scared in her life; moreover it often seemed to Zai that other people were often scared around Sonia. What was Sonia's secret, if she had one? Did she know something Zai didn't? Of course, she knew a lot, more than anyone Zai had ever met. But what exactly? And where did this knowledge lead, this freedom she lived in? If she was a person in the sense that Zai understood the word, then should Zai follow her lead? At this point Zai lost her train of thought. Maybe Sonia's path couldn't be anyone else's. Maybe there wasn't any path at all.

Sonia often gave off a chill. Wasn't it the same chill as in the draft, the draft that had made her wish "she had never been"? Sometimes Sonia lay at home all day without leaving her room, and her face, which she hid in some book opened at random, exuded a heavy melancholy. She probably didn't really know anything and lived at random, and sometimes did wicked things, and never did good ones, and was so distant from everyone. You would never learn anything from or through her. God help her!

There were people in the world, of course, who might help Zai. There was Jean-Guy. He didn't know much of anything, was afraid of infectious diseases (rather strange for a future doctor!), liked himself and said he was good, intelligent, and special. And that was so comforting to hear, she was prepared to listen to it always, only it would be embarrassing if others heard it. They might decide Jean-Guy was conceited and vain. They wouldn't understand he was just saying it to give Zai pleasure. Although, what did she care about other people?

And suddenly she remembered a certain book. She couldn't say whether she had actually seen it or had dreamed it. It was a small fat book, maybe a dictionary or a prayer book. And it had something in it about everything. A man she had once met on a train had held it in his hands and referred to it from time to time. It took the place for him of an address book or a train schedule, and then and there the image of that mysterious and weighty black book became a symbol of the complete and final, free and wise answer to all life's questions.

But there was no such book, nor were there the kind of people she needed. She was utterly alone with her thoughts, and life was slowly floating through her, looking in a way like the waning moon.

CHAPTER FIFTEEN

In the new life Dasha had begun that spring, what struck her most of all was the number of weddings, births, christenings, divorces, funerals, and inheritances she suddenly found herself involved in. She had never seen anything like it. She named the dresses hanging in her wardrobe: the funeral dress, the wedding dress . . . Actually, she had several of each kind and they were overseen by a slender Arab maid who wore high heels and played a small harmonica in the evenings under the palm tree in the garden so exquisitely that, listening, you could lose yourself in it. The music didn't last long. The maid's Arab cavalier would come for her and they would vanish, taking the harmonica with them. It was an instrument Dasha had never held in her own hands, and she imagined it completely different from the way it in fact was. Dasha's dresses hung in a spacious, pleasantly scented wardrobe, and in another one, her boots were hung on sticks made expressly for this purpose. Here there was the pleasant smell of leather.

There were lots of cabinets in the house. An entire wall in the hallway was fitted out with cabinets, and in the big room downstairs where the piano was and where there were always flowers galore, there were also cabinets: glass-fronted cabinets for porcelain and a radio cabinet where one could listen to the whole world. There were cabinets in the nursery and the bathroom. There were almost no tables in the house other than the dining room table. Instead, here and there, there were low metal and glass pedestal tables adorned with heavy crystal ashtrays, polished and gleaming.

The large living room windows were kept shuttered and the canvas curtains drawn until nightfall; people stayed inside their houses in the cool half-dark. In the gardens above the city a dry heat quivered and one had to make sure it didn't penetrate the house. Mornings, Dasha remained alone in her large bedroom. A tea cart with a coffeepot and cups rolled noiselessly over the carpet at the slightest touch, and its movement made the flowers in the vase at the opposite corner of the room shed a few petals and the door of her vanity table open slowly, with a soft sigh. Inanimate objects rustled delicately in this house.

It was as if three months ago, on one of those black, windy evenings, the life here, which had been shut up tight, opened wide for a moment to take her in and then closed the door behind her. The next morning, she already felt at home here, the mistress of the house, Moreau's wife, a part of this life and this house. She had walked through it then several times. Moreau wore his usual grave but newly happy and calm face. Before she had time to think about it he embraced her by the window of the dining room, kissed her hand several times, and said: "I hope you always have the calm, happy face I saw today for the first time when you woke up."

She didn't dare promise him anything, but she had a feeling this was possible.

The boys appeared. Now Dasha knew them well, but that day she couldn't tell anything about them. What was most important on such occasions was to be perfectly natural and that was so hard! Later the elder boy turned out to be sentimental and lazy, not overly principled and not averse to tattling. The younger liked to fight, was willful and rude, once broke the radio, and nearly lost an eye playing with a dog. But that first morning they stood before her sullen and withdrawn. The governess eyed her warily. But it all worked out both with her and the maid. And the days flowed by.

Running a house turned out to be an entire science. As was conducting oneself in this house. And in this new world as well. How to choose new gramophone records, dresses, and wines, how to drive an automobile, try on hats, think up a dinner menu for twenty, get used to the people who came to the house, danced, played bridge and tennis, and talked about their airplanes and yachts, about fashion and Paris, but not the Paris she knew and loved. Their Paris seemed to overlay the one she knew; they did not coincide at all. Entire blocks that Dasha knew seemed to be missing altogether in this other Paris. And she began to think that in addition to these two Parises there might be yet another, third Paris, and maybe even a fourth. The city she was now living in was gradually revealing itself to her in the blinding white heat and severity of its streets. It might also have an overlay, but she would never find out about it. You couldn't find out about everything.

In the evenings, they would drive out of town—either alone or with several of their friends—winding down the white roads, frequently without any destination in mind, under the big, low-slung moon. Beneath an awning, at little tables, they would drink a lot and talk very little. Or they might go to the seashore, where an orchestra of twenty exotic instruments played and they listened to this music and the surrounding silence in a state of strange inner stillness.

In contrast to the colorful, exotic, and ill-assorted world in which Dasha had lived up until now, the people here were more homogeneous, with their hauteur, their humor, their reserve, with their own harsh, practical world, which was convenient but not very comfortable. Love and money, progress and the impending war were their main topics of conversation. There were others, but these four formed the basis of their discussions. You could penetrate deeper into the various lives and find in any one of them a whole series of petty crimes, a chain of truths and deceits, unfulfilled desires and incomplete actions, but Dasha didn't do that. Once recently Moreau, gazing at her with admiration, had said: "I think I'm seeing that calm and happy face on you more and more often. And that makes me happy."

And it was true. She saw herself in the many mirrors of her bedroom and the large mirror in the hall. She did have the kind of face that should please him. Everything here and around them was just as it should be.

It was as if all the furniture in her soul had been rearranged: everything had changed. In Paris she had had a habitable, well-worn, not always comfortable, not always well-swept room, an old bookshelf over the sofa, a window looking out on another building. Now everything was different. Out her window were eucalyptus and orange trees, books lay on a pedestal table, though she didn't know how they'd gotten there, the carpet was rolled up to reveal a beautiful waxed parquet floor that you could slide on. The day was meted out so that there was no time for self-contemplation. And at night sleep was sweet in her low, fresh large bed.

She wrote home rarely; her letters arrived without a greeting, as if she were writing to everyone at once. "It's already quite hot here," she wrote, "and in the garden they have put up a magnificent colorful umbrella (see the photo). We swim every day, at sunset, with the dog, who is not at all like what a dog should be. First of all, its name is Lola, although it's male; second, it's old; and third—it's crazy about me for some reason. The children swim too and study (but rather badly). We have guests daily. We have old friends and young friends, some sympathetic and some repugnant, none of which matters much, though I can't say why."

And so on, as much as would fit on an ordinary sheet of paper.

The old Arab cook was undoubtedly more intelligent and courteous than most of the guests who sat around the dining room table in the evenings. Moreau was quite amazed when Dasha remarked on it one day, although this was not of great importance. The old cook had once been in German captivity; he had seen a lot and knew how to talk about it. The guests, the women and men, spoke disjointedly, on random subjects, armed with a vocabulary of about five hundred words, and they all entertained themselves the same way: either with some game or a new "at the edge of the desert" restaurant with music, or the Lambeth Walk. They differed from their children primarily in their lack of restraint or propriety with regard to their passions, which dominated their lives. This was their entertainment, and their torment, and it used up the time and means of the men and the tears of the women. Those who were impervious to these passions seemed rather lifeless and gave Dasha the impression of being ill or retarded.

The men differed from one another in their tastes and the nature of their business. The women differed primarily in age. At thirty you could predict what they would be like at forty— exactly like the present forty-year-olds; at forty you could guess unerringly what they would be like at fifty. Imperceptibly Dasha felt herself being included in this chain. It seemed perfectly natural to her. She actually liked the calm, logical order that had been established here.

A completely different example of the human race was the children's governess, Miss Mill, a woman of no age one could determine who wore modest dark dresses and never said an unnecessary word. You never heard her footsteps. Her eyes, which were a little too wide open and lacked any expression, looked straight ahead. She did everything asked of her, and on her days off she sat in her room, never went out, but closed the door and looked through the illustrated magazines that had accumulated over the previous week. Her room was always clean and empty. On her table there was an empty pitcher, a glass, and a clothes-brush. No other objects of any kind anywhere, nothing of her own—not a nail file or a darning egg or an old letter or the most basic necessities, it seemed. The bed was made as if no one had slept in it for weeks; the mirror was polished, the cloth on the table had not a spot on it, and the air was cleaner than anywhere else in the house. You could picture her there clearly, in the evening or during a free hour: sitting on a chair at the table, still and lifeless, expectant, hands folded, for the time to come when . . . for something only she herself could say.

"What an odd woman," said Dasha to her husband one day. "I've never seen anyone like that. You might think she was un-happy with us."

"She's delighted to be with us. She's been living in the house for eight years and she knows she's set for old age. I think that the great majority of people on earth live that way, or almost that way," he replied.

It was odd. But evidently only Dasha was surprised. So she got used to the governess, too, as she did to everything in the house, which she now spoke of as "our home."

"Our home," "our bedroom," "my favorite vase," "my boys and your boys want to go for an outing on their bicycles," "don't come to dinner tomorrow, our cook is on vacation," "my hus-band ordered a new Packard." That was how Dasha spoke now with her calm, happy face. "They must have an opinion of me. What is their opinion of me?" she asked Moreau sometimes. "You've known them for a long time. Tell me, what do they think of me?"

"They like you very much," he replied, admiring her. "It couldn't be otherwise. I knew it. Look at yourself!"

She looked at herself and saw that everything inside was still in terrible disarray, like the room left untided the day she left Paris. But what did she need that room for now, with its faded upholstery and old rags in the dresser drawer? What use had she for that unswept, uninhabitable corner when she now had an entire house, spacious and comfortable, gleaming with cleanliness and comfort, where everything was in its place, and Rome and Cairo and London came through on the radio, where a little Arab woman carried a tray with tall glasses in her slender hands, where a fat novel was open to the first page—*A Brooklyn Violet,* or *Prater Something,* or whatever it was called. You had to be Miss Mill not to read a single book in your life!

In the final analysis, what had changed? Very little. She had always been in tune with everyone and everything, and now she continued be in tune with herself, other people, the world. She was not the only person like this. If you took a count, you might find that the majority of people on earth were like her. Not all would feel identically, of course. Some would say, How beautiful God's world is and I live in it as a small part of it! Others would say, God damn it, let's try not to throw the world out of kilter. And a third would shout, A thief's not a thief unless you catch him in the act! Poets would rhyme *earth-worth* and in the grand harmony of the world everyone would freeze at a wonderful landscape, a harmony somewhat indifferent to man, of course, but Mother Nature's nonetheless, which gives us her dairy products, picturesque sunsets, and other joys, including good luck. In the end, Miss Mill would reform the stormy little boy who continued to break everything around him with great glee; the tattling little prig would find his place in the sun. It was good to feel young, healthy, loved, untroubled about the coming day, with dresses for every occasion in life, beautiful cabinets full of necessary and lovely things, a gleaming refrigerator in a gleaming kitchen where the water turned into ice cubes to the quiet ticking of an invisible clock—day and night—which was so handy in the hot season.

The days passed quickly. Moreau left for the city at eight.

The cook and Miss Mill took up the greater part of Dasha's morning. Someone would drive by before lunch; life's little joys and life's little cares rushed past Dasha, barely grazing her. At two o'clock, the long black car would drive in the gate and Dasha, tanned, straight-backed, wearing African sandals and a fresh dress, would cast one last quick glance over the table, which was set in the dining room for lunch, under the broad blades of the fan that swooshed quietly just under the ceiling.

Moreau would take a shower and then come down. The boys had their lunch early and at that hour were usually already on their way back to school. At the table, when there were no guests, they spoke little—it was one of those habits that Dasha considered a throwback. From the beginning of their acquaintance she had noted that Moreau combined the receding age with the coming one. He observed certain precise rules, following the example of his father and grandfathers, but at the same time modern life freed him from so much in quick bursts. He sensed no conflict between the old and new, willingly surrendered the old for the new, and accepted the new the way he did his existence in general—without a great deal of thought.

Once Dasha asked him: "I'd love to know who you vote for when there are elections to the chamber. Would you tell me?"

He smiled mysteriously. "One can tell right away that you come from a land of barbarians. How one votes is a strict secret and no one has the right to ask those kinds of questions."

"But still?"

He wouldn't tell her, though.

"Fine. I'm going to have secrets from you, too, I'm not going to tell you who I vote for, either."

But it never occurred to him to be curious about things like that. She could vote for the socialists if she wanted; he was voting for Maurras. *It would be impossible for us to quarrel, though. And thank God!* Dasha had thought at the time.

"It would be impossible to quarrel with you," he told her

once, in regard to something else. "I consider life with you the greatest happiness that has ever befallen me."

After lunch, life settled down in the house, as it did in town. This was a sacred hour in the day, the siesta, when all activity came to a halt. The blinding sun, which scorched the town, raged motionless outside the house walls, and in the lazy silence the clocks chimed delicately every quarter hour. Later, the tubs were filled with perfumed, greenish water. Husband and wife drove to the shore to play golf and admire the freshly watered lawns. Then they ate dinner at home and relaxed on the broad terrace.

At that hour, the sounds of the harmonica came in from the garden.

"That music doesn't irritate you?" he asked once, taking her into an embrace with his one arm.

"Of course not! What about you?"

"Not in the slightest."

In the half of the house where the boys lived, the day's activities gradually wound down. For the last time, wearing just his shorts, the younger boy rode the banister into the hall with a crash, punched the old copper gong hanging by the door, let out a deafening screech through a whistle he had, and, repeating some word that had captured his fancy over and over a hundred times, scrambled upstairs on all fours. The door slammed; Miss Mill ran off to attend to something. The older boy, who had recently turned thirteen, was often ill with fever and had gone to bed long ago. Usually Dasha went up to see him at nine o'clock. Sometimes she wanted to sit next to him and put her hand on his forehead, concentrating for a few minutes in silence . . . but that was out of the question. She had tried it once, but he had looked at her so strangely and indifferently that she had snatched her hand away while the younger son, who had pulled out all his bedclothes and finally settled down, laughed mockingly: "Me too please! I want my milk of human kindness!"

The next day she lingered by the younger one's bed. This one was always healthy and sharp-tongued, and she was a little wary of him. The elder, who was sickly, might get better if she wanted it very much and if everything were different. But why wish something to be different when life was so calm and happy? This was all just some nonsense she was embarrassed to recall. She lingered, straightening the embroidered sheet; he followed her movements and then with one great kick reduced everything to disarray again, and when she went out he laughed. All this was perfectly harmless and naturally she could not change anything here.

If there were no guests and they weren't going out of town in the car, into the open countryside, which looked like the desert, she would go into the garden, where it was quiet and dry. Gray palms lined up in a dense row, one after the other, as if they had been brought here and placed standing in the harsh, rusty soil, where something alive was running across the sand, something invisible in the darkness, something that came to life only at night, lizards that were invisible in the day and that might have vividly colored bellies and sly, merry little eyes but were hidden from human sight. The stars, unusually large and green, were burning in the sky in an out-of-the-ordinary picture. The Great Bear had barely peeked out from beyond the horizon, so it was quite indisputable that the earth was round.

In the living room, which looked north, the windows now were half-open. His legs crossed, Moreau was reading in his easy chair by a wide window. The candelabra were lit. He would only allow mosquito netting in the bedrooms. Now he bobbed his head softly and rhythmically, chasing off the tiny blue moths that circled around him. At first, Dasha had been amazed in the mornings at the color of the sweepings from the ground floor. They were blue. The moths had turned to dust by morning.

From the garden Dasha watched Moreau for a long time. He raised his head several times and cast a quick glance toward the windows open the length of the wall, but of course he could not see her in the darkness. She lowered herself into a canvas chair without making a sound, stretched her legs out, and threw back her arms. *People played noughts and crosses. . . . It would be interesting to know whether there were cross-spiders—garden spiders—here. . . . The Southern Cross—that's not here, it's much farther, on the other side of the equator. We might move there, where we could see it. The Southern Cross and Eridan, which the public was starting to get good and sick of . . . No Bears there . . . White people living on ice . . . Tomorrow they were bringing twenty bottles of Champagne in the morning. Would there be enough ice? For the most part it was good that she was cold with the boys: that was how it should be. Everything would work out, everything already had. She knew that everything would always work out for her.*

Dasha stared up at the sky and thought about her inner world. Deep down, where her thoughts anchored, everything was new, not at all the way it had been. There was some new kind of order over everything, and a stillness. No more melting in rapture, no merging with some immensity, no reflection of a starry sky. Inside her, everything was calm, clear, and prosperous. In the transparency of Dasha's unclouded conscience and her frozen thought lay simply . . . sleep. Nothing else would ever again shine from there. She had lost her sense of up and down. Slowly and seamlessly, from void to void, her mind summoned up today's accounts from the old, wise courteous chef, which she still hadn't checked. The kitchen expenditures for the week . . .

"Dasha," said Moreau, leaning toward her. "Have you fallen asleep? I thought you were standing at the window looking at me. . . . It's too early to go to bed. Let's go have supper somewhere . . . if you're not too tired."

"There's no doubt about it. The earth is perfectly round," said Dasha, rising to her feet.

CHAPTER SIXTEEN

Sonia Tiagina's Notebook

I don't hear a certain voice in what's going on around me. I'm waiting—I need it. I've been waiting for it for years, but everything is silent there. My anticipation has become so acute, so painful, it won't leave me be. It fills all of me—my days, and nights. I don't need books. I don't need operas from Russia or people and their old and new conversations. I need a word that could be an action. . . . I don't know what it should be. How could I? No one could. Maybe most people don't care any more what it's going to be like, that word, spoken, at last, to our whole planet, but in my mind I have linked my fate to this word, this act of will. If it doesn't come, I'm lost.

Feltman, dear old Feltman, whom I love so much, though no one guesses, of course, because I answer him brusquely and leave the room when he comes. Once, looking at me with his intelligent, beaming eyes, he said, addressing my mother: "No, there's no point in judging her that way, Liubov Ivanovna, because you're wrong. Sonia isn't a foreigner at all, she's extremely Russian. Dasha is much more of a foreigner. Or Zai."

My mother, however, insisted on her opinion: "If Zai were a foreigner, that would be normal, just think about it! Dasha is one hundred percent Russian, she couldn't be more Russian. Her name is Russian, her hairstyle is Russian, her temperament is Russian. But this one! Where she gets it all I simply don't understand. She has nothing from me or Tiagin in her."

"All three of them are foreigners," my father said conciliatorily. But Feltman didn't agree, and he peered at me again. My father launched into his pet theory about us being like citizens of the Canton of Uri. I gave Feltman a hostile look, but he never takes any notice of my expressions or he chooses to ignore them, and keeps on beaming with satisfaction. I worry about him. How could he have survived this long and what's going to happen to him?

So—I'm waiting. I live by this insane and secret hope that there won't be a war, that the war the world has a presentiment of won't happen. If a war begins, it may go on for so long that it will seem like forever. Cut off from everything, I clutch at this last hope, which holds a vague yet decisive absolute.

For the twenty-nine years I've been on the earth, my life's been spent in search of some absolute. At first everything was shapeless, then the contours appeared along with the goals of existence. I sought out people going my way and thirsted for a single completeness that alone would make life worth living. I sought out feelings that might give me an awareness and sensation of being complete, and I walked proudly past everything that couldn't. In essence, the joys of life didn't exist for me, because the joys of life didn't bring even a whiff of an absolute. Among the joys of life, by the way, I include friendship, which I've never known. The irresponsibility of friendship has always dampened my ardor. Friendship is a half-measure in human relations. There is not nor can there be an absolute in friendship.

You like something, you don't like something else; you turn a blind eye to certain things; certain things you forgive, others you don't. In general, you forgive a lot because you waste only as much of yourself as suits you, retaining your freedom over your conduct, time, and will. If you forgive, you'll be forgiven, so why make any special effort? But if your services (material or moral) are needed, just remember they'll be returned in kind when you need them, which means everything is just mutual insurance against everyday disasters. Satisfaction, no risk. No one ever compares strengths: equivalence in what is given and what is received; contact only when there is the desire for it: once a day, once a week, or once a month, by tacit agreement and without compulsion.

Between friendship and love there is one phenomenon I've often thought about. It doesn't even have a name; meanwhile it exists. This was what there was between Ludwig of Bavaria and Wagner, between Brahms and Schumann. What do you call that? It encompasses deification, apprenticeship, friendship, love, freedom, enslavement, one personality growing into the other, and the image of the one outstripping the image of the other. I have never experienced this. If I had, maybe everything would be different. But how could I? These times don't allow the individual to strike that kind of spark Without God and being enamored with the idea of social equality already acquired or gradually being so, man has lost the way to this kind of love, this type of friendship, in which one gropes toward completeness. But there's a barrier that hides the great, eternal secret of relationships between two people and it won't let itself be discovered.

Yes, the way to this kind of friendship has been lost, and there is one more important reason why—we're so terribly changeable. In his lifetime modern man undergoes so many metamorphoses that in the end he can't recognize himself and his beliefs are increasingly less commanding. We never really know where we stand.

My romantic experience is not so great. There were two times and with both of them it was as if an orchestra was starting out at full blast with a *tutti* and a *forte*. Things started right in the middle, beyond any doubt that this was it. The moment I realized it was love, there was no turning back. And I didn't think about it—I lived, I flew, to hold on, to pin down my happiness, because an absolute is not in an instant but in its duration. When things ended, I felt done in and barely alive. How did they end? Not in a storm or an explosion but with just a small fracture. That was enough for me to put an end to my love crudely and pitilessly myself: a spoiled thing ready for the trash heap, a cracked plate tossed into the garbage. You shouldn't ever try to glue, heal, or fix anything.

Fly, fall, send to hell and gone everything even just grazed by corruption! There isn't going to be perfection, and the beautiful and integral are unattainable. There isn't going to be an absolute along this path, which means don't go one step farther. The absolute turned out to be rotten to the core.

What else can you expect? The last romantics, those closest to us in time, left us with this thirst for the absolute: "Comme si quelque chose de la réligion se mélait aux douceurs d'un amour, jusque à la profane, et lui imprimait le caractère de l'éternité," one of them said timidly, in the end hanging himself in the building near that same bench by the Seine where B. and I sat so often. We moved toward the absolute but took our own paths, our own ways.

Oh, that thirst for completeness and wholeness! The secret wish to keep from falling apart, to keep the world from breaking into a thousand pieces with a clap of thunder. The secret wish to bring about harmony in oneself, to find it in the world, to save the world and oneself. Crazy ideas, insane goals. Unattainable? But if you don't have them, how can you live? How are you supposed to put something back together if not inside yourself? There is no other choice now. The old one had once been so temptingly simple, always at hand, consoling, convenient: if something inside you isn't well, if the wheels are screeching, the clamps squeaking, the screws rusting, take a look around at the whole wide world and remember that you are only a part of something universal, integral, wise, and beautiful, and even good, and as you merge with it, thank the Creator! The old choice turned out to be—well, not false, but senseless, because suddenly in the place of this picturesque road there was an abyss, a chasm as deep and dark as the ones Gustave Doré liked to draw in his Bible illustrations.

Now we have to start from the opposite end—with ourselves. And the task is much more difficult. We have to find inside ourselves not just our own but the world's equilibrium. My absolute has to connect me with the world itself, justify everything, resurrect everything. That was the dream: to glue a broken object back together, to create world harmony ourselves. But I never did find anything that tied me to the world and I don't know anyone who has. For a long time I loved the world, but it never responded and a desperate sense of abandonment fell over me. There was still a small place—the last place—for a tiny hope. If I couldn't do it maybe my country would glue things back together. B. once asked how I could expect a concrete answer to my abstract questions. And Dasha told me not to read so many newspapers. But there's no answer; if the world is falling apart and beyond repair, if *all is lost,* then I am lost too.

Life is lonely, not death; choosing one's end means being free and connected—life means being disconnected. Isn't it a fact that the universal is dead, the spirit has flown away, and we are living beside a corpse and don't know it and we still want (oh, holy simplicity!) to be one with it? I thought about how to live, studied how the world lived, but everything in me is backwards—I'm still seeking some kind of connection—my connection with it—in oblivion.

For someone else it may not be in oblivion in the literal sense of the word but in relative oblivion: in not-thinking, torpor, the "what is passed would be sweet" of foolish lazy people, in the "dig and build" working class. It doesn't matter what concrete forms it takes from day to day: the hard, crowded life of the worker or the easy life, the empty meaninglessness of the parasite; the fear and oppression of the pariah or the boredom and power of the scoundrel. But I'm still alive and free— I won't give in to relative oblivion. Oh, what happiness to be able to say it loudly, out loud: I am still alive and free and I am choosing the only accessible absolute for me: I am choosing absolute oblivion.

Having lost my faith in everything once and for all, I'm like a simple peasant woman. I await a miracle. Miracles sometimes occur, of course, but only in an intact world. What kind of miracle can one expect in ours, where everything is backwards: people are silent when they should speak out and speak when they should be silent; the sole act that can lead them to harmony is considered suicide. By leaving the world, I will merge with it.

CHAPTER SEVENTEEN

That summer Sonia felt herself to be alone in a state of tension. Everything seemed changed from the previous year. Now it was June. Jean-Guy almost never came by any more, Zai was recovered.

But here was Jean-Guy visiting Sonia again in her room.

"What is it that you want?" she asked, looking at his sullen, possibly angry face.

"For everything to be turned topsy-turvy."

She laughed. "Well, that's definitely going to happen, and soon. But I doubt you'll be happy about it."

"Then one will be able to think of something."

"What irresponsible words! Why do you have to think of something? Is your life so bad?"

He leaned on his thin arm and a wistfulness crossed his big dark eyes, where each of his moods was marked.

"She doesn't love me enough," he said and Sonia thought: *Why is he telling me this? Do I really unintentionally inspire people to open up to me?*

"What do you want from her?" she asked.

"I want her to love me. But she doesn't. That is, not the way

I expected. She's constantly slipping away from me in her thoughts, talking about other people, laughing about something private. In short, she lives without me, apart from me, even when I'm by her side. I don't have any real power over her. That's not what I wanted."

"What do you want?"

"Me? I want to be loved. I can't bear it any other way. If it doesn't happen, I don't know what will become of me."

"I don't understand you," Sonia said perfectly sincerely. "You're not a stupid boy, you're even handsome (you know you are), and you're afraid no one will love you? How old are you?"

"Twenty-five."

"And no one has loved you yet?"

"No one. That is, not the way I'd like, as if it were in fact forever."

"Very well said: 'as if.' Don't you think, Jean-Guy, that we have all reached an end point? The highest point, a kind of apogee?"

He stretched in the chair but didn't answer. They were silent.

Pale and skinny, wearing her gray robe, a fourteen-year-old girl once again, Zai walked in. In the past two weeks she'd become used to Jean-Guy sitting in Sonia's room in the evenings, she didn't protest as she had the first night, and now she came to hear what they were talking about. For a couple of minutes she sat on one of Jean-Guy's knees with her back to him; then she quietly moved over to the bed, and since no one was talking, she began humming something very softly. The sorrow, discontent, and gloom all vanished from Jean-Guy's face; it became agitated, and he, self-conscious.

"Every day," said Zai, not looking at anyone, "really ought to bring something. The sun rises in the sky with such effort, and then—nothing. We drink and eat and go to sleep. But now there are books. And then there was my illness, which gave me time to think about so much. Tomorrow I'll get up in the morning, and the day after that I'll go to work."

Sonia said nothing. Jean-Guy stared at Zai.

"I came to hear what you're talking about," Zai continued. "But you're both silent and I'm talking. Did you have an argument?"

"That never crossed our minds."

"I'd like you to be allies, not necessarily against anyone, just allies. You might agree with each other about a lot."

"What?" Sonia asked, and naturally Zai sensed the ridicule in her voice. "What could we agree about? And why should we be allies?"

"The most important thing is to know," Zai said very quietly, "who is an ally and who is an enemy. Smart people always know that."

"And then?"

"And then nothing. . . . I'd like to go far away somewhere. . . . No, I'd like live my whole life in Paris and never go anywhere. It's so nice here."

"Yes, it is nice here."

"I'd like to experience everything, understand everything, and see no one and know nothing. I'd like to break into pieces and always be whole. Don't laugh! Oddly enough, all this is going on inside me at the same time."

"It's not funny at all."

"I'd like to love one person all my life and at the same time I'm afraid of missing some other happiness."

"A double?"

But Zai didn't answer. Jean-Guy broke into the conversation with a quick temper, passionately: "There, you see? You see? I knew it all along. I told you, you don't even know what you want. You don't love me one bit."

"Couldn't you two work this out without my presence?" Sonia asked.

"Of course, we'll leave. You both provoke me into discussions I want no part of. How can we discuss these things with the three of us here? These things are discussed in twos."

"But everything in the world has to be balanced out," said Zai, not budging. "Do you agree that everything that exists in the world has to be balanced?"

He shrugged.

"I'd like to know," he said angrily, "what exactly we three are balancing here, in this room, with this discussion. I think one thing is indisputable, but I categorically refuse to talk about you and me in front of other people. What is it with this habit of yours of bringing everything up for discussion!"

"Get out of here, both of you!" Sonia said dryly. "Zai, see him out."

CHAPTER EIGHTEEN

Sonia Tiagina's Notebook

Zai and Jean-Guy had a quarrel in my room. I have nothing to reproach myself for. Did I make them quarrel? Of course not! But if it hadn't been for me they would both have been calmer. Happier. Everything around them is moving, and so are they. He's upset and doubting, and she's searching for something, growing. It's all like the movement of the planets in the heavens, like everything all around us, because everything all around us is alive. I don't live alone, I wait from day to day, from night to night, for something to happen. A voice to reach us, a word ring out. And this word must change everything and resurrect me.

"Sonia is the most Russian of the three," repeats Feltman, dear Feltman, with his tender, intelligent soul that is always smiling at something. There aren't many like him left. Yesterday he was telling us about the death of some friend of his whom he'd buried recently, and it felt as if he were telling us about his own funeral. For some reason I can see his imminent death so distinctly, and for some reason I don't think it will be easy. My father is older and often sick, but I don't see death over his shoulder. He may even be getting more and more frivolous, to my mother's great distress. I wouldn't be surprised if one fine day we find he has another daughter or son somewhere. He's fooled a lot of people in his day.

Volodia Smirnov, in his idiotic Russian-French, admitted to me today that "if anything happens" he will be mobilized the very first day. I couldn't restrain myself: "You think something is going to happen?"

"I think sooner than we suppose. I've decided to marry Madeleine, so that if anything happens everything will be in order."

I praised him for this foresight. Saying goodbye, I asked him what had happened to his brother from Prague. It turned out that, once he had gotten a visa, no easy matter, he had finally left for America, in fact just a few days ago. That man and I had such a fine silence that evening. I won't forget that hour for a long time. It is one of my best memories of the entire year. Others have conversations; I have silence. It's no surprise that I feel out of step.

For a long time I've noticed this acute disjunction, which has made my life especially hard and not very sweet-smelling. From time to time I've seen myself too distinctly, soberly, and in those moments everything else seemed to be in the fog of a thickening dream, and I was alone, caught in a searchlight beam. And the opposite: when I saw what surrounded me in its naked-ness, in its reality, I myself vanished in a barely earthly guise, barely discernible. I felt a painful disjunction between dreaming and waking, when the world around stands so firmly and simply and I am wavering somewhere out of the focus of my own vi-sion; or as if I were seeing the world through a veil, a fluid world, elusive, while discerning my every vein, my every faint feature.

I have no harmony. And without harmony or measure, noth-ing can exist. There has to be harmony in each person. And so I don't exist, I never existed. I have enough strength to admit that.

In some people one encounters this awareness of their own nonexistence. But alongside it there is a frenzied pride: I'm proud I'm not like everyone else, that I'm broken, lost, that my world is like this, my age is like this, that I don't have or need anything. Why don't I experience any pride at these thoughts? Any fierce joy? Pride and joy would blind me to my whole life and I wouldn't see that terrible spiritual poverty, that drifting I've wandered into. The fact that I see it doesn't give me any satisfaction. Yes, I see it; yes, I have no illusions; yes, it's a void.

But couldn't it be different? Sometimes I think that maybe sometimes it is!

CHAPTER NINETEEN

August came, hot and windy, with the dust and rumble of emptied streets. Liubov Ivanovna and Tiagin had left Paris for the countryside nearby, counting every last franc; Zai was going to the bookstore (she didn't get a vacation the first year) and coming back in the evening worn out by the heat and work; Sonia had written and sent off her application for a teaching position and spent entire days lying in her room and smoking. Once every couple of weeks a letter arrived from Dasha, like clockwork, with no greeting—about Africa, the boys, the maid, the dog, the weather, Moreau, and herself. Zai opened and read them, stacked them on the dining room mantel, and moped over them.

Feltman didn't stop by any more. He'd come only once since the Tiagins' departure, bringing a clock he had taken to some acquaintance for repair. It was nine o'clock in the evening and for some reason he thought the "girls," as he called them to himself, had finished supper long before. But Sonia and Zai were sitting across from one another at the dining room table, at one end of which sat Jean-Guy chewing on a piece of bread and refusing to eat anything else. The lights were on in every room in the apartment and for the first few moments Feltman thought the house was full of guests. But it wasn't; everything was actually too quiet in a way. Even in the dining room, evidently, no one had been talking before his arrival.

He sat down. Zai asked him if he wanted to eat, but he'd already had his supper. He set the Tiagins' clock on the table and inquired whether everything was all right. Yes, everything was all right. Sonia seemed thinner to him.

"Aren't you going anywhere?" he asked just to make conversation.

She looked at him indifferently.

"Where am I going to go? The dacha? No, I'm not going to the dacha."

"Pity," he said, "it's dreadfully hot and dusty in town."

"It's hot everywhere," she replied. "But next year I will certainly go to the dacha. I'll even set aside money for it in advance."

Zai took the plates into the kitchen and came back with a bag full of apricots. In passing she stroked Jean-Guy's wavy black hair with her free hand.

"Here are the apricots," she said, putting them on a plate. "Eat them and put the pits on the paper."

Everyone obediently started in on the fruit, even Feltman.

"Did you bury someone again today?" asked Sonia.

"Do I really bury people so often?"

"In my opinion, yes."

"When did I bury anyone? Only last week. Oh no, there was that time in early July, and in the spring, poor Peter Semyonovich. . . . It's true, you're right. I do go to a lot of funerals. Many people I know have died. Why is that? But you can't even imagine how many people I don't know who have died."

After a pause, Sonia said: "People you do and don't know. But there are even more nameless people."

Feltman came to life: "Nameless: you've put it well. I've known you so long, Sonia, and you've never spoken so well."

Slowly Zai cleared the table again and clutching the salt and pepper to her chest, went into the kitchen and started rattling the dishes. Jean-Guy followed her. There he sat down on a stool and began waiting for her to finish the dishwashing. "That lady with the diplomas might help you once in a while. After all, she doesn't do a thing all day and you work all day long!"

"And you grumble all day long!"

"If we were together, you could move in with us and we could make my mama do everything in the house. Enough of her combing the dog for fleas and laying out cards."

"Tell me, Jean-Guy, is it true she does something she could go to prison for?"

"You've gone mad! Who told you that? That business stopped at least two years ago."

Zai gave him a kitchen towel and the forks and knives, and he started slowly wiping them, his mind on something else, yet carefully putting the cutlery away in the open drawer.

In the dining room, her chin resting on her palm, Sonia looked at Feltman and thought, *Why doesn't he leave?* And he—examining the dry, crinkled apricot pit—was asking himself the same question: *Why don't I get up and leave?*

"I could tell you so many interesting things," he said meanwhile, "about all kinds of nameless people. All the ways and places they disappeared. Imagine, recently there was this case: a gentleman was living at the sea shore, a Russian, of course. He loved children and treated them to sweets. He was suspected of perverting minors, but only suspected, not accused. He came home from the questioning and hanged himself. And no one ever found out who he was or where he came from. There were only initials in the newspapers."

"There's an ending for you!"

"And what about that other nameless emigrant who threw himself out a window when President Doumer was assassinated?"

"Really?"

"He left a note that said, 'I can't go on living. I feel responsible for this crime.'"

"How bizarre!"

"Can you imagine, Sonia," Feltman was getting livelier, and when he leaned under the lamp, his gray crewcut shone the purest silver, "can you imagine in France your concierge feeling responsible for something, a robbery, let's say?"

Sonia was silent.

"Or Paul Valéry suddenly announcing that a shadow had fallen over him because of someone else's stupidity or meanness?"

"Of course not."

"But you, you understand it, don't you? That is, the fact that one person can burn with shame for another?"

Sonia turned away from Feltman.

"No, I don't," she said. "Why do you ask that? I have no opinion about that."

Feltman leaned back into the shadows. "No opinion? Then why are you interested in nameless people?"

"Did I bring it up? Didn't you?"

The Tiagin clock—a round, flat gold clock which Feltman had put on the table in front of him—was ticking very quietly, so that only he could hear it, and it reminded him he should go. He would return in a week, when the Tiagins were back. At the end of the month.

He stood up, coughed, and went up to Sonia.

"Goodbye," he said, smiling his calm, childish smile. "You have to thaw out, Sonia, thaw out. When are you going to thaw out?"

She stood up, too.

"A thinking nail," she said dryly. "Have you ever heard of such a thing?"

"Is that you?" This spooked him.

"No, not me." She chuckled. "But it happens." She thought for a second. "I'll go out with you. Wait for me."

They walked down the street. Feltman was on his way to the Metro. He lived far away, but he traveled to all ends of the city with enviable ease. Distance never deterred him and he always had enough time.

He asked her which way she was going. She didn't know what to say. The simplest would be to tell the truth—I'm seeing you to the Metro—and so she did.

"You want to see me to the Metro?" he exclaimed, touched and amazed. "What surprises there are in the world!"

Laughing a little, he strode boldly alongside her. She didn't laugh, she didn't even smile. She was occupied with her own thoughts.

"I'd like to tell you many different interesting cases. There's not much I haven't seen! Life passes, mine's already passed, actually. Another year or two, maybe three. Sometimes it gets you down when you think you don't have anyone to pass your experience along to, all those trivial facts, interesting and funny, there are so many of them, in essence, I mean, and they'll be lost. Enough baggage for a train car of people! You couldn't fit it into any book."

"Or ballad," said Sonia.

"What ballad! There's only one important note in a whole ballad. No one ever finds out which note that is, only the composer can hear it. Behind that note there's an entire five-act play."

"But still, something gets said in that one note. It would be worse if it never was."

"To be honest, the difference isn't all that great. Infinitesimal. Actually, I feel infinitesimal."

They said goodbye, he descended underground, and she went home. She had never felt infinitesimal, but now it seemed to her that between the infinitely small and the infinitely large the difference was not that great. *These arms, these skinny fingers, the lightly waving hair circling this face, the feet stepping evenly—what a small body, frankly, barely tied to the ground— here is where it begins, there is where it ends, and around it is an infinite space, billions of miles and billions of years. But what was inside this small, weak, and fragile object, what was locked up inside it and trying to break out, was enormous, powerful, and terrifyingly explosive.*

The neighborhood was quiet at this summer hour. All you could hear was the city breathing, alive, all around and in the distance. In August not only the Tiagin alley but all the streets nearby began to resemble the silent rooms of a large structure built entirely of stone. They became halls and passageways, the guardroom of some castle, the formal residence in some unfamiliar palace, the prison corridor that once appeared in the brain of Piranesi, and finally a square, like the winter garden of a manor house where at this by now totally dark hour of the oncoming night the plane tree and cedar, the acacia and lilac, seemed like otherworldly, tropical, maybe even artificial plants.

Sonia passed through the gate and down the alley sidewalk. Jean-Guy was walking on the other side, almost at a run. She had only to shout out, call to him. . . . *Run away, Jean-Guy, run away as fast as you can. She doesn't love you. You were just a means for her, a way to learn about life: she's already left you. She has only one desire: to grow. It would be hard to come to terms with her. And why try? Let her grow, let her go on changing until she finds what will free her completely.*

Sonia watched Jean-Guy duck out into the street and disappear. It seemed incredible now that she had knocked at those doors. Of course, Jean-Guy hadn't answered. Maybe he hadn't understood her correctly. Her intentions had been absolutely "pure," the same intentions she had knocked on Feltman's door with today. They were all the same to her. Actually, what are "pure intentions"? How could anyone possibly know how all this would end? To think of the question meant she had more on her conscience than Ladd now.

Zai was standing in the dining room by the mantel, lost in thought as she sorted through Dasha's letters. They were all the same. Maybe it was all untrue. No, of course, Dasha didn't know how to lie, and why should she? It was all the truth because there was more truth than fabrication in life, generally speaking. Zai was making herself more and more miserable. She leaned her elbows on the mantel and looked in the mirror: no prettier! At that moment Sonia walked in and stopped by the table. "What, you're alone?"

Zai didn't answer.

"Good night!"

Zai did not even look around. Sonia played with the light switch.

"I believe in miracles," Zai said suddenly. "Once in my life I saw a miracle. But nothing ever came of it."

Sonia walked up to her and looked closely into her face.

"Exactly nothing ever came of it. It all melted away, forgotten. As if it had never been."

"You mean you wanted there to be a chain of miracles? That doesn't happen."

Zai repeated softly: "a chain of miracles." That was true, that was what she wanted. But that didn't happen: Dasha turned out to be incapable of a chain of miracles. But still, there was a miracle! "There wasn't a chain, but there was a miracle. Just one. Nothing ever came of it."

"And who's to blame for nothing ever coming of it?"

"I don't know," said Zai, looking in the mirror, where she could now see Sonia's half-turned face. "Maybe you. Actually, that was almost a year ago. There's no point belaboring it."

"Me?" Sonia said in amazement. "There's no beast stronger than a cat. I hope you don't blame me for your failure with Jean-Guy?"

"That was a success."

"Thank God! So at least I have nothing to do with that."

"You wanted to, Sonia," said Zai, moving away from the mantel. "But it didn't work out. You don't have anything to do with anything in life."

"Do you realize what you're saying?"

"Yes. And it's the truth."

"So you don't think I can do whatever I want?"

"Yes, that's what I think."

"Or achieve my goal?"

"I don't think so. After all, you've tried, Sonia, and it hasn't worked. Not with Jean-Guy, even though I tried to help you, because after the first evening in your room, when I was still sick in bed, he was already wrong for me, he was already free. But is Jean-Guy really the point? It's all over, it's all past, one day we'll even enjoy recalling it. But it doesn't exist any more. Being around you is so hard, Sonia; it's so hard to breathe."

"Yes, I know," Sonia replied, continuing to stand, motionless, in the middle of the room and watching Zai slowly and noiselessly begin lowering the blinds "But it might change someday. Then you'll tell me you noticed. There's nothing but hope ahead. It should happen soon, very soon. Before winter, in any case."

"You say 'nothing but hope,' but in a voice that sounds if you were talking about something hopeless, some catastrophe. You make me uneasy. You know, Sonia, I'm almost not afraid of anything any more, but those 'hopes' of yours scare me."

"You mean all your childish fears have passed?"

"Childish and not childish. They've almost all passed. I have so much courage now that sometimes I can scarcely believe it myself. But of course I can't do everything I want, either."

"And there are people who can?" Sonia laughed grimly.

"You're laughing at me. So I don't want to talk any more at all."

"You're still a child. Look how easy it is to offend you."

It was dead quiet.

"You've grown so much, Zai. How old are you now? Twenty?"

"Nineteen and a half."

Sonia walked around the table and came close to Zai. She looked into her face intently and gently touched her hair, straightened a lock of it, and suddenly pulled her hand away. "You're going to live your one and only life no worse and no better than anyone else."

"And if it's not my one and only, what then?"

Sonia just smiled slowly and tensely. She walked away, examined something for a moment on the sideboard, an old salt-cellar that hadn't been used in a long time, and left. Zai picked up a napkin that had been dropped under a chair, turned out the light, hid her father's clock in his bedroom dresser, and went to her room. There she undressed quickly, got into bed, set up a small lamp with a shade over her book, and plunged into her reading. It was silent throughout the house.

The world in which Zai passed her days now was a magical, captivating world that had thrilled her completely in recent weeks. She got up early, drank coffee in the kitchen, dressed, and, trying not to make any noise slipping past Sonia's door, went off to her job at the bookstore, which was also the warehouse for a large publisher located in the Latin Quarter. She went on foot, taking quick, businesslike steps. Downstairs, in the old building's large lobby, where sculpted ornaments were still intact on the blackened ceiling (and plywood booths had been built in the corners for the telephones), was where the books were packed. Two fat women in gray aprons worked there tying up the packages, and a young man, lean and near-sighted, pasted on the labels. An old employee, evidently quite an expert at his business, register in hand, received the customers, and in the window of the booth you could see the telephone operator's fluffy curls. The walls were lined with bookshelves from floor to ceiling and posters hung between the windows. Once fine authors of the nineteenth century were published here and now they looked out from the walls at everyone dashing by, their expressions pleased as befits people who spend their leisure to some purpose. An archway led to the store, where three clerks and a cashier sold books. A grand broad staircase went up to the offices on the second floor, to the reception room, which had two large couches and a table with an ashtray, to the secretary's office, to the director's office, and finally, to the owner's office. Privately, adopting Sonia's habit, Zai continued to call him "B."

Going to the third floor, the stairs were narrow and dark. They led up to a row of rooms where typewriters clattered, the copy editor sat, and so many employees worked cheek by jowl that Zai still didn't know them all. Her place was in one of these rooms. It was "the smallest place in this whole big business," as B. once expressed it. She had to glue and use scissors, run downstairs to the packing room, frank envelopes, and go to the post office. Zai was paid eight hundred francs a month. She had a future.

Behind this whole visible world, nestled in the old building, there was yet another world unseen by the naked eye. On the landing of the first staircase a narrow, easily overlooked, almost secret door opened up, and an electric light illuminated long rows of bookshelves, cramped rooms, one after the other (the doors had been removed and how many rooms there once had been was long forgotten). Passing through them all one might end up surprisingly back in the first, as if it were a labyrinth of wisdom—in which Zai nearly got lost every time. The place smelled of books because there was nothing in the room except books: no windows, no furniture, just shelves.

Every time Zai stepped into this mysterious place she had the same feeling she had had the first day, as if something similar had already happened to her in her life: surprise, curiosity, fear, delight, the sense of one's own insignificance. The first time she saw it was when the director and B., extremely pleased with something, were there paging through the neat white volumes, and bringing samples for future covers up to the light. Soon the director left and B. turned his attention to Zai, who, perched on the moving ladder, was removing volumes of Goncourt from the top shelf and checking them against a list. He smiled and caught her intent gaze as it roamed over the shelves.

"Elizabeth," he said. "If you'd like to take books home to read, then you can get cut copies from Mademoiselle Painson. Tell her I asked her to give you whatever you want."

Zai blushed. "Upstairs they don't call me Elizabeth because one of the packers is Elizabeth. They gave me a different name."

"What's that?"

"Lilly."

"Fine. Lilly it is."

Zai thanked him. He went out, and a few days later, upstairs on some matter, he himself put on her desk two volumes of Van Gogh's correspondence, which smelled of fresh ink. That day was the beginning of a new life for Zai.

She realized suddenly what the overwhelming sense of déjà vu she had had that first time she crossed the threshold of the book storeroom meant. Not the one small, important book in the hands of the stranger on the express train from Warsaw to Paris, who was lost in the past, but hundreds of books standing in tight rows beckoned to her, revealing a new and precious life, and each one seemed like a part of something great and essential that the mysterious book in the train car had hinted at only vaguely. She felt there was a treasure close by; if she touched it, it became hers. And she surrendered to it all at once, without hesitation.

It never occurred to her that she might work anywhere else. Everything she needed, it was all here, and only here, and it was owned by B., not that funny traveler who looked like a minister but B., a grave, tall, reserved man with an ugly and special face whose gaze now made her tremble. When he smiled, which was rarely, she seemed to fill with happiness and freeze, afraid to move and break this mysterious spell. He was the master of this new world she now lived in, and she didn't need any other.

Mademoiselle Painson calmly unlocked the door to the tall built-in cupboard in her office and left Zai standing in front of a row of books. She looked at the spines, pulling one book or another out. During those moments Mademoiselle Painson, examining herself in her pocket mirror, put on her hat with the grapes and pulled on her Irish lace gloves.

"I'm putting Montaigne back," said Zai. "And I'll take Anatole France, if I may. I still have the last volume of *Temps perdus*. I'll return it tomorrow."

No reply was required, Mademoiselle Painson merely said: "Put the key back in the drawer" or "Goodbye, Lilly." And Zai walked out of the room, already in a daze, carrying these new pages.

There were days when B. didn't go upstairs and Zai didn't go downstairs, and then she tried to catch a glimpse of him from afar, in the stairwell, for example, or to hear his raised voice when he was seeing a visitor out. B. inhabited this world where Zai now lived and grew, where everything was filled with such portent, a world she entered every morning with a fluttering ecstasy she concealed from everyone and which she later took away with her to her own nighttime room.

Elizabeth and the other fat woman wrapped and tied up the packages; in the store, customers flipped through pages; Mademoiselle ran down the stairs; the telephones rang; a long-armed, thin-necked author sat in the reception room and studied the ash-tray as he awaited his fate. The small wallpapered door opened and the light turned on. With list in hand and a storm of thoughts in her head, she felt her legs buckle at the thought that today or tomorrow he might smile at her again and say: "Ah, Lilly! So, are you getting used to things?"

Or, if they were alone, something longer, as had already happened once: "Ah, Lilly! So, is everything all right? You don't regret your freedom? You're not like Sonia, that means. And how is she? Give her my regards, tell her to stop by one day." But before she could reply he had left the room.

When they were together, Zai felt no fear of B. She was only afraid in front of other people. He made her feel good, as if she had never been afraid. And now it didn't feel as if her sense of security would pass. Now she accepted everything in a completely new way, guessing that someday this acceptance would prove to have been very important, decisive. Yes, to be honest, she had changed, she wasn't at all like she used to be.

CHAPTER TWENTY

The Tiagins returned from the country at the end of August and a few days later an alarming letter arrived from Dasha. She wrote she was sick at heart, she had been having bad presentiments. She felt there was no doubt that some awful event was imminent and she asked Zai to come to her while it was still possible. She said Zai would have a good time, she would visit for a month, and then they would see. Dasha herself could not, as she had promised, come to Paris any time soon. "At our house," she wrote, Zai would not sit idle. There were language classes, for example, and Zai could study Spanish.

"I don't want to study Spanish at all," said Zai, and she was reminded of how she had once said, "But I don't want to go to Paris at all!"

At the end of the month the city started filling back up with people as usual, but there was no one left from Sonia's tight little circle and she lay in bed for days on end, numb. Liubov Ivanovna, wrapped up in her own worries and domestic matters and experiencing an unrelenting irritation at Sonia and partly at herself, didn't talk to her at all. *You can't go against fate,* was what passed through Liubov Ivanovna's mind several times a day. *A lodger! Who is she like? Who made her like this? Is she lazy? No. A fool? No. What are we to do with her? And she seems to lack what men like, despite her beauty. I'm so afraid of her I don't dare ask whether she had an answer to her application and if so, what it was.* Liubov Ivanovna got angrier and angrier at herself, but she didn't ask Sonia any questions.

Tiagin was still working. In his old age he was getting fonder of long discussions on international politics. Feltman and Sipovsky resumed their visits, and they would spend hours deciding matters of war. It grew dark early. In the dining room where they usually sat, Liubov Ivanovna sewed and darned, listening to their unhurried conversations. Sometimes they'd turn on the radio and listen to the sweet, peaceful music and to voices that were either martial and ominous or weary and sinister. Unconsciously, Zai fenced herself off from all this with books. She now had her own mysterious, broad existence that very much resembled happiness. The world of books and B. himself—it was all tied up in a single knot. She had not seen Jean-Guy for a long time.

Once in a while Sonia would come into her room and disturb the enchanted atmosphere Zai continued to inhabit at night. Zai noticed, as did others, how Sonia had changed over the summer. She was so skinny she avoided wearing dresses with short sleeves so no one would notice her arms. Dasha wrote: "I have utterly ceased to understand her. All this is simply unwise! Doesn't she understand (read this to her please) that she is becoming a burden to everyone? Papa is far from young, Zai is working and supporting herself. Who is Sonia counting on? If she hadn't played the fool last winter, she could now be somewhere near the seashore and have a calm winter ahead of her. That's what you get from writing about Xenophon! She might just as well . . ." and so forth and so on.

"How sensible she's become," Zai said softly, reading it.

When Sonia came into Zai's room, very often Zai would regretfully tear herself away from her book. But there were evenings when she kept on reading and Sonia would sit down with her at the table, cross her arms behind her head, and stare into space. Half an hour or so later Zai would ask: "Sonia, why are you like this today?"

Sonia would invariably reply: "You asked me the same question yesterday or the day before."

"Really?" Zai set aside the book and leaned toward her.

Once she felt like hugging and kissing her, but Sonia pulled away. "What is this tenderness? Please, I can do without it."

There were days when Zai felt a heightened tension both in the store and at home. Liubov Ivanovna looked distraught and Elizabeth the packer's eyes looked like she'd been crying. Dasha wrote again: "Have Zai leave immediately and come here. You're all living in some kind of denial. You have to understand that we could be cut off from one another." But Zai firmly stated she wasn't going anywhere.

Tiagin, yawning and sighing, tore off the last page of the calendar and looked gloomily at the back. It was the same kind of Russian calendar they'd been buying every year for the last seventeen years. Bits of Tiagin's life were gradually falling away: the regimental dinners, the regimental funerals, the Russian habits, such as polishing his boots to a high gloss every day, sleeping in a nightshirt, fasting during Lent, going for a steam in the Turkish if not the Russian baths. One of the last old habits to go was the calendar: an aphorism about the vanity of vanities, a quatrain on "What passes will be sweet," and a menu for the next day. The saints: Flor and Lavr, Illarion, Serapion. . . . Liubov Ivanovna had already brought him a hot water bottle for his belly. It was bedtime.

Zai was still sitting by her table in her room. Sonia hadn't come in yet. Zai was partly happy about that because today the conversation would inevitably touch on events, world events, that Sonia was so good at sorting out. Whereas Zai did all she could to block them out. Before her lay a letter from Jean-Guy written in his illegible, crooked script, the letters coming one after the other to form words, and the words forming a decisive and final question: yes or no. She didn't want to answer. She thought of the day just spent; B. had met her on the street when she was coming back from lunch: "Hurry, hurry," he said with a stern look. "If you're late for work, the boss will fire you; he won't care that your polka-dot dress suits you so well." She was gong to think about that for many long days. Life was wonderful! You could live in reality as if were a marvelous dream. You could block out everything and create a marvelous world of delight, youth, and hope.

Sonia wasn't going to Zai's room today because she had locked herself in her room long before. For the past few days she'd been wandering around the house like a shadow, as if something had happened. But nothing special had happened apparently, not yesterday, not the day before yesterday, not last week. At work, Zai had a great deal of work (half of the employees were on vacation) and there weren't any special conversations. She didn't dare ask B. whether he was going away anywhere; evidently he wasn't. To see him every day. To see him. To see. That was all she needed.

Behind Sonia's door everything quieted down at about half past ten; in the crack of the door, in the hall, there was a light. It didn't go out all night, and for many days afterward Zai would recall going to the kitchen the next morning and seeing that light from under the door but not paying any attention to it. Actually, in the morning it could be sunlight: in the mornings during the summer months a narrow sunbeam reached Sonia's small room. Meanwhile, Sonia was in no hurry to undress, she just took off her shoes and paced barefoot around the room. The disorder on her desk bothered her for some reason, and she set about stacking the books, putting the familiar objects away, and tossing certain papers into the wastebasket.

The many newspapers accumulated in the last week gave the room a look of disarray. As soon as they were stacked up, the room looked spacious and clean. Sitting down on her bed, Sonia bundled the papers neatly together. So many words! All read, learned, and digested. Not the arguments of sly and clever people but facts; not predictions or presentiments but reality. A month ago she had stopped reading books altogether. Books seemed to have a hint of dishonesty, of playing games. You couldn't just say, Ivanov put a bullet into his head, you had to surround the action with clouds that now and again sailed across the moon or a locomotive moaning in the distance or occasional dripping from the kitchen faucet. All this was perfectly correct, of course: locomotives moan, faucets drip, and the moon frames the suicide with the clouds moving across it. But sometimes you don't feel like knowing that. Newspapers involved less playing around, sometimes none at all. The issue from last Friday, the issue from Tuesday . . . All that had passed. Tomorrow a new day would come—or, more precisely, wouldn't.

It was quiet in the house. She was glad it was quiet. If Sonia's hearing had been a hundred times sharper she could have heard the quiet murmuring between the Tiagins in their bedroom, the rustle of the pages of Zai's book, the sleepy ramblings of feet, the light clacking of the knitting needles of the woman upstairs. . . . People. Sonia lived as if they weren't there, or rather, they lived as if she weren't. They didn't care that she now felt her full responsibility to them—and for them. For them and everything that was happening. It was that one last hope that had lived on in her for so long, the secret, unuttered hope that had come crashing down. That hope had stolen into her soul, and when it died from the savage force, the fateful blow (about a week before), she knew: we will be completely honest, we will not be afraid to answer for everything and in one fell swoop! We will not ask pointless questions (which have a certain tradition): Who is to blame? What is to be done? I alone am to blame. I am to blame for everything, and I am answering for everything.

She put a glass filled to the brim with water on the chair by the side of her bed, threw back the blanket, took off her blouse, and stepped out of the skirt that had fallen to her feet. Her garter belt had worn out completely; it was good no one could see it. Her narrow bare feet were cold, her brassiere had been taken in twice in back—so skinny had she become. Wrap herself up; tightly in the blanket, press her head deep into her pillow. What kinds of dreams would she have, if any?

After lengthy altercations with Liubov Ivanovna and her father, Zai had got her way: she would not come home for lunch any more. Instead she would go to a small café near the Church of Saint-Sulpice and eat there—a ham sandwich, a cup of coffee. Sometimes Thérèse, the typist, came and together, in the square, on a bench, they ate apples and fed the birds bread crumbs. There Zai read until the very last minute, when she had to run back to work. "It won't matter," he said today, "that the dress is polka-dot." He said this, making a strict, alien face. "And it suits your face very well." Sometimes he looked one way, with those good and very sad eyes of his, but said businesslike, dry phrases. "And it suits your face very well," he had said today.

The next morning, as usual, she rose early, but Tiagin had risen even earlier. He was now working in Clichy as a book-keeper and he left the house at eight. Liubov Ivanovna was busy in the kitchen. Sometimes they had arguments there in the mornings: she suspected he was not indifferent to a certain desk clerk. He got angry and denied any interest in the feminine sex, now or at any other time in his life (which at this point he himself sincerely believed). He recalled some recent flirting of hers with Sipovsky. And not only did she serve Feltman tenderly, but she served him the part of the dish he liked best. Zai walked in and the conversation broke off. Tiagin drank his coffee, said good-bye, and looked significantly at his wife, who threw herself on his neck. Content with one another, they parted until the evening. Zai slowly drank her coffee, holding a book under the table. She heated the iron, pressed her dress, made sure there weren't any spots on it, got dressed, and left as well.

Everything at the pale-faced flower seller's on the corner of the boulevard was fragrant from having been watered. She had just opened the stall and hung out her blackboard, on which she had scratched in chalk: "Today is Friday, 1 September. Saint Gille's Day." Little and big Gilles would be expecting presents and flowers. A happy day for all the Gilles in the world. At the jeweler's the pearl jewelry had long since crawled back into its shell, and now fat rings were sitting on a grate and watching the passers-by. The electrical appliances store, the furniture store, the fabric store. All this so that life could be wonderful, easy, and happy. People's goal was to make life ever more pleasant. Man devoted his entire existence to creating comfort every-where—for himself and his own. This was chiefly what Dasha was doing. "Dasha, what have you done with yourself?" It did not sound smart and it was time to stop saying this all the time— on the run, in the morning, on the street, crossing the pavement.

That day B. did not say anything to her and everyone was very reserved, both with her and with each other. Zai understood that people were thinking about the coming war, but she wasn't particularly. It was clear to her now that the little book which contained so many different things had at last turned into the thousand books among which fate had sent her to live and work, just as she herself was no longer that little girl who kissed the flowers in the garden but had turned into this slender, efficient young lady in a relentlessly clean dress, with long polished fin-gernails and a fine gold chain around her neck.

At lunch hour, the square was completely empty. The first yellow leaves rustled on the paths. They had probably been here yesterday, too, but she'd been thinking about something else and only noticed them today. Ahead lay two nonworking days, two long days when she wouldn't see B. That meant, See you Monday, leaves and birds, yellow on the paths and green in the trees, swallows and pigeons!

In the evening she came home with her pay in her pocket. She always gave half to Liubov Ivanovna and kept the other half for herself and spent it immediately, so that later sometimes she had to economize on apples. People were milling around the newsstand. Evening was gathering. The distant boulevard, in the direction of the Seine, was plunged in a softly thickening violet-gray haze not yet pierced by street lights.

She ran up the stairs and rang twice. Everything was quiet. There were no steps behind the door, no voices. At this hour Tiagin was usually home already, dinner was on the table, the pots were banging in the kitchen, and the radio was turned on in the dining room. Zai listened closely. Not a sound penetrated to the landing where she was standing. She strained to listen and waited for something to jingle or steps to start scuffling. She rang again, two short rings, but the silence continued. And then all of a sudden she felt a vague unease, certain images flashed like lightning through her memory, images that had nothing to do with this minute or each other: the crowd milling silently around the newsstand, the lonely evening over her book, the absence of B. this afternoon, and the innumerable telephone calls for him from the provinces; the emptiness of the birds' square; Sonia going to her room early the night before and the key turned in the lock. She leaned on the bell and the long, insistent sound rang through the house. Zai pulled back her hand and put her ear to the door. Somewhere in the back of the apartment she could just make out steps. Her heart started pounding. The steps died down, and on the other side of the door there was whispering: two whispers were arguing about something. Zai beat on the door: "Why don't you open up? What's happened?" Back in the vestibule someone was whispering to someone and again steps approached. The door shuddered. Feltman's face appeared in the crack, and behind him stood Tiagin. And suddenly Zai felt like screaming, screaming in a terrible voice and throwing herself on both of them. Her entire body started quaking and she dropped her books and purse, from which something rolled out and across the floor.

She rushed to the bedroom. Liubov Ivanovna was lying on the bed. Her eyes were red and unblinking in her pale face. She did not look at Zai or change her expression.

"Don't go in there," she said very quietly. "Don't look at her."

Tiagin sobbed. He started in hurriedly, muttering about how it would be good for Zai to go somewhere else, to friends, until the morning, but Zai didn't catch his words. Feltman was standing somewhere in the background.

"Don't go in there," Liubov Ivanovna repeated. "You shouldn't look at her. You can't fix anything."

But Zai opened the door to Sonia's room. The lamp was burning yellow and no one was there. By the right-hand wall, on the narrow bed, lay Sonia. She was dead.

The parquet, smooth and gleaming, which you could go a long way across in total safety, sliding and capering, was gone. There was nowhere to put your foot, there was no floor, there was nothing at all to hold onto: Zai faced a chasm, one step and she would fall in, and that was the reality, whereas the parquet her foot was stepping on was only a dream. Everything else was a mirage, and she was living in it—living in something that simply wasn't, it didn't exist, people had banded together and dreamed it up, colluded to deceive her, and she had gone along in touching acquiescence. She had invented poetry, theater, love, *joie de vivre,* the lamp that shone in the evenings over the open page, she had invented the notion that liberation from fears is possible, that every person has a bright, proud, and strong soul, free and maybe even eternal. One night someone, she thought, had wagged his finger at her ominously, as if she were a child:

Careful, young lady, watch your step, young lady! It was by the garden fence where the dead dog had lain, its legs spread wide, and it was raining, not a joking, playful spring city shower but rain that had whispered something important and ominous that she had not been able to make out. Her whole life was a mirage, and all her efforts to make a person out of the quaking insect she had been were in vain, because she was quaking again, only harder. It had all been in vain, the joys had been a trick and if there was death, the hopes had not borne any genuine content.

Even in books everything wound around and about. The city where she lived was a mirage, too, of something wonderful and false: a desert, a prison. The buildings and rooms were like cells, and everywhere you looked people were swarming, quaking, fluttering around the loudspeakers and newsstands. The whole world was divided up; into these cells, without air or sun; people were crawling over one another and piling up. And the moon shone over the world—also imprisoned in a cell, in an iron cell over Paris, the way it sometimes is at the full moon, when you look at it from the Place du Trocadéro and it goes behind the Eiffel Tower for a few minutes.

She had stood there once with Jean-Guy. All that was over, though, the pointless childishness. Ahead lay—nothing. Only fear. If there were ever hints at something that wasn't a mirage she would cover her ears and squeeze her eyes shut. She had been thrown back into that weak and inert state of trembling she could never overcome a second time. The world where lights burned in strangers' windows was falling apart, the world where Zai came out on a tiny stage in a funny wig and backless shoes. . . . *We laughed a lot. We wanted to live. I wanted to protect myself, to fence myself off from things, to keep from knowing or hearing anything. But who am I? What am I here for? If I can't do anything and never could . . .*

Everything had been carefully neatened on the desk, the shelves, the cupboard. Who had done this and when? Liubov

Ivanovna would not have dared break down the door. Tiagin broke it down when she summoned him over the telephone, with the concierge, and that had been at eleven o'clock in the morning. The doctor arrived first, then Feltman . . . or vice versa. No one could remember anymore, not even Feltman. The doctor demanded that they give him the empty packet of sleeping pills lying under the bed; they had upset the glass of water—spilled what was left in it—but in the course of the day it had dried and someone's foot had crushed the glass.

They called to Zai from the bedroom. She closed the door softly and went back to Liubov Ivanova's room.

"Why are you shaking like that? Go into the kitchen and drink some water. Papa, look at how she's shaking," Liubov Ivanovna said mournfully, her arms thrown to either side of her on the wide bed, all in tears. No one answered her. The light was on in the dining room: it seemed to Zai that her father wanted to be alone and was actually hiding from them; she didn't know what to do with herself. She stood in the hall for a moment and then went back into Sonia's room, trying not to let the door creak.

Had she tidied everything up here, so neatly and cleanly, herself, last evening, or had others cleaned up after her today? She was lying on her narrow bed, her head covered by a sheet. This was the truth, this was the reality, everything else was the insignificant, miserable human imagination. In the corner was the chair that was usually by Sonia's desk, and on it hung a pair of stockings—probably her only pair. There were newspapers folded on the chair, a big stack that had accumulated over the last ten days or so. On the desk lay a pen, pencil, scissors, and slim paper knife—in unusual, lifeless order. Once again they called to Zai and she stepped away from the desk, took the stockings off the chair, held them in her hands, and threw them down. A white sheet covered Sonia's long narrow body in stony folds. "No, it's impossible, impossible, impossible," Zai suddenly spoke. "It can't be, it can't happen, what is this? Get up, come back. . . . I can't go on like this. Does this mean it all was, is, and will be a lie? What am I saying? Who to? Who can hear me?"

Mechanically, she gathered up the pile of old newspapers and went out, closing the door, walked down the hall to the kitchen, and threw them under the table. And suddenly she saw Feltman in the corner of the kitchen, on a chair. Why was he here and how long had he been sitting here?

Tiagin was pacing around the apartment. You could hear the light creak of his steps, his muttering and sobbing, first in the dark entryway, then in the bedroom, then in the bathroom. Something fell somewhere. Zai returned to Liubov Ivanovna's room. This pacing would continue the entire night, for ten nights, a hundred nights. There was no reason for it to end. Liubov Ivanovna asked her to turn off the lamp; she felt like lying in the dark. Zai turned off the light. In the kitchen Feltman sat over the newspapers, mechanically sorting through them.

"I don't understand," he said. "I don't understand anything. Where is the logic?"

Zai sat down on a stool across from him, by the sink. "Why try to understand it?" she asked.

"You have to understand it. But there's no way. Why? Does anyone understand anything? Do you understand?"

"No."

"You just tremble. You're afraid of everything, like a little girl. You have to be courageous and firm and try to understand. Find the logic."

"There's no point," said Zai.

The newspapers fell from his arms, he picked them up, looking around, dropped them again, and automatically began smoothing them out. Flat, dull, identical faces had been drawn on them here and there, with straight hair and narrow eyes, noseless, with a wavy line for a mouth.

"Does it really matter?" said Zai after a long silence.

"Can't you see that there was something here we need to understand? How could it possibly have been for no reason? That's illogical, impossible."

"Why is it impossible?"

Feltman didn't answer.

Zai closed her eyes. "We have to start all over from the beginning. But there's no point. We had illusions."

Feltman didn't understand what she was talking about.

"Of course," he said. "Life in general is an illusion."

"Everything was all wrong."

"Yes, of course," he responded again, unable to guess her thought.

"And now everything is much scarier than it ever was before. . . . Do you know if they sent Dasha a telegram?"

Feltman nodded. Zai went to the doorway. Somewhere, maybe, everything was otherwise, but right now it didn't matter whether they'd sent Dasha a telegram or not.

She couldn't hear Liubov Ivanovna in the darkness, but Tiagin kept pacing around the now darkened dining room, around the table; in the kitchen Feltman was softly shuffling newspapers.

A corner was torn off one; another had been drawn all over. Yesterday's was folded in such a way it looked like it hadn't even been read. All across the front page, across the big headline, ran a line made with a thick pencil. He tossed everything into one pile. "Understand, understand," he kept repeating to himself. "The main thing is to understand. There was a reason! Find the logic."

He left after midnight. By that time Zai, all in tears, was lying next to Liubov Ivanovna. Tiagin was still shuffling around in the dining room and hall; mechanically he went to lock the door after Feltman. *Why is he doing that?* thought Zai. *There aren't any locks or walls, there's nothing, no defense. I'm going*

to bed here, not in my room, so we can tremble together. People,
let's all tremble together!

"Papa, come here!"

Tiagin walked in and Liubov Ivanovna opened her eyes.
"All three of us can be here together," said Zai, making room for
him on the wide bed. *It might have comforted them a little if I'd
said, Let's tremble together! But they wouldn't understand that,
they still have traces of their past courage, when he fought and
she followed him blindly; traces of their past faith. . . . All I
can do is tremble like I used to. I used to think my fate was this
or that. How I dreamed! But my destiny is trembling. It's all I
have. They crushed me at the very start. Everything else was a
mistake.*

At that moment something flew across Zai's face, but she
couldn't have seen it. The bedroom was dark; only in the entryway did the light Tiagin hadn't turned off continue to burn. It
was a moth, or a little fly, some sort of insect, but Zai thought it
had touched her hair, so she raised her hand with an effort and
drew it across her face. It was wet, and her hand got wet, too. Zai
wiped it on the pillowcase.

Hemmarö—Paris, 1948–1950